A Day In The Rough

A Day In The Rough

Salvatore J. Bommarito

ISBN : 1-4196-0883-5
Library of Congress Control Number : 2005905396

To order additional copies, please contact us.
BookSurge, LLC
www.booksurge.com
1-866-308-6235
orders@booksurge.com

A Day In The Rough

I want to thank J. D. Salinger for inspiring me to think about Holden Caulfield as an adult.

Additionally, I owe a debt of gratitude to the countless men and women I've met over the years in the investment banking business. Although most were professional and great to work with, several were obnoxious, overly aggressive, totally self-centered, and conspiratorial. I dedicate Stoke Spencer at his worst moments to all of you. And, you all know who you are.

Finally, I want to thank my family. I'm the luckiest person in the world to have so many fantastic people to love.

BEING A BEHIND

This is a story about one day in my life, a bad day. Some events were significant and some trivial, but together they drove me into an emotional black hole. I'm going to take you on this one-day odyssey without mincing words, and perhaps, you won't judge me too harshly.

My name is A. Stokley Spencer II. The "A" stands for Alexander. Most people who don't use their first names are snobs. But I'm not like that. I just hate the names my parents gave to me. My father was named after Alexander Hamilton, the Secretary of the Treasury at the birth of our nation, and wanted to do the same for me (as if it's some kind of honor). My ancestors, who date back to the Mayflower, believed that success is best measured by the amount of money in your brokerage account. Hamilton was honored with his picture on the 20-dollar bill and the Spencers hope to have a picture of one of their own on U.S. currency sometime in the future. Fortunately, I only received Hamilton's first name. You'll understand why, when you read on.

In any case, I insisted that everybody call me "Stoke." It's a stupid name too, but better than Alexander or Alex. I thought Stoke sounded athletic. My athletic prowess was nothing to write home about, but sometimes my name helped when I tried to pick up women.

Have you noticed that my initials form the word ASS? I asked my mother what the hell she and my father were thinking when they named me. She said I was named after my father and nothing more (I guess she isn't too happy about having an ASS for a husband and an ASS for a son). I suggested that they must have been high on drugs. My mom's very proper, a high society debutante. She was mortified when I accused her of using drugs. Yeah right, mom, I never used drugs either.

I asked her whether my father (ASS I) partook of weed, but she ignored me. I could just see my old man toking a doobie in his Brooks Brothers suit. Then it struck me, since my father was ASS I, he wanted to string together a long line of ASSes, so that's how it all came about. Needless to say, my father was very disappointed when I didn't name my first son ASS III. I broke the chain.

Now, back to the Alexander Hamilton thing. Has it occurred to you that Hamilton's initials are AH. Still don't know what I'm talking about? Ass Hole, get it? My father should have been a proctologist, not a banker.

I'm 48 years old and in fairly good health, but I have an enlarged prostate gland. You're thinking that's more than you need to know, but it's an important issue in my life. In recent years, I haven't slept through the night because I have the urge to piss about every three hours. I read all of those scary stories in the health section of the newspaper about prostate cancer and decided I better discuss my situation with a doctor (about peeing too often, I mean). Bottom line is that my PSA (I have no idea what it stands for) is elevated. In the words of my urologist, it means that I'm a candidate for prostate cancer. Great, it sounds like I'm running for office, ASS II, a.k.a. Senator Prostate Gland. For the rest of my life, I'll be visiting a urologist every six months to take one more PSA test. If it goes higher, I'll be subjected to a biopsy procedure that is purported to be so horrible that my doctor refused to describe it to me.

The real kick is that each PSA test costs about 100 bucks. So, if I have a test semiannually for the rest of my life and I live until 80, I'll spend $6,400 on PSA tests (This does not include the cost of each visit to the doctor, which is another 100 bucks. So the real cost is $12,800, assuming the cost of this test does not increase, which of course is an unrealistic assumption in today's healthcare environment).

I told my father about my prostate situation. He said he's had the same problem since he turned 50, and has been taking PSA tests since they were invented (he's a real pioneer, my father). I think the ASSes collectively might break the Guinness record for money spent on this tiny gland situated behind the family jewels.

I went to the right schools, the type of schools that all ASSes are expected to attend, Buckley in New York, Andover in Massachusetts, Dartmouth in New Hampshire, and HBS. You don't know HBS? Well, it's Harvard Business School, loser. My educational background was made possible because I was a legacy (my father went to the same schools) and my dear old dad gave each school six figures, which ensured my acceptance. After HBS, I landed a job at Gregg Yorke & Peters, one of the most prestigious mergers and acquisitions boutiques in the country. I'm a Managing Director, but I don't manage anybody and I'm not a director. The title makes absolutely no sense but it's widely used by financial services companies.

I worked my way up to be one of the top four partners in the firm and really bring home a lot of bread. Have you noticed that the initials of my firm are GYP? I can't seem to avoid being saddled with initials that are the butt of jokes (no pun intended). In the case of GYP, the name is justified, since my partners are a gang of ruthless dealmakers, known to take no prisoners and cut the hearts out of the competition. We'll do anything to win business and make large fees no matter what, even if we have to skirt the edge of the law.

By the way, you did know that gyp is a racial epithet? It refers to eastern European gypsies, who steal to support themselves. In Rome, they swarm over tourists and steal anything they can with every deception known to man. The women actually use their children to perpetrate their larceny. Their expertise at ripping people off is quite amazing.

I was going to tell you about my two boys, but decided to save that aspect of my life for my next book. Their exploits have reached epic proportions among the young people of New York City.

My wife's name is Sharon, Sharon Spencer. Her initials, SS, are apropos, as she often employs many of the psychological tactics of the Gestapo when dealing with her family, our domestic help, and all sales people. I once told her not to put her initials on her luggage because it might offend some people (like Jews, for instance). If she had to use her initials, she should include her middle initial 'O' as in Olivia. She said that she often felt she needed to be saved from her life with me, but SOS would be worse than SS, and I should just mind my own business.

Now that you have some background information, I'm going to tell you more about that crazy day. My wife will play a prominent role in the events that transpired, as will some of my colleagues at GYP. It seemed like there was a conspiracy among a number of unrelated people to ruin my life. Of course I take full responsibility for my behavior and want you to know I was only trying to defend myself against a vicious onslaught of those with bad intentions.

A FALLEN MAYOR AND WET T-SHIRTS

New York City in July can be a torture chamber. It's sunny and humid, cloudy and humid, rainy and humid, or humid and humid. During the rest of the year, the weather is pretty good except when it's cold and humid.

Personally, I enjoy the changing seasons. But between June and September, the city becomes a rain forest sans trees. It doesn't have any poisonous snakes but has almost as many bugs and rodents as the tropical forests in Brazil.

I've lived in the city for the past fifteen years and always dread the onset of the summer. Life becomes more expensive in the summer, as my dry cleaning bills skyrocket and the air conditioners in my apartment run at full speed enriching Con Edison.

NYers aren't exactly the sweetest people in the world when the weather is pleasant, but during the monsoon season, we're irritable 24/7. Perspiration stains appear like grotesque tattoos on our clothing reminding us to feel uncomfortable every second of the day. I'll bet divorces increase in the city during the summer months. Somebody should commission a study of marital breakups between the months of June and September.

The numbers must be staggering and elevated by male misbehavior relating to the proliferation of half naked women walking on the streets (and at the bars). Nobody looks well dressed in the summer, as our clothes are always wrinkled and body odor is hard to control regardless of how much antiperspirant is applied to armpits.

To make matters worse, most companies try to decrease their electric bills by ratcheting down the air in the guise of conservation. The working stiffs suffer, but senior management doesn't give a shit. Large companies conspire with city governments in this regard. The latter publicly announce that all companies must decrease energy usage or face brown outs and black outs. But really, government weenies are just trying to help large companies save money. Have you ever walked into the office of the chief executive of a company and been hot and uncomfortable? CEOs are exempted from perspiring like normal people. They're self-centered egomaniacs who want to be comfortable in their offices even if every other employee is not. Most are old, unattractive men who want to make everyone else look crappy, so that they look better in their fresh clothes.

The day that changed my life began as I arose at daybreak. I was out very late with a client reliving the 1980s, when drinking and eating to excess followed by innocent sexual pursuit was not politically incorrect. I stumbled into my apartment at about 3 a.m. after having been turned down by several teenyboppers at a joint where I was at least 20 years older than anyone at the bar. It was all honest fun that had little chance to evolve into a serious sexual encounter. Most of the women at the bar were girls who had recently reached puberty and were not old enough to drink legally. They gained entrance only because they were cute, had great asses, or both. The last thing they wanted to do was to make out with an old fart like me.

My client pursued a number of young beauties and predictably struck out every time. His potbelly and triple chin offset the attraction of his gold Rolex, Zegna suit, and Hermes tie. Even an exposed wad of c-notes didn't help, and he went back to his hotel alone, drunk, and horny, just like me.

As I tiptoed into my bedroom, SS ambushed me. Actually, she was asleep and was startled by the smell of perspiration (it was 90 degrees with 90% humidity outside), alcohol (I drank too much) and garlic (we ate at an expensive Italian restaurant). When she screamed, "You're disgusting," I responded, "I suppose a blow job would be out of the question?" SS spun onto her stomach as I climbed into our underutilized love nest. When we used to have sex, SS told me regularly that I wasn't a great lay, so I guess she figured I'd be even worse after a night on the town.

It felt like 30 seconds passed before the alarm went off at 6 a.m. I wanted to get an early start because I was scheduled to go to Chicago to meet with Gil Richards, CEO of my largest client, and eat too much, drink too much, and try to get laid. The clock radio was set on a hard rock station and I heard "… I wanna give you my love … every inch of my love … oh, whole lotta love, brrr …" Robert Plante (of Led Zepplin fame) was screaming at the top of his lungs. Brrr is supposed to represent the sound that Jimmy Paige, the lead guitarist, makes with his guitar after that verse. In any case, it scared the crap out of me. I jumped up from an alcohol-induced coma, "Oh my God."

SS, of course, answered, "Shut the goddamn radio and get up." I hope you don't have to share your life with a bitch!

I followed orders and dragged my tired ass into the bathroom to relieve myself, noting that I managed to sleep from three until almost six without having to piss. This was close to a record for me this year. Maybe excessive amounts of booze are good for your prostate. I'll have to ask my urologist about this the next time he gives me a digital exam. I changed into running shorts and put on my sneakers. It's very important to exercise the morning after an eating and drinking orgy, lest you become a fat slob. I almost puked when I bent over to tie my sneakers but recovered in mid gag.

As I exited my building, I said good morning to the doorman. "Tough night, Mr. Spencer?"

"Do I look that bad?"

"Not so bad." He didn't want to be too honest and jeopardize his holiday tip.

My apartment is located at Park Avenue and 80th Street on the west side of the street. It's also known as the WASP side of the street. The rich ethnics live on the east side. The benefit of living on the WASP side is that you don't have to cross Park Avenue to get to Central Park. It sounds like a big deal, but it's not, and I regret paying more for the honor. It's only important if you have young children and you want to decrease the number of times your nanny crosses Park with a baby carriage to get to Central Park.

Anyway, I made a right turn out of the front door and headed to 79th Street, which would lead me to the Central Park. After I turned right off of Park, but before I reached Central Park, I had to make my way past a small army of men protecting the Mayor's home between Madison and Fifth Avenues.

I heard Mike B. likes to get an early start to his day at Gracie Mansion and commutes from 79th Street. I can understand why Mike lives here rather than in Gracie Mansion. Recently, I attended a fund-raiser he hosted at his brownstone, and it's one fabulous place. I read that Gracie Mansion is getting a little old and rundown because the City can't afford to refurbish it. Most former mayors didn't care about the condition of the Mansion and lived there in spite of it deteriorating state. They just wanted the free rent. Mike is loaded and would rather live his own palace with his own toys.

Just as I got to the doorstep of his brownstone, the Man himself popped out and I ran into him. Before I knew it, I was on the ground with one of the Mayor's gorillas holding me down. They frisked me and determined that I wasn't a terrorist with a bomb taped to my chest and allowed me to get up. I sent the Mayor flying when I hit him, and his suit ripped when he landed on the ground. All of his gofers rushed to pick him up and brush him off. Oh oh, the Mayor will be late today. Certainly, he couldn't go to Gracie Mansion in a ripped suit after having rolled around on the urine soaked sidewalk.

I approached the Mayor, and his bodyguards started to draw their weapons. I said, "Easy boys, I just want to apologize for bumping into hizzoner."

Mike was a real sport. He realized he wasn't in any mortal danger and started to laugh about the incident. "That was quite a hit you put on me."

"I suppose I should introduce myself, Mr. Mayor. My name's Stoke Spencer. I'm a real fan of yours." I figured he'd think I was a jock because of my name.

"Nice to meet you, Stoke. Give your name and address to my people, and I'll send you a bill for my suit."

He's a goddamn billionaire and he wanted me to pay for his suit? All of a sudden his entire entourage began to laugh out loud when they saw my reaction. "You really got me, Mr. Mayor. How about I buy you a drink sometime and make a contribution to your favorite charity?"

"Sounds good to me. Take care, Stoke. You must have been some athlete with that name." He walked back into his brownstone giggling and shaking his head. I don't know why he was so amused, as he had a ripped suit and was going to be late for work. No one would believe that some middle-aged dork in running shorts ran him down outside his home.

It was already 75 degrees and guess what, it was humid as hell. I was already drenched in my own perspiration. I proceeded up the path adjacent to the Metropolitan Museum onto the inner road of the Park. It's 6.2 miles of agony in this type of weather. Usually, I cut off before I get to the hilly part near Harlem. But I was invigorated by having almost killed the Mayor of New York. Today, I'd go the distance.

I used to jog a lot. In fact, I ran several marathons ten years earlier, but no more. I had to decrease my mileage because my knees and back couldn't take the pounding. And I was too lazy to do the training required to get ready for a race. I used to spend hours running loops in the Park. You have to run 18 miles at least one time before the race to prepare yourself for "the wall." Most runners have heard of the wall, but few ever experienced it. It rises up from the running surface after 18 or 20 miles and makes you feel sick as hell. In the New York Marathon, the wall rears its ugly head sometime after you cross the 59th Street Bridge and run up First Avenue. Usually you're so psyched by the screaming crowds that the damage you're doing to your body doesn't hit you until you approach the Willis Avenue Bridge (where the crowds thin out). That's when I started to feel like shit and really had to gut it out. People of all sizes and shapes run marathons, but many good athletes can't complete it because their bodies can't take the abuse.

Theoretically, your body can only run so far, and you'll literally die after some number of miles. I think that was what happened to the first guy who ran this distance during a war in Greece a few thousand years ago. He ran from one place to another about 26 miles to deliver a message from one commander to another, and dropped dead. I can assure you that I felt like I was going to croak every time I ran this race. The first time, I finished near the end of the pack just as dusk approached. SS and the boys were waiting for me for a long time near the finish line. I finally staggered in and found them in the family waiting area. Every single spot on my body was screaming in pain, but none worse than the bottom of my feet, which were bruised from pounding on the pavement for such a long time. I could barely walk the three or four blocks to my apartment.

When I arrived, I fell into a hot tub, which really felt terrific. After soaking for about 30 minutes, I tried to get up, but no dice. My body didn't respond and I was stuck in the tub. I called out for SS, who, by the way, thought the whole marathon thing was a colossal waste of time. She attempted to drag my body out of the water but couldn't (I outweighed her by 70 pounds). Ultimately, I was able to scale over the wall of the tub and crawl across the floor to my bed. I fell asleep for a while and woke up fairly refreshed, but walking was a problem. During my nap, SS looked in on me and I had a bloody nose. She thought I was going to pass away in my sleep (no such luck for her).

For the next few days, my thighs hurt so badly, I couldn't walk down stairs because the jolt from every step made me scream out in pain. So, I descended backwards. At GYP, I received some very odd looks as I navigated down the stairs connecting our two floors.

After I got into the runners' queue on the inner road, I established an easy pace. That means that most everybody was zipping past me. I'm not a very fast runner. In fact, I finished 22,582nd (out of 24,000) in the last New York Marathon I ran.

The great thing about running when it's so warm out is that all the women get really wet with perspiration and you can see through their clothes. Half of them are running in my direction, so I get to look at their wet asses as they pass me (it pays to be slow). And I get a wet t-shirt experience from the women running in the other direction. From time to time, my competitive juices start to flow and I won't let another runner pass me without a fight. It's usually a chick, because I really can't run with the men. I want to tell them that my name is Stoke as they ultimately do pass me, so they know they were in a battle with a real athlete.

One of the interesting things about running is that it stimulates your bowels. So, my morning jaunts have two purposes: one, to keep me from becoming a fat blob, and two, it enables me to put a major bathroom event behind me (so to speak). Guys carrying newspapers fighting for bathroom stalls dominate the morning hours at work. I think it's really gross to shower and then go to the bathroom (clean as a whistle and then you're not).

I heard a good story about a large investment bank that had a bathroom crisis. They built a gigantic trading floor with hundreds of people on it. Apparently, nobody gave enough thought to the daily bathroom rush. Traders usually arrive early and have a bite to eat. Like clockwork, after taking coffee (the principal way most guys get their bowels stirred up), they head directly to the john. Well, just imagine 50 or 60 men lined up in the lavatory nervously dancing in place waiting for an open stall. Even worse, think about how gross it must be in the bathroom after several hundred men have relieved themselves. The firm's janitors had to do their magic two or three times each morning.

Let's get back to the Park. I usually get the urge about half way through my jog. A tiny stirring grows slowly into severe spasms, and on some days it's a struggle to get back home in time. Accompanying stomach pain is gas. So, as I putter around the jogging route, I usually pass wind (I'll bet most people do, including the women). This isn't a suave thing to do, especially for someone trying to impress the babes, so I try to pick my release points carefully. On occasion, it's impossible to hold it in, and I get dirty looks from the runners who are unlucky to be downwind. The doormen know I'm usually in distress, and are on the lookout for me. If I'm sprinting back, they hold the door open and get me into the elevator as quickly as possible.

When I arrived back at the apartment on this fateful day, I was under control from a bowel perspective and casually walked into my building. The doormen were relieved. They're concerned that one of these mornings I won't get to a bathroom in time and will do the dirty deed in the lobby. It'd be horrifying. So, it's in their best interests to get me upstairs as quickly as possible.

It was almost 7 a.m. and my wife was in the kitchen drinking coffee. SS is a thin, blonde-haired Irish gal. When dressed up she's attractive, but in the morning without makeup she looks like a skinny teenager. Her attributes from a purely sexual perspective aren't great. When I try to feel her up, sometimes I miss, get it? Not much up on top. But her legs are slim and her ass is tight. It doesn't matter any more because I seldom got to touch anything on her body. The boys were still in bed and wouldn't stir until one of us literally dragged them from under the covers. "Good morning." I tried to be pleasant.

"You came in late last night." SS didn't look up and she didn't say it in a nice way.

"Important client, who likes to have a few drinks after dinner. Pretty innocent stuff."

She stared straight into my eyes. "When are you going to grow up? Why must you go to bars with young girls and make a fool out of yourself?"

"I didn't make a fool out of myself. I was just entertaining my client." I guess I wasn't too convincing.

Rage filled her face and SS didn't look great when she was angry. "Are you looking to end our marriage? If so, you're doing all the right things. I'm not going to put up with this anymore. You come home drunk every night. It's not something I want the boys to see. You're not setting a good example."

"You act like I'm abusive or something. And I don't get drunk every night."

"Stoke, you're such a loser. You stopped making me happy a long time ago. You don't care about my needs. You only focus on work and going out to bars."

"I'm sorry you feel that way. Frankly, your attitude and lack of interest in me is creating much of the problem you so ineloquently described. You're a cold woman."

"And you're a rotten husband. You're not an attractive person, so I don't want to be close to you. Is that so hard for you to understand?"

"No, because I feel the same way about you." I went to the counter and poured a cup of coffee. It was too weak. "Something else. Your coffee tastes like crap."

"We need to talk about our relationship. If things don't improve soon, you may have to leave." What struck me was how coldly she said the words. It was as if she practiced her little speech.

I wanted to think about my next move and not say something dumb but couldn't control myself. "Listen, you better be careful because you just might get your wish. I work my ass off and earn a terrific living. You and the kids benefit by my efforts. Not once have you contributed to this family financially. You depend on me and I can make your life miserable. Hell, you may even have to do your own nails to save money."

"Don't threaten me, Stokley." Holy shit, she never calls me Stokley. I guess I'm not much of an athlete in her eyes. "I'm entitled to your money. I've already talked to my attorney about that."

"You talked to an attorney, about divorce?"

"Yes."

"Well, I suppose we're already on the slippery slope." I was feeling really mean at this point and decided to say something to really infuriate SS. "I'm pretty horny. I didn't get laid last night. How about one last fuck for old times sake?" You never know.

"Get out of my sight."

I showered and left as quickly as possible wondering what happens after you have a conversation like that with your wife. When I got off the elevator, the doorman knew I needed a taxi. It was amazing how service from doormen was directly related to the size of your holiday tips. I give them relatively large holiday gratuities And in return, they hold the door open for me. What a deal.

The doormen on Park Avenue and in all of the high-end buildings have an attitude. Have you ever noticed it? It's like they're providing some kind of special service that requires an advanced degree. And it pisses me off when they threaten to strike, which seems to happen every two years. Just how much do they think they should be paid? Is it $100,000, or $200,000 for opening doors and hailing taxis? I think these not-so-hard working men should ask their union leaders why they are always striking, causing them to lose pay.

After that repartee with my wife, the last thing I wanted to do was to get into a taxi with some sleaze ball that hadn't bathed in a week. Maybe my taxi would be air-conditioned. Right! A taxi pulled up to the curb just as the humid air hit me. A layer of haze hung over the city and blocked the sun. I got in the taxi, no air and the body odor almost made me barf. I almost opened the door and got out, but with my luck I wouldn't get another ride. And besides, I had a short trip down Park Avenue to 52nd Street.

A few years ago, the TLC (Taxi and Limousine Commission), endorsed the installation of security walls between the drivers and the passengers (the Berlin Wall of taxis). In any case, the walls are too thick. Normal people don't fit in the taxis. In fact, dwarfs and children don't fit either.

The problem is that there isn't enough room between the wall and the seat for your feet. You have to turn your feet diagonally (pigeon-toed or duck style) to get in and out of the car. On more than one occasion my very reasonably sized feet (size ten) have gotten wedged between the wall and the seat.

To make matters worse, taxi companies once enlisted cartoon characters, athletes, comedians, and opera singers to suggest that you buckle up (fortunately this has ended). N Yers don't need to be reminded that driving in the city is one of the most hazardous experiences known to man. Considering that New York cabbies only have driving experience in lesser-developed countries, the danger is understood by all. Nevertheless, I don't need a red puppet screaming in my ear.

When I got in the taxi, the driver mumbled something and I said, "52nd and Park please."

He mumbled something else and I said, "Excuse me."

He repeated himself. I said, "Sorry I can't understand you."

He said something else and the only word I understood was "fuck." I said, "Did you call me a fuck?"

The driver stopped the car, as he recognized the f-word and probably thought I was cursing him. He turned around and I said, "Please take me to 52 and Park" in the clearest English I could muster. I said it loudly thinking that volume would offset his inability to communicate in English.

He said, "Okay," and proceeded. After getting the shit kicked out of me by SS, I was worried the cab driver might do a number on me as well.

The car ride was uneventful except that I was drenched and wrinkled by the time we drove a few city blocks. I looked like shit, the same as everybody else who commuted to work on days like today.

When I arrived at my building, the sun had broken through the haze and the temperature felt ten degrees warmer. My feet got stuck as I tried to get out of the taxi and I had a thought. Maybe the cars were designed to trap your feet, so that you couldn't run away to avoid paying the fare. That's it. I feel better now that I solved the feet and taxi wall enigma. I dragged my small travel bag and myself into the building to face new challenges at GYP.

THE THONG

I entered my building dripping with perspiration, looking as if I had worked a full day as an attendant in a sauna bath. It was great to feel the cool air on my body.

My next adventure was getting past security. Our building is no different than any other major edifice in New York. After the 9/11 attacks, security was ratcheted up to combat terrorism. I've always been a tad skeptical about the effectiveness of these security measures, as they served more to inconvenience building occupants than discourage the scumbags that want to kill innocent Americans. But like everyone else, I am trying to live with this new reality. However, I wasn't in the mood to cooperate today. I walked up to the guard and he said, "ID please."

"My ID is packed in my brief case. You know who I am?" I had worked in the building for the past ten years, and the guard had worked in the building for the past ten years. Why the hell did I have to show him my ID? If I wanted to blow the place up, I'd have done it a long time ago.

"Of course I know you, but we have to follow the rules."

I wondered if Norm Cohen, our CEO, had to show his ID when he entered the building. I doubt it. So I asked the guard, "When I become CEO of GYP, will I still need to show you my badge?" It was a trick question because I'd never be CEO of GYP or any other company for that matter. If the guard said no, I was going to raise hell, but he knew how to respond to obnoxious people like me.

"Mr. Spencer (The guard used my name, I told you he knows who I am. Does he need practice checking employee IDs?), when you become CEO you can change all the rules to suit yourself. If you want us to check every person but you, tell us, and we'll comply. Mr. Cohen is the CEO and he wants everyone's ID inspected before they enter the building."

"Did he tell you to check his ID each time he comes to work?"

"I'd have to kill you if I answered that question." He smiled at me.

"You're not funny."

I decided to drop it, along with all of the crap in my briefcase. When I opened my bag to dig out my ID, all my papers, pens, tissues, coins and condoms fell on the floor. I really didn't have any condoms, but it would've been funny to see the looks on everyone's face if a dozen prophylactics flew across the foyer. "Godammit, this is bullshit. I'm going to have you fired."

"Please, Mr. Spencer, no profanity. When you reach the top spot, you can fire me. I'll leave without protest. I promise. Now just show me your ID and move along."

"Wiseass." I found the ID and flashed it at the guard in a way that he couldn't have seen my picture or my name, then stuffed everything back into my briefcase and stormed towards the elevator.

Nothing of note happened between the elevator and my office, other than the tingle I felt as I walked through the investment banking bullpen and saw Laura. Laura Ward is the resident

Grace Kelly look-alike, five feet eight inches of heaven. Her blonde hair and long legs made her the fantasy of every guy at the firm. The growing bulge in my pants proved she was my fantasy as well. Most of us would cut our pinky off to see her walk around in a thong, the outline of which was visible when she wore white pants. She wasn't wearing pants today, darn it. She wore a little mini skirt that was hiked up to the top of her thighs for all the men to enjoy.

Josh Aaron is her boss and he arranged her work area in such a way that he got a treat every time she spun around (assuming she was wearing a skirt, otherwise he had to settle for the outline of her thong).

Josh is the most popular guy on the floor, not because of his personality, but because of Laura. Actually, Josh is a dork, who's also a pervert. All my partners arranged to have meetings in Josh's office whenever we could, so we could ogle Laura. In fact, we tried to have meetings in his office even if he wasn't participating in the meeting. The clerical staff would always ask why we wanted to use Josh's office rather than a comfortable conference room. They finally figured it out, and it really annoyed them. The women were all jealous of Laura's looks and the attention she received.

As far as I knew at the time, nobody at GYP ever went out with Laura (I later found out this wasn't the case). Sometimes I wondered whether she was just an attractive gal, who dressed fashionably, or whether she intended to drive all the men crazy. I sure would like to see her in that thong.

I approached my office and good old Liz was waiting for me. She's been my secretary—sorry my assistant—for the past seven years.

Such bullshit, you had to call an airline stewardess a flight attendant, and a secretary an assistant. What warped feminist mind concluded that it was a form of sexual harassment to be called "stewardess" or "secretary"? Maybe SS was part of this conspiracy. She has a warped mind.

Anyway, Liz Palmer was your typical BBQer. She was born, raised, and currently lives in the same neighborhood in Queens. Every day she takes the number 7 Subway into Grand Central arriving at the office at 8:45 a.m. and leaves at 6 p.m. Nevertheless, she's a great assistant.

I suppose I should define the term "BBQer." That's 'Brooklyn, Bronx and Queens' girl. First of all, you know a BBQer is approaching by the way she speaks. BBQers have a Bronx or Brooklyn or Staten Island accent and they never stop yakking. Let's put it this way, Henry Higgins (of my "My Fair Lady" fame) would be appalled by the way these women enunciate words. Moreover, BBQers curse a lot and don't give a shit if it's not ladylike. Liz has a mouth that would make a sailor blush. Further, they all have big hair. It's at least shoulder length, teased and poofed up with a blow dryer, or however women achieve that effect. Liz has really big dirty blonde hair. I'm sure a physical inspection would prove that she isn't a real blonde. In fact, she's had several hair colors while working for me. Most BBQers are either anorexically skinny or chubby. Liz is on the heavy side. And these women are NY fashion plates. There's a way they all dress that makes them immediately recognizable. It's sort of a contemporary slut look.

But most important, they're sexually available to high-powered male professionals. The pool of BBQers who have satisfied the prurient needs of New York executives has been endless. They get dolled up every year for holiday parties and look to dance (and grind) with guys earning six figure salaries. Sex is on everyone's mind at these events. I'm not degrading this group of New York females. Rather, I want to thank them on behalf of all male investment bankers for the service they have provided to our industry over the years. I hope all female BBQers get married, procreate, and deliver the next generation of BBQers to us.

You're probably wondering whether Laura is a BBQer. Not on your life. She's not ethnic, she has long straight blonde hair, and she lives in Manhattan on the Upper West Side.

"Stoke, how's it hanging?"

I can't believe she speaks to me this way. "Liz, a little professionalism please. Cohen would've had a fit if he heard you use that language." I smiled.

She smiled back at me. "Screw 'um. You're the biggest producer at this place, and I know you'll protect me against any harassment accusations made against me."

"Damn right I will. You're mine, you're protected."

She followed me into my office with some black coffee and said, "Why don't you ditch that skinny brat you're married to and take a tumble with me." She started laughing. Liz often listened to the screaming matches I've had with SS over the phone. She's not shy about speaking her mind.

"If I got a divorce and hooked up with you, I wouldn't be able to afford your makeup and hairdressing expenses." She laughed even harder.

By the way, Liz has been married twice and was not serious about sleeping with me. She's only attracted to BBQ men who have big potbellies and can drink and have sex all night (I sort of have a pot-belly, but I wouldn't be able to perform the other service). She thinks bankers are wimps, and would rather have a man who could slap her around and survive her counter attack.

"You still going to Chicago today?"

"Yes, I'm meeting with Gil Richards at his office and then out for a night of debauchery. God help me. If I had more clients like Gil, I'd have to check into detox."

"You know, you have a meeting with Cohen in five minutes?"

I groaned. The guy's such an asshole. I can't believe he hasn't fired me. He's always on my case and I'd like to strangle him. "I've been trying not to think about it."

"That guy walks around here like he has a stick up his ass. Does he think he's so much better than all of us?"

"The simple answer is yes. Not only that, he thinks he's better than all his partners and treats us like we owe him a debt of gratitude. I suppose I should head over to his office."

I turned away from Liz and reluctantly made my way across the huge investment-banking floor towards Norm's office. My relationship with Cohen has always been a stormy one. He's the consummate nitpicker, and I'm a big picture guy. Norm gets furious when a colleague travels first class on an airplane even if the client is paying for the ticket. He thinks it sets a bad precedent, and the person might try to get away with flying in the front of the plane when GYP is paying the bill. I keep telling Norm that GYP's policy is clear: economy class and no exceptions. If someone violates the rule they can be fired. No one is going to risk his or her career for something as trivial as a larger seat on a plane.

I believe that if the client is paying, do whatever the hell you want so long as it's legal. Cohen always gets crazy when I espouse the libertarian perspective. In any case, Norm is the managing partner and I'm accountable to him.

More importantly, he decides how much I get paid every year with the approval of the compensation committee of the Board. To his credit, Norm tries to deal with differences between his bonus number and individual partner expectations beforehand.

Having said this, never in the history of investment banking has a boss and a senior banker agreed on a compensation figure. It's always a knock down, dragged out fight. Millions of dollars are at stake, so conflict is inevitable. I couldn't perform this aspect of Norm's job. For the last three months of our fiscal year, which ends on September 30, he spends nearly 100% of his time engaged in the compensation process. I'd be reluctant to negotiate with each person and would probably bankrupt the company by paying everybody too much.

I took the opportunity to walk past Laura's area again. I was hoping she'd get up and show me something, anything, upper thigh, panties, anything. No such luck. She was engaged in a heated conversation on the phone. Josh Aaron wanted to talk, but I was so disappointed about Laura that I just walked away from his office.

When I reached Norm's office, his secretary told me to go right in even though he was on the phone. Investment bankers are always on the phone. It's a wonder we get any work done and we all don't suffer serious neck injuries. A phone is always planted between our head and shoulders. GYP should pay for chiropractic services.

Cohen quickly dismissed whomever he was speaking with and greeted me with a big smile. I'm fucked. A smile means he's going to try to screw me. I hadn't given my compensation much thought because it wouldn't be paid for several months, so I was at a real disadvantage because Norm always gives administrative crap a lot of thought very early on. "Come on in, pal."

I wanted to tell him to shove it because I wasn't his pal, but there was too much money riding on the conversation.

"Hello Norm, how's it hanging?" I used Liz's line.

"How's it hanging? Is that what you asked me? What the hell kind of greeting is that?"

"It's supposed to be a male bonding sort of comment. Forget it. I was just trying to be friendly."

"Stoke, you're one of the top partners in this firm, and your behavior is so bizarre at times. I hope you don't speak to any of our junior people in that fashion."

"Look, we're not getting any younger, and I think it's refreshing to at least attempt to communicate with the young people at their level. Why do you make such a big fucking deal out of every inconsequential thing? Chill out."

"Would you please shut the door?" I complied. "You must represent the firm internally in a way that you want our subordinates to represent the firm to outsiders. Speaking like a homeboy isn't the right way to accomplish this. Using profanity is unacceptable. Honestly, you make it difficult for me every time we get together. It's as if you want to incite me to say or do something not in our collective best interests."

"What are you talking about? Do you think I sit at home and think of ways to annoy you? No, I could care less. But when I see you and you start talking to me in a condescending manner, I have the urge to say something that will hopefully ruin your day."

"I was hoping to have a productive conversation with you. I want your compensation discussion to be an uplifting experience. Considering we're here to discuss your bonus, it's puzzling why you'd choose this moment to bust my balls."

"I thought you said profanity was unacceptable. Isn't 'bust your balls' profanity? As far as my bonus is concerned, I'm the leading rainmaker at this firm. You're not going to fuck with my compensation. If you do, I'll walk across the street with every one of my clients. So, don't threaten me."

"Why don't we just start over? I'm not interested in having a love fest. I know you don't care for me, personally, and to be frank I think you're unprofessional. So there you have it. Nevertheless, I set compensation levels, including yours. So let's get to it and end this meeting as quickly as possible. Okay?"

"Good idea."

"As you know, the 20th Century is over and times have changed for all investment banks. We can no longer pay out every dime we earn to our employees. We must save for a rainy day."

"Please, Norm, save the bullshit. I am the investment banking business in this firm. I know how tough it is out there. And I'm not just an employee of this firm, I'm a partner."

"I'll skip my introductory remarks and get right to the point. Last year you were paid a $5 million bonus, the highest bonus in the company except for mine. I told the Board that it would be prudent to hold back a portion of everyone's compensation just in case the business does not return to previous levels."

"Is the Board holding back any of your compensation?"

"That's none of your business."

"Wrong, and your response is the answer to my question. It's one of the primary problems I have with you. You're willing to dish out pain, but not willing to share in it. You're the worst kind of manager. Take all the credit, and transfer risk to others. Let me be blunt. I'm not willing to have any of my compensation held back unless you do the same. If you have a problem, I'll go directly to the compensation committee."

"You're a brave fellow. I'm on the verge of throwing your ass out of here. Your insubordinate attitude is unacceptable. You had better choose your words carefully from this moment forward."

"I told you not to threaten me. I'm in the deal business, and I know how to negotiate. Since I'm directly or indirectly responsible for nearly 50% of the revenues of this firm, neither you nor the Board will take any action against me."

"Well, I'll let the Board know how you feel. In the meantime, your bonus will be $4 million in cash and $1 million in subordinated debt. The latter will mature in five years and carry a 4% deferred interest coupon. The principal and coupon of the debt will be forfeited if you quit or are fired for cause. Do you understand? I'm not negotiating. If you have a problem with this arrangement, you can go fuck yourself."

"Just so you know, I don't have any problems with any of the provisions. My only problem is that you have not agreed to the same arrangement. And I intend to discuss this issue with the Board."

"Get out of my office."

I walked out of Norm's office as fast as I could, expecting something to hit me in the back of the head. The man's a putz. Great start to the day. A divorce conversation with my wife and fuck-you contest with my boss, what could be better? I better avoid sex. With my luck, I'd come down with venereal disease.

Realistically, I didn't think I was at risk. My contributions to GYP were so great that insubordination on the grandest scale wouldn't result in me being axed. And as I indicated to Norm, I could easily take my revenues and my clients to a competitor. Also, my partners were comforted by the fact that I wasn't interested in moving up the corporate ladder.

My career aspirations for higher office ended a few years ago, so the only thing my colleagues had to do was to put up with my anti-social behavior and pay me an amount of money reflective of my annual business accomplishments. In other words, I didn't compete with anybody internally for power or position.

My office duties were not yet complete. Senior bankers are responsible for the behavior of junior people, and we sort of adopt young professionals when they're hired. No specific associates or analysts are assigned to me, but a few work with me regularly on certain clients. If a client is comfortable with a particular junior person, that person will likely work on all future deals.

Anyway, I was getting some of my own medicine from the best associate in the firm. Rob Viand graduated from the Wharton School at the University of Pennsylvania. He didn't return to school to get his MBA because he didn't need to. I'd bet a year's salary that he has the highest IQ in the firm. His ability to understand the finer points of the mergers and acquisitions business is uncanny. Not only is he technically proficient, clients love the guy.

He's a six-foot two-inch Greek-American. As the first person to ever go to college in his family, he's a hero. When he told his father that he earned a million dollars a few years ago, the old man went crazy, organized a party, and told every single relative about his salary. Of course, Rob was mortified, but it would have been disrespectful not to tell his father about his success.

Unfortunately, Rob wasn't respectful to any senior partners at the firm, except me. From the start of his career, he was always correcting managing directors, and calling them morons when they asked him stupid questions. He's right, some of them are morons, but you just can't say these things to senior people. Some MDs would come to me whining about how Rob raked them over the coals and that I better do something about it.

The first time I spoke to him, I told him I'd throw him out the window if he insulted any of my partners again. The irony of that statement should not escape the reader. Rob could crush me without ever breaking into a sweat. The threat was metaphorical.

Usually, I ignored the crybabies because Rob was just an outstanding young banker. At our compensation meetings, I always recommended him for bonuses significantly greater than his peers, which also pissed off my colleagues. They longed for the day that Rob would resign and go to graduate school like 90% of the young people in our business.

Every bulge bracket firm required analysts to resign after four or five years to complete their education. After a long dinner two years ago, which included many martinis and a bottle of wine, Rob convinced me to make him an associate. "Fuck the MBA," he said in a drunken stupor at the time. "You know I'm better than most of your partners. I don't need an MBA."

He was correct, and I was drunk. "Right, fuck the MBA."

When I told my partners that I granted Rob dispensation from the MBA requirement, they were outraged. I told them that I was making him a permanent part of my team, and he was no longer their concern. You really can take advantage of your business colleagues when you're more successful than they are. So, for the past two years, Rob and I have churned out fees together. He's still pissing people off, but usually I let it slide, until now.

Rob works 80 or 90 hours a week. He has little time to, how shall I say this, get laid. Please understand. Rob could be a movie star with his slick Mediterranean looks, wavy hair, and incredible physique. He gets up at 5:30 every morning to run and lift weights. So, he doesn't hesitate to take advantage of all sexual opportunities, even if they involve fellow employees.

For the past few days, he'd been taking long lunches. And on a couple of occasions, I saw him walking into the office a few minutes after some of the secretaries. At first I ignored it. He wouldn't be stupid enough to bang a secretary, I mean assistant, would he? But I could see a trend developing. I decided to confront him today.

Rob was standing in the bullpen and I yelled to get his attention. That's the area where all of the analysts and junior associates work. Rob has an office, but he's often with the junior people giving them instructions about one deal or another. "Rob, I need to speak with you. Come to my office when you're done."

"I'll be right over," he hollered back to me. The bullpen is a noisy place with a lot of activity and piles of papers all over the place.

In about three minutes, Rob knocked and walked into my office. "What's up?"

"Shut the door and sit down." It wasn't unusual to close doors because we frequently work on confidential transactions, so Rob wasn't suspicious. "I want to talk to you about a personal issue."

"Did I screw something up?" The man is so engaged in the business. He was going to be a gigantic success, if I could only keep him under control.

"Sort of. Are you banging any secretaries?"

"What?"

"You heard me."

"Why is that any of your business?"

"This isn't the time for your wiseass attitude. I've always protected you from the jerks in this place who would like to set you loose, even though you're the best associate we have. But interoffice sex isn't defensible. It's stupid and dangerous."

"I'm seeing Laura."

I was speechless and jealous and my jaw nearly hit the floor. I tried to rally. "I want you to end it now. Or, if she wants to quit, you can have a relationship with her." I should have known it was Laura.

"Come on, Stoke. We're just having a little fun. I work my ass off around here and it's hard for me to get out socially. She's convenient."

"Trust me. When you dump her she'll sue you and GYP for sexual harassment. That's where the problem lies. My partners and I can't depend upon a happy ending to your romance. And we can't have you dating any other females at GYP either."

"What if I refuse to comply? Will you really take action against me?"

"Afraid so. Your running roughshod around the firm makes my partners very edgy, but it's an internal issue. It doesn't threaten the firm in any way. Egos are bruised, but lawsuits unlikely. What you're doing with Laura and the other women at the firm is really dangerous."

"I didn't mean any harm." Suddenly he stood up and swiped his hand across my desk knocking several things on the floor. I couldn't believe my eyes. He was starting to tear up.

"Why is this such a big deal? Are you in love with this woman? She's a knockout, but she's just a secretary."

"It really has less to do with Laura than with my family. The Viands have historically worked with their hands. We're a middle class, Greek family, and everyone gets married early and has a boatload of kids. I'm 30 years old and I don't even date. I have no time to date and fall in love. My family is putting a lot of pressure on me. One of my uncles asked me if I was gay. Can you believe it?"

"Are you? Only kidding." I tried to lighten it up, but Rob ignored me. "Seriously, ethnic families have a hard time dealing with the success of their young people. Most professionals are marrying later, and so the little ones come later. No big deal."

"You don't understand. My relatives think there's something wrong with me. I haven't brought a girl home to meet my family since I was in college. I haven't had a real relationship with a woman in five years."

"What does this have to do with Laura? Is she a person you want to bring home to your family?"

"Are you fucking kidding? My parents would disown me if I brought a woman home who wasn't Greek. I'm just banging Laura. By the way, she's amazing and has an incredible body."

"I'm getting excited. Let's get back to your situation. How do we get you back on track?"

"I'm going to quit. I need to get a job that gives me more time to concentrate on starting a family. I'll go nuts if I wait much longer."

"What did you say? You're going to quit? You must be kidding. This is a joke, right?"

"It's no joke. I'm working too hard. I've made enough money to buy the biggest house in Queens. I'm giving you notice right now. Two weeks and I'm gone. You've been great to me over the years, but I have to build a real life. Investment banking isn't a life, it's an obsession."

"You're ruining my business, Rob. You can't just walk out without advance notice."

"I'm giving you notice. Two weeks."

"Please reconsider. Think about it for a few days. You won't be happy as a ditch-digger. You're an investment banker. You make millions of dollars each year."

"I already thanked you for that. But I really did earn every nickel. I haven't been out of the office for more than a week in half a decade. I need rest and relaxation. I need to find a spoiled, black-haired Greek woman, who wants to have six babies. I'll be too old to have children if I wait much longer."

"What the hell are you talking about? Some old farts sire kids when they're seventy."

"Stoke, please understand. I must start now. I'll tell you about the things I did with Laura if you stop giving me a hard time. Okay?"

"I guess that's something. I'll wear a diaper when you tell me so I don't stain my trousers."

I came around the desk and hugged Rob. I was about to start crying. What a fucking day this was turning out to be. Rob walked out without another word.

As I emerged from my office, Liz asked me, "Is everything okay? I saw you guys kissing each other. I was concerned."

"Very funny. We were hugging, not kissing. Don't tell anybody, but Rob's resigning."

"You're kidding. What the hell brought that on? He's a terrific banker with a promising future."

"You're right. He's gotten himself crazy about starting a family and settling down." It's not easy being an associate in this business. Late hours and short vacations prevent many of the young people from developing relationships.

Women are the ones who suffer the most. Raising a family and working in this crazy industry is next to impossible. That's the reason why there are so few senior women in the business. Investment banks are always criticized for not promoting females to senior positions, but the reality is that they all quit before it can happen.

"I'm sorry, Stoke. I know you're close to the kid. He'll sure be missed. I may have trouble coming to work without his tight ass around here. Sure would've loved to bed down that young stud."

"Aren't you a little old for him, Liz?"

"Turn the lights off and he wouldn't care about my age, I can assure you. I'd give him a ride for his money."

"You're starting to gross me out. And besides, he's doing Laura."

"You're shitting me. What a pair they'd make. Their babies would be amazing."

"Don't get yourself nuts. Rob is only visiting with Laura. It's mandatory that he marry a Greek woman. His family would disown him if he created a mixed breed child."

Liz was about to get worked up about intermarriages. I could see it in her eyes. "What's with all this ethnic purity crap?"

"What are you getting at?" I pretended that I didn't know what she meant, and let her present her thoughts. I needed something to cheer me up.

"This is America, the melting pot of the world. Everyone should be fair game. There should be no limits about who can marry whom. Ethnic purity was a Nazi concept, and should not be condoned in this country."

"Hey, you're preaching to the choir. I have no problems with the races mixing it up. I think the kids are better looking when the parents are from different groups."

"Damn shame, in my opinion." Liz walked away to answer my phone. I walked back to my desk.

"It's your lovely wife on the phone," Liz screamed out. She hated using the intercom, and she hated SS.

Terrific, I'm going to have another confrontation with the bitch. I picked up the phone, "Hello."

"Stoke, we need to talk. We need to do it now."

"I'm leaving for Chicago and can't focus on our marriage right now. You'll just have to wait until I get back."

"That's bullshit. If you want to save our relationship, you should be more willing to talk and try to understand my side."

"We always talk about your perspective. We never talk about what's bothering me. You're a nagger, a total fucking pain in the ass." I said this a little too loud, and Liz closed my door. I smiled at her in appreciation.

"Stoke, do you want to be married to me or not? I have to know. I have options you know."

"Already have another sucker lined up, do ya? I thought you were planning this for some time. Your speech to me this morning sounded rehearsed."

"I've been unhappy for a long time. You don't satisfy me anymore."

"You don't give me a chance to satisfy you. When we first married, we had a good sexual relationship. Marrying you was the beginning of the end of all that. We should have just dated for the rest of our lives."

"That's nonsense. I tried very hard to please you. I agreed to do things that I had never done before, things that were uncomfortable."

"Like what? Having intercourse once a week in the missionary position isn't trying very hard. You're a prude. So don't give me any more crap about that. I really think this is the wrong time to get into our sexual compatibility."

"I want you out of the house now. This is the last straw." She was getting hysterical. "I tried so hard to make a nice life for you, but all you cared about was your job."

"This job enables you to dress like a queen, to have two homes and to drive around in fancy cars. After we got engaged, your father told me that I better make a lot of money or you'd drive me nuts. I should've walked away right then and there."

"You always hated my family."

"They're just like you, selfish, insular, dishonest, naïve, and arrogant. You're right. I hate their guts, every one of them."

"I never told you this, but I was abused as a child."

"Oh shit. Spare me. Are we on Jerry Springer? I could care less about what happened to you 20 years ago. It doesn't surprise me that one or more of your family are sexual deviants."

She was crying loudly. I'll bet she thought she could just walk away from me without feeling any remorse. But it doesn't work that way. There's no such thing as a smooth breakup. Shit, when I was a kid, I hated every girl I ever broke up with, regardless of who instigated the split. That's how I got over a relationship. It's impossible to be friends with someone you were formerly intimate with. "I don't want to talk anymore. We can get into this when I return."

It's interesting how things get pent up in a relationship. When you're trying to make a relationship work, you look the other way when your partner does something wrong. But you never really forget. You save it up and wait for the right moment to drop it on them. Sometimes these things come out when you argue. Ever notice how an argument over something stupid causes you to bring up an unrelated repressed feeling from the past? Happens to me all the time.

My life with SS has been shit. I allowed her to push me around for years. I went to work to escape her constant whining. I bought her whatever she wanted. I acquired peace and quiet. If she was shopping, she wasn't bugging me. These things have been building up inside me for a long time, and I suspect they'll all surface again and again during our conversations in the coming weeks.

Keep in mind that I'm really capable in this area. I'm an expert negotiator, and will rip her to shreds. SS will try to respond in kind, but she won't be a match for me. I was never mean to her or my children. They may think that I didn't give them enough time and all that stuff, but I never abused anyone verbally, mentally, or physically. I tried to be a good husband and father, and maybe I wasn't, but I wasn't unkind. My wife is a miserable bitch, and today is the day that this realization finally hit me. Our relationship was over, and I was going down the slippery slope no matter what.

The same holds true for relationships at work and friendships. We change every day during our lives. The changes happen slowly, and at some point, you experience an epiphany when all the seemingly insignificant things that happen to you give you new perspective.

Since this process takes so long to develop, I believe it's impossible to reverse. You can't force yourself to trivialize drops of water, when collectively they're like a tidal wave. So when the epiphany takes place, you feel obligated to put your issues on the table with your wife, co-workers, or friends. If the issues are serious enough, relationships are in jeopardy.

As far as marriage is concerned, the ubiquitous reasons are the welfare of the children, financial concerns, and personal insecurity. It's ludicrous to think that a shitty marriage is better for the children than termination. Similarly, it's naive to think that a couple can keep their problems from their children.

I believe focusing all my efforts on making the children happy, and not wasting any time on a broken relationship, is the best course. Sometimes two people can't break up because they can't decide who should get what. And sometimes, dependence comes into play.

Laws relating to marital dissolution are supposed to create a comfort zone for husbands and wives, when one is financially dependent on the other. But it never works out that way in real life. For goodness sake, some wives never balance a checkbook during their marriage. If their husbands leave or die, they're incapable of even paying the bills. In any event, when the initial sore is opened, it won't heal. People don't get divorced after one argument.

I was feeling pretty rotten about my conversation with SS. I can't pinpoint what bothered me the most, the inevitable breakup of my marriage or the hassle related to a divorce. But I felt weak. I thought that ogling at Laura might perk me up.

Now that I knew Laura was an active heterosexual female, I was even more excited about seeing her, and any of her underclothes. I sashayed over to Josh's office. Fortunately, Laura was at her desk, and fortunately, Josh was in his office and not on the phone. I knocked and walked in and said, "How you doin, pal?"

"Look what the cat dragged in. You look like shit. What's the matter?"

"Marital problems. I'm gonna break up with my psychotic wife."

"Is that right? I'd say I'm sorry, but I'm not. She's a first class c... Oops I almost said the "C" word. I'm trying to not to use it anymore. I was out last week and the word slipped out of my mouth and my date went berserk. And I wasn't even referring to her."

"You got that right. Of all the names you can call a woman, that single word makes them the craziest. From a man's perspective, the guttural sound of the word is fantastic. It's without a doubt the most descriptive word to characterize a miserable woman."

"What happened between Sharon and you?"

"Got ten hours? It's a long story that's now coming to an end. I'm sick of her. Our relationship has become a living hell for me. We don't even have sex any more." Josh wasn't really a close friend and I didn't know why I was telling him all this, but I needed someone to talk to. I probably should've made an appointment to see a shrink.

"Why would you stay married to a woman who doesn't put out? Sex is repayment for all the abuse men have to take."

"Precisely my thoughts." For a moment, I considered the importance of sex to a marriage. It's inconceivable that a marriage can be strong without sexual interaction. Not that every happy couple swings from the chandeliers and has explosive orgasms every night, although that wouldn't be so bad. But intimacy is the glue that holds a marriage together.

The need to be physically close to another person starts at birth and wanes to a certain extent, as you get older. But it's very important to alleviate stress and to express affection for someone (like your wife or another woman). Sexual activity is the ultimate gratification for men and women, no matter what women say.

Sexual problems often occur when men are more concerned about their own pleasure. I could understand a woman being disenchanted if every time she had sex, her husband had an orgasm and gave his wife nothing in return. Guys, you can't climb on, hump, and have a cigarette (smoking after sex is gross, but it used to be fashionable). You gotta give something if you want her to come back for more.

"Well the process is excruciating. Take it from me. I've been divorced twice. In fact, I should give you my attorney's name. She's an animal. You'll love her. Plus she's good looking, so the whole time you're fighting with your wife, you'll be thinking of boning her."

Josh is an okay guy, and an excellent deal person. He comes from a traditional Jewish home in which economics are paramount. In that regard, I'm sure his own family gives him an A+, after all he earns a few million dollars annually. However, Josh's current home life leaves something to be desired. Basically, he doesn't have one.

His first marriage lasted about three years and yielded two daughters. He met his first wife at Dartmouth, where they were in the MBA program. Her background made her a perfect catch, as far as Josh's family was concerned. She was from an Orthodox family. Their lives together were built around traditional Jewish values, which were a little too conservative for

Josh's taste. His family was Orthodox as well, but he eschewed the rules and regulations of the truly faithful.

Anyway, the happy couple had a ceremony that would've made the most fundamentalist Rabbi rejoice. They consummated their marriage in the old fashioned way, sometime between the ceremony and the gefilte fish course in a backroom at the synagogue. It must be the official sex room of the congregation. I wonder if they have mirrors on the ceiling and porno available to turn on the happy couple.

Of course, the ceremony started after sunset on Saturday and included the glass stomping ritual. The synagogue is located in a lower class part of Brooklyn, and so the affair was a major disappointment to Josh's parents. They were hoping for a several hundred thousand dollar extravaganza at the Pierre, but yielded to tradition and humility. It all ended very late with dessert, coffee, and the *New York Times*. Every good Jew reads the *Times* religiously (so to speak).

Josh agreed with his parents about the venue and hated every second of the affair. He was disappointed by the meager gifts from the attendees. What did he expect, considering the location of the ceremony? After all, you aren't going to receive $1,000 gifts when the meal at your reception costs $58 per plate and tastes like shit.

The couple had just completed their graduate education and had no money, so cash would've been helpful. The food was Kosher and I'll say no more about that. And it was all done on the cheap, even though Josh knew his wife's family was loaded.

Immediately thereafter, marital issues began to surface. At first his wife was relatively cooperative in bed, occasionally touching the good parts of his body and allowing him to do the same. But she didn't have her heart in it. There was no passion, and Josh sensed that his marriage wasn't going to make him forget the fun he had in college with more promiscuous "reformed" Jewish women and the horny southern Christians.

His wife wanted to get pregnant immediately, which he now believes was a conspiracy to end all sexual relations. In fact, Josh didn't get laid for seven months, nor did his wife do anything to assist him during the gestation period. Several months after the first baby and maybe ten or fifteen boring sexual encounters later, they were working on a second child, which put him in the preverbal penalty box for several more months.

Josh then did what any horny, deprived man would do. He sought relief outside of his bedroom and shower. The "palm sisters" can only bring a man so much pleasure. This was the beginning of a slippery slope. Once Josh transcended the guilt of his first encounter, future trysts were a piece of cake. Being with a woman who wanted to please him and have an orgasm was too much to resist. One year after the birth of his second daughter, he moved out.

Since this all took place long before Josh had a pot to piss in, his separation agreement responsibilities were minimal and mostly directed towards caring for his daughters. He sees his daughters regularly, but they're encouraged to hate him by his ex-wife, who by the way is a successful investment banker at a competitor of GYP.

Spiteful women who are scorned by their men often use the children as a weapon. They create guilt and hard feelings by speaking about daddy in the worst way. I suspect SS will be just as effective, and make it difficult for me to have a normal relationship with my boys. But who knows, maybe she'll surprise me.

Josh went 180 degrees in the opposite direction with his second wife. Frankly, Josh isn't the most attractive man. He's about my age, maybe a few years younger. The good life, fine food and wine, has caused him to become slightly obese. His second ex-wife is a former paralegal he met during a transaction he completed three years ago. They worked late and copulated like two wild dogs after every working session. Unlike his first wife, this woman is very good-looking with a body to die for. She loved sex and was completely uninhibited.

My colleagues and I know all this because Josh used to come in every morning and give us the "blow-by-blow" details about their sexual adventures. He never told one story about his first wife, but he was very proud of his exploits with the second. As you might expect, Josh was only able to keep up with his wife for about a year. After burning the candle at both ends during that period, he had to slow down or give up his job and service her full time. But then, he wouldn't have enough money to satisfy her hunger for material things. As we expected, wife #2 dumped him. He was able to get away cheaply because she just wanted her freedom. Lucky guy, I'm sure I won't be getting away cheaply.

"Give me your attorney's name and I'll call her this week. I think the writing is on the wall. By the way, your assistant is really looking sensational. If there were a 'Miss America in White Pants Contest,' she'd definitely win. I just love to see that thong through her pants. Too bad she's wearing a skirt today. Oh, well."

Josh smiled, "Yeah, ain't she adorable. You gotta admit the skirt is really cute too. I'd love to undress her some time, but she doesn't ever respond to me in that way."

"You're a fat old man. Why the hell would she want you slobbering all over her?'

"Do you think you're more attractive than me? You're a fat old man too."

"Fuck you. She'd pick me in a heartbeat, if the choice was between you and me."

"Five hundred bucks says you're wrong," Josh was getting really wound up now. He wanted to defend his property.

"You want to bet that she'd rather have sex with you than me? You must be kidding. You gotta bet. What if she sues us for sexual harassment?"

"Who cares? We're just going to ask her a hypothetical question. And besides, it's the word of two partners against a mere secretary. Right?"

"Right. Get her in here. $500. Okay?"

"$500 it is." He picked up his intercom, "Laura, would you please come in for a sec?"

"Be right there," she responded. She floated in like a cloud. This woman's presence was staggering. I couldn't wait to tell Josh that Rob was banging her. He'll just die.

Josh led the conversation. "Laura, please shut the door. We want to ask you a question in private." She complied, but knew that something was going on. Boys will be boys, she thought. "Stoke and I'd like to ask you a hypothetical question. We mean absolutely no disrespect. It's just in good fun. Okay?"

"I'm not sure what to say." She knew this was going to be something juvenile. She had to make up her mind whether she was going to play along or not. If not, she should leave the office immediately.

She decided to be a good sport. "Ask your question. I hope you aren't going to say anything gross."

"We're never gross," Josh smiled at her. "Actually, there's a lot of money riding on your answer, so you must respond truthfully."

"I'll do my best."

"If you were trapped on a deserted island and Stoke and I were the only guys on the island who would you more likely be inclined to have sex with, assuming you were horny and needed sex, that is?"

She caught herself before she burst out laughing. "Well, if I were on a deserted island with the two of you, and I hadn't had sex in a long time, I'm not sure either of you could satisfy me."

Josh and I were dumbfounded and just stared at her. "So, what I'd do is take you both on at the same time. Maybe after having sex with both of you, I might feel satisfied." Laura turned around and walked out.

I stood there and looked at Josh. She was too much. I wanted to marry her right on the spot. I said, "I have a hard-on."

"So do I."

"She's so sexy, I could die. She played us masterfully. I feel like an idiot. I'm going out there to tell her I love her."

"I'd have to kill you if you did that. She belongs to me. I want her. She's my secretary." We started to laugh hysterically. Laura could hear us bantering through the door. She turned around and smiled.

"On a more serious note, Rob Viand is resigning."

"What! That guy owes you everything. I can't believe he's doing that and leaving you."

"Take it easy. He's not going to another firm (that would be the ultimate insult). He's quitting to find a wife, a Greek woman. He wants to get married and have Greek babies. His family thinks he's gay because he never brings any women home. It's a matter of masculine pride."

"That's pretty heavy, but I understand. I guess he must be burned out after working with you all these years."

"Wanna hear something else?" Josh nodded, thinking how could anything top what's already transpired. "Rob is banging Laura." I walked out and Josh slumped in his chair with his mouth agape.

When I returned to my area, Liz told me that an emergency meeting was starting in five minutes in the large conference room on our floor. "What's going on?"

"I have no idea. Cohen's assistant told me that you should go right over."

"Does it have anything to do with me?"

"She wouldn't tell me anything. She's a bitch."

As I entered the conference room everybody's eyes were glaring at me. Apparently, the meeting started some time before I arrived. "You guys look awfully grim. What's going on?" This was a pathetic effort to lighten up the meeting.

Cohen responded, "Sit down. We have some bad news for you"

I'll bet the shit head was really enjoying this. Maybe he's going to fire me, I thought.

Cohen proceeded. "I just received a letter from the SEC's Chief Council (that's Security Exchange Commission for all of you not familiar with Wall Street lingo). They're investigating Crucible Corporation and Gilbert Richards."

"What the hell for?"

"Apparently that LBO (that's leveraged buyout) you orchestrated for Richards has some problems."

"I know it has problems. I'm working with Gil to restructure the deal. In fact, I'm seeing him tonight to discuss the matter in detail."

"The SEC indicated in the letter that the forecast in the prospectus was misleading and incomplete. And the new investors were duped into the deal by your buddy."

"Don't be a wiseass. That's all a bunch of horseshit. The deal was bulletproof from a due diligence perspective. I'm not going to stand for any SEC harassment."

"Settle down, boy." The booming command came from Antun Smith, GYP's outside counsel. Antun is an imposing African American man, a former pulling guard for the Fighting Irish of Notre Dame. At six foot five and two hundred eighty pounds, he could pounce on most any man and squash him in a second. I've gotten along well with him over the years, but I'd never fuck with him. "When the SEC investigates, you'll respond in a timely and professional way, lest they put your sorry white Anglo Saxon ass in jail."

"I didn't mean to say I'd defy them. Rather, I meant to say that we put the deal together with the utmost care. In this environment, to be anything less would be idiotic."

The big man spoke again. "I'm glad we got that straightened out." Whether he was a friend or not, I'm sure he'd break both my legs and leave me to die on the street if it would save GYP money or embarrassment.

"Did the SEC provide any details?"

Cohen again. "They indicated that they're going to subpoena our records and put us on notice that you and the firm are targets. Nothing specific beyond that was provided in the letter."

"So what am I supposed to do?"

"Antun and his people will collect the information, review it with you and the others at the firm who worked on the deal, and send it to the SEC."

Antun jumped in at this point. "Let's be clear about what's happening here. The SEC has an inkling that certain information provided by Crucible was misleading. They want to see your work papers and notes from meetings to ascertain how the information they believe is misleading got into the prospectus. Therefore, if you did nothing wrong, you don't have anything to worry about. If you assisted Richards in cheating his new stakeholders, then the SEC and GYP will hang you. Understood?"

"I understand. Unfortunately, the company is struggling as a major contract with the government has fallen apart. Is there anything special I should be doing now?"

Antun said, "Nothing, we're on the case. You go see Richards and tell him you know about the SEC investigation. It's okay to talk because he knows the SEC is going after GYP's records."

"If that's all, you can leave." Norm Cohen dismissed me with a smirk on his face. I left and he and Antun resumed their conversation. Antun had to be respectful to Cohen because he was the one who approved his invoices.

Fortunately, I couldn't think of anything I did wrong. But it wasn't out of the question that Gil misled me and his new stakeholders to get them to agree to the deal. If he knew the contract was going to be cancelled before the deal closed, it would be damaging evidence. I didn't know this to be the case. He made me believe his dealings with the government were proceeding smoothly.

Crucible manufactures advanced radar systems for fighter jets used by all the branches of the military. Its technology is cutting edge. Notwithstanding Gil's outrageous personality, he's a gifted engineer. Sometimes his style rubs the military bureaucrats the wrong way. If the military shit-canned the deal, it might have more to do with Gil's attitude than the technical ability of his radar system.

During the course of my due diligence, some government procurement people warned me that Gil was driving the brass crazy. I just didn't believe that the military would allow a personality issue to interfere with its desire to find and destroy the enemy.

The world of investment banking along with the corporate world has changed drastically over the past few years. The scrutiny in the financial world has increased exponentially because of the precipitous drop in the value of stocks since the late 1990s. Making matters worse were the numerous instances of corporate misbehavior uncovered during the same time.

As far as the stock market is concerned, I was always amazed how people could invest in companies that didn't generate revenues, like the dot com companies. True, a few of these companies warranted investor consideration. Companies involved in the R&D business that had possible cures for diseases and better mousetraps might be reasonable gambles.

Internet investors became wildly speculative encouraged by the new breed of stock analysts, who flogged stocks of de novo companies that only had an idea how to do business with or through a computer.

But the analysts were not solely responsible for the billions of dollars lost when the bubble burst. Investors wanted a quick profit. The stock market is a long term trading pit. Traditionally, it rewards investors who select companies that have potential far into the future. Ultimately, it punishes those who are looking for short-term gains. Fundamental analysis was abandoned for momentum investment, or the greater fools imbroglio. If you buy something that is worthless for one dollar and you sell it for two dollars to someone who's more of an idiot than you, you made a good deal. The guy who bought it for two dollars will make out only if he finds someone even more stupid.

Every day on CNBC, I watched new companies with unproven operations issue stock. Virtually every new issue increased in price out of the box. We all wanted to be a part of it. If you could get in and get out at a profit, why should you give a shit whether the company standing behind the stock would be in business next week or even the next day? But if you were the schmuck who owned the stock when the bad news hit the market, you cried foul and said you were cheated.

Unfortunately, the aforementioned scenario occurred frequently in the past and involved millions of people directly, or their pension funds. Even professional fund managers were drawn into the feeding frenzy. So, the regulators had to respond when almost every self-respecting person claimed Wall Street had fucked them.

To claim that it was the brokerage houses that caused all these losses is nonsense. To begin with, investors never really earned profits before the bubble burst. If an investor buys 100 shares of a stock at 20 dollars and it goes to 40 and then goes to zero because it's really worthless, what did the investor loose? Not 4,000 dollars, he lost 2,000 dollars.

I always got a kick out of the crybabies appearing before Congressional committees telling lawmakers how they lost their entire pension worth millions of dollars. They inevitably failed to point out that they invested only 50 thousand dollars, and it increased to one million for no justifiable financial reason. Then the investment went to zero.

Whose fault is it that the investor made the bet on the stock? Is it the broker, or the analyst? Why would anybody invest his or her life savings on a flyer? If the investor were inclined to make a big bet, why would he listen to a 25 year-old high school graduate? Brokers make recommendations and many investors accept their advice without independently studying the underlying companies.

For some reason, the investing public has a hard time understanding that brokers make money when they churn investor accounts. The more you buy and sell securities, the more these people earn. I didn't say the investor had to make profits for the brokers to earn money, only that they bought and sold securities.

I can't resist telling you about an experience I had with a retail broker. I hope I don't offend anybody, but many brokers aren't the brightest lights in the room. Every "financial consultant" must pass standardized tests given by regulatory agencies before they can advise investors. I don't want to come across as arrogant, but if I didn't get at least a 90% on all the tests, I'd have jumped off the Brooklyn Bridge. Moreover, if my colleagues knew that I received a score below 90%, they would never let me live it down and would've pushed me off of the aforementioned bridge. By the way, the passing score is 70. So, if a moron can somehow get a 70 on this test, he will then be "qualified" to recommend stocks.

On the day I took the test, I was sitting in a huge auditorium with a few hundred aspiring brokers, who were cramming like crazy because they would be in business tomorrow if they could somehow get past the test. If they failed, they would have to be retested and wait to help their clients lose money in the stock market. One young fellow sitting near me was particularly concerned. I told him to relax, and that it wouldn't do him any good to cram at this point. I told him the test wasn't difficult and I was sure he'd do just fine. What a stupid thing for me to say to him. I shouldn't have gotten involved. He looked at me and told me that he didn't think he had a chance to pass, and if he got half of the questions correct he'd be ecstatic.

Can you believe this guy? When he finally managed to bring his score from 50 to 70, he'd be recommending stocks to widows and orphans! Would you invest your life savings with this person?

It's illegal to know information about a company that's not available to the public and invest in the stock. Brokers may not pass on to investors inside information about a company. If they tell you they know something that isn't public and you invest, you broke the law. It's a simple concept. But brokers constantly feed their clients with the "inside scoop."

The regulatory agencies are flooded daily by complaints involving the misconduct of brokers. Generally, the tips received from brokers aren't true and investors lose money. Investing involves risk, and "sure bets" are usually illegal transactions or bullshit.

Corporate malfeasance has created a tremendous amount of mistrust in the investment community, and along with the "irrational exuberance" (the now famous Alan Greenspan description of investment without fundamental justification) of the late 1990s, foretold huge losses of value in the stock market. Mr. Greenspan was right. Because of what happened, investors no longer have confidence in financial statements issued by companies, nor do they believe CEO comments about their companies' prospects.

Many investors are now convinced that companies are operated to enrich management, not shareholders (Enron is a perfect example where the managers allegedly propped up the stock for personal gain). And short-term performance is the principal goal of corporate executive, rather than long-term performance.

As stated earlier, this is counter to the way the stock market has rewarded investors historically. Sophisticated investors would rather buy stock, hold it over an extended period of time and earn long-term capital gains, than constantly trade stocks to make short-term profits. Managers who operate their businesses to maximize profits in the short term are doing their stockholders a disservice.

Some investors say these managers are only concerned with increasing the price of their stock so they can exercise stock options and then sell stock for a profit. This is a naïve perspective and a huge exaggeration.

Of course, the liberal press is all over the greed issue. You'd think that every corporation in America cheats, and that every CEO is a felon. The number of alleged securities related crimes by corporate executives is starting to be of great concern. At first the illegal stuff was limited to just a few isolated instances, but it seems every day another scandal about exaggerated earnings or creative accounting pops up in the news.

The illegal things that corporate types sometimes do, astounds me. Did the CEO of that communications company really think he could overstate revenues by billions of dollars, and nobody would figure it out? Did those fellows at the Texas energy company think they could steal tens of millions of dollars from the company using bogus special purpose companies? Or how about that New England conglomerate that paid its executives outrageous bonuses without clearing them with the Board of Directors? And what about the CEO of the same company who bought over ten million dollars of art and didn't pay sales tax? Is he kidding? What idiot earning ten million or more each year would risk everything to save a million in sales tax?

As I returned to my office, I wondered if this Crucible problem with the SEC was a result of one more stupid decision by management to cheat the investing public. If so, it would surely change my life.

When the feds want to take you down, they usually do it. Outside counsel that protects my firm has great legal skill and often exonerates clients who are accused of crimes, but only at great expense. On the other hand the Feds are staffed with many young attorneys, who aren't that experienced. They're idealists who want to put the bad guys in jail, reminiscent of Eliot Ness and the Untouchables. But the government has the biggest club of all, unlimited resources. They can pound on you until you just run out of money to defend yourself.

It's the same thing with taxes. If you get a notice from the I.R.S. that you owe a few thousand bucks, do you fight it and waste more than that on accounting fees, or do you just pay the damn bill to avoid the hassle? I really hoped Gil didn't bullshit me.

As I approached my office, Liz asked, "Is everything all right?"

"Just fantastic. Get Gil Richards on the phone, please." She knew things were not okay.

My intercom lit up. "The maniac is on the phone." Jeez, that woman was a piece of work.

"Hi Gil. What the fuck is going on? I just found out I'm the target of an SEC investigation. How come you didn't tell me this was coming down? Why did I have to hear it from my boss?"

"How're ya doin pal? Stay relaxed about the SEC. There's nothing to their investigation. What the fuck? You were involved during the whole buyout. You know I wouldn't do anything illegal."

"Don't take me for a fool. You wanted that deal completed more than anything. You made a fortune. You would've done anything to close."

"Look, the complaint has nothing to do with my the former shareholders. They're happy because they got their money out of the company before we ran into a few minor problems. The current stakeholders instigated the complaint. They think I fudged on the projections. They think I exaggerated the numbers. You put the numbers together for me. You did the diligence. They were accurate at the time."

"Gil, you had trouble making the first interest payment because the radar deal has been delayed. You don't have a chance to ultimately hit your numbers without the radar sales."

"Godammit. That's not true. You asked me a million fucking questions. You and your minions were a total pain in the ass."

"Maybe we didn't ask enough questions. I hope you didn't lie. If you did, you've put us all in jeopardy. Who turned the SEC onto all this?"

"I think it was John Applegate at United American Insurance. That rat drove me nuts. He's a vindictive Napoleonic prick."

"Don't underestimate him. I know of situations where he thought a borrower screwed him, and John went after him with a vengeance. He will spend anything to get even. That's his reputation. He's not afraid of tanking a company and putting in new management after it goes bankrupt."

"Slow down partner. This guy isn't taking Crucible from me, no way. I'd put out a contract and have him killed."

"Come on Gil, don't even kid about that."

"I'm not." Now that response really made me nervous and was prophetic (you'll know why soon enough). I changed the subject.

"What are we doing tonight after our meeting?"

"We're gonna have dinner at a great restaurant I'm sure you never heard of called Salute. Then, we'll go to this great club. It's filled with beautiful sweet things. If you get laid you'll be more relaxed."

"For a 60 year old guy, you really are a sex machine. I hope I'm as frisky as you later in life."

"Later life? Whatdaya mean? I got rid of three women because they couldn't keep up with me. And each one of them was progressively younger. I'm not in later life. I'm in my prime. By the way, my daughter wants to join us. I told her about you and she's really interested in meeting you."

"I'm married. Remember?" I reminded Gil.

"So what. She just wants to have dinner with you, that's all."

"I'm leaving the office in a few hours and will get to your place at about 5. We can talk more about the SEC thing."

"Then to dinner and dancing."

"Right, see you later." The man is truly out of his mind. Investment bankers have to deal with all kinds of people. Some guys are conservative; some guys are like hired assassins with their competition and with their vendors (including investment bankers); and some guys are nice people, who just want to make an honest buck.

Gil isn't like any of these guys. He lives life to the fullest. Having a lot of money enables him to seduce women, drink expensive wines, and fly around in private planes. He works hard so he can play hard. I guess I envy him to a certain extent but couldn't be like him.

He was a running back on the Indiana football team. He once told me that all he did in college was play ball, drink, and fuck. Well, he had sex one time too many, and made a girlfriend pregnant. Gil did the honorable thing and married the woman, but it was just the beginning of a carousel of wives as he built an enviable career at Crucible.

The guy has had three wives and has worked at only one company. Go figure. In any case, he's one good-looking sixty-year old man. He works out regularly and dyes his hair. Frankly, women can't resist the guy.

POOP AND PHALLIC SYMBOLS

It was ten minutes to eleven, and my plane was scheduled to leave at 3:30. I wanted to buy a new pen before I left on the trip. Most bankers used felt tip pens. I hate them. It was like writing with a crayon.

Our firm went through $1.99 felt tips like water. Our employees used them with abandon. The pens were never used until they ran out of ink. What the hell, why should they be? The pens were free. My colleagues brought them home to their wives and kids, along with pads and all kinds of stationary products. GYP's earnings would be a million dollars greater, if we just kept tabs on this stuff.

I buy expensive pens that are commensurate with my status in life. Mont Blanc, Dunhill, Aurora, Penguin, and Cross are some of my favorite brands. And I never lose pens. When someone tries to steal one of my fine writing instruments, I'm tempted to chop their hands off. And be clear on this, people are jealous when they see you writing with an attractive pen. Most are too cheap to buy them, and they'll steal from you if you give them a chance.

I told Liz I'd be back in an hour and if anything came up, I wasn't available until then. I needed to concentrate when I bought pens. I scurried out before anybody could stop me with another dumb problem. My day was already a fucking disaster.

I walked out of the building and would you believe I stepped in a mound of dog poop. I work in a fancy Park Avenue building and there's dog shit at the entrance. Some of the mailroom guys were standing nearby having a cigarette and saw what happened. They began to giggle among themselves. I don't know why they weren't more sympathetic towards me, as I always treated them respectfully.

Underdogs love to see the higher-ups get their comeuppance, I suppose. Let them have a good laugh on me. I earn millions and they can barely pay the rent. Of course, your compensation doesn't make any difference in situations like this. If you stepped in dog shit, it's going to smell, regardless of socioeconomic status.

Sort of reminds me of a few other adages: We all put our pants on one leg at a time. If it ain't broke, don't fix it. If you smelt it, you dealt it. I'll be dipped in shit (this is an appropriate adage for the situation I found myself in).

Learning American English (as compared to the Queen's English) has to be one of the most difficult things to do. You can't understand what the hell Americans are talking about until you have a grasp of hundreds of adages and idioms. Take, "I'll be dipped in shit." It means a person is surprised about something. Mostly people from the South who are always stepping in horseshit use the phrase. If someone from Japan was trying to learn English and heard that expression, he'd be puzzled to say the least. And yet, it's an innocent comment.

I scraped off as much as of the feces as possible on the curb. It seemed that my plight was the source of considerable amusement to all the passersbys.

One time I was watching a late night episode of Al Goldstein's television program. You know him, the publisher of "*Screw Magazine*." Al was on a rampage about how some people didn't pick up after their dogs.

Stepping in dog shit was a common occurrence in the city and he wanted to make a point and encourage dog walkers to do the right thing. So, he dressed up in a military uniform and drove around with his head protruding out of the top of a limousine. He combed the streets looking for people walking dogs who left crap on the street.

When he found these felons (he was using actors), he pointed an unloaded rifle at them and forced them eat the poop (naturally it was fake). Say what you want about Mr. Goldstein, but if I could find the jerk that left the poop outside our entrance, I'd make him eat it too. But I did the next best thing. With crap still on my shoe I went back into the building and sought out the guard that tortured me earlier in the day. There he was getting ready to ask me for my ID again.

"I'm not going back into the building. I want to report a crime that took place outside of the building."

"What happened, Mr. Spencer?" The people standing around were all ears.

"Somebody's dog shit at our entrance and I stepped in it." The snickering started, but the guard played it straight.

"I can't believe it."

I lifted my shoe to show him the evidence. "If you were more diligent, you'd have caught the perpetrator and spared me this ordeal. But you inspect every ID, even those of people you've seen every day for the last ten years."

"Let's not get into that again. I'm doing my job. I'm trying to protect the occupants in this building. I'm sorry you stepped in dog droppings."

"Well, I think you better arrange to get it cleaned up. There's a much greater chance that someone else will step in the shit, than someone will blow up this building."

"We'll take care of it right away, Mr. Spencer." I know that the gathered crowd was laughing behind my back as I walked away, but I had to make a point.

While I'm thinking of it, I should give you my feelings about those who spit their gum on the ground. It's not as bad as dog shit, but damn close.

The Sanitation Department has strategically located garbage cans throughout the city. You can't walk a block without passing one. I'll admit that when I'm finished extracting the flavoring out of chewing gum, I need to get it out of my mouth as quickly as possible. But is it too much of an inconvenience to walk a few steps to a garbage can before you spit it out? I don't think so.

When gum attaches to your shoes, your foot sticks to the ground with every step. It's so gross. The most outrageous place I ever stepped in gum was inside a Broadway theater. A wad of gum was under my seat. There I was in the orchestra where the seats are $100 apiece, and difficult to come by I should add, and some fucking slob spit his gum on the floor. It was during "Hairspray", a comedy. Maybe the gum spitter was a comedian. The idiot! Our housekeeper also thought this guy was a rat because she had to remove the gum from my shoe when I got home.

It was like an inferno outside and I could smell the shit on my shoe. I did more scraping on the curb to no avail and hailed a cab. My favorite pen store was a ten-minute cab ride away. I prayed for an air-conditioned taxi, but no luck. I managed to squeeze my feet into the inadequate space between the wall and the seat and saw that some of the poop was now deposited on the wall. After about 45 seconds, the driver turned around. You stink, mon."

"Now you know what it's like every time I get into a taxi," I said to the driver. I don't believe taxi cab drivers ever shower, and I was surprised that my driver was offended by the smell of dog crap.

"You stinkin' up my cab, mon."

"I stepped in dog shit. I'm sorry."

"My cab gonna smell, mon."

"Your cab already stinks, and you stink because you're too cheap to use the air."

"Get out Mr. Dog Shit. Get out of my cab."

I got out and walked away without paying. I thought the driver might pursue me, but he was concerned that my shoes were a biohazard. I walked into a shoeshine store that appeared as I exited the taxi. I approached the proprietor and asked, "Do you clean dog shit off shoes?"

He gave me one of those looks. All of the shoeshine boys looked away. They didn't want the job, for sure. "Are you some kind of joker?"

"No, I'm not. I stepped in dog shit and even cab drivers won't take me anywhere."

"Mister, we're not in the dog shit business. Sorry."

I left the shoeshine store and spotted a shoe store. I went inside and young man greeted me. "Can I help you, sir?"

"I need a new pair of shoes. Mine have dog shit on them and nobody will clean them for me."

"No problem. Let me get those things in the garbage and we'll fix you up."

I finally had shoes that didn't smell, but they needed to be broken in. Moments after leaving the store, I started to feel blisters on my heels. But it was better to have blisters on my feet than shit on my shoes. I didn't want to be out of the office for more than an hour, and 45 minutes had already elapsed.

I finally arrived at the pen store. During my career, I had amassed a huge collection of pens. I dabbled for a short time in old fountain pens, but couldn't handle the mess and their large girth. To protect my valuable writing instruments, I keep a large number of Parker T-Ball Jotters throughout my office. When the pen thieves arrive I never leave them alone with my priceless beauties. If they need something to write with, I offer them a Parker. It pisses me off when they steal any of my pens including the inexpensive Parkers, but at least I minimize my losses this way. Some people are very jealous of my amazing collection.

Every week I change pens, although for heavy-duty writing I use Crosses and Mont Blancs. At business meetings, I draw out my pens like swords and lay them next to a legal pad for all to admire. Some of my fancier writing instruments have in-laid features and elaborate metal designs that attract the eye. What sense does it make to wear Zegna suits, Hermes ties, Gucci loafers, and Ascot Chang shirts and write with a Bic, a pencil, or a crayon?

SS believes my obsession with pens is a homosexual trait (not that there's anything wrong with that). It disturbs her when I fondle my pens and touch them to my face in deep concentration. One time, she walked into my study and I had a pen in my mouth. SS said that sucking on a pen was tantamount to fellatio. I told her that I wasn't sucking on the pen, and I was surprised she even knew what fellatio was based upon the frequency and content of our sexual intimacy. That shut her up. The bitch. In any case, I'm not gay.

As I approached the counter in the store, the owner, a Frenchman named Jean Claude, warmly welcomed me with a pronounced Gallic lisp. I know he wanted to hug and kiss me on both my cheeks because I spent so much money at his store, but he thought better of it. "Mr. Spencer, so good to see you. How've you been?"

"Getting along, Jean Claude." What is it with Europeans? They insist on being addressed with two first names, one of which is always effeminate. I could have suspicions about Jean Claude considering his two names (the first being a girl's name) and the pronounced speech impediment. His open silk shirts and gold chains didn't dispel my suspicions either. "I want to find some new pens to add to my collection. I'm tired of the same old stuff. What have you got that's new and different?"

"It 'ees difficult to show you pens you don't already have. I suspect you have at least two of every major brand in ballpoints, roller balls, and mechanical pencils."

"You're right. I don't see a pen I don't already have in my collection."

"Would you finally consider building a fountain pen collection? It's a huge untapped category for you."

"They're a mess, totally impossible to use at work."

"I wouldn't recommend fountain pens for everyday writing. They're to be savored like a fine wine. You're supposed to sign important documents and large checks with these magnificent items. We carry wonderful pens with large gold nibs. They perform beautifully." This guy was also very emotional about pens. He referred to writing instruments as if they were living creatures.

"The idea doesn't excite me, but maybe I have no choice if I want my collection to grow." This whole conversation was ridiculous, but I really am serious about pens. I intend to pass them down to future generations, assuming SS doesn't get them in a divorce settlement. She wouldn't want the fountain pens because you can't sign credit card chits with them. Then it occurred to me, fountain pens would be like a hedge against our impending divorce. "Okay, I'll have a look at some fountain pens."

"Wonderful," the Frenchman cried out. "Wonderful" is a feminine word. It sounds strange when a man says "wonderful." "Allow me to show you my favorites. Some are brands in which you have already invested. You'll know the names."

"Sounds fine. Please be quick, I'm running behind schedule."

Jean Claude was back with three of the most ornate, ostentatious pens I have ever seen. They were like fat cigars. If SS ever saw me with one of these in my mouth, she'd be convinced I had a penile fetish. "They're beautiful, no?"

"Yes beautiful," I responded sarcastically. I picked up the first pen. It was a Mont Blanc. Not like any of the ubiquitous MBs you see. This one had gold inlays and pearls in the cap. The nib looked like a golden sword. You could use the pen as a dagger and kill someone with it.

I attached the cap to the bottom of the pen and wrote my name. I wouldn't use it for anything other than signing my name. I couldn't. I'd be exhausted from moving it across the paper. It felt like it weighed a pound. "This thing is very heavy."

"The weight gives it perfect balance, no?"

"Actually, the weight gives me a cramp in my hand." I recapped the pen and slipped it into my suit pocket. The pocket was on the inside of my coat. I wanted to see if it ruined the fit of my suit or caused me to list to the side from its excessive heft.

"Mr. Spencer, that pen commands respect. It's made for the Chairman of the Board. In fact, it's named the 'Chairman.'"

What a fucking joke. The pen had a name. "How much does it cost? I hate to ask."

"Nine-hundred, seventy-five dollars."

"Come on, really?"

"Really, it's one of the finest pens ever made. It contains more gold in the nib than any other pen in the world."

People are starving and I'm considering the purchase of a one thousand dollar writing instrument. What excess. I pulled it out of my coat and it exploded, spewing ink on my hands.

"Godammit. What happened?" The ink was staining my skin. It must be extra thick (and expensive) like the pen. When you write with this ink, it will never fade.

Jean Claude was going ape shit. He was about to go into shock. I was probably his largest customer and one of his pens assaulted me. "I'm so sorry. This is a disaster."

"I told you I hated these fucking pens." I said "fucking" very loud and some women in the store looked at me askance. But I could care less.

"I have to go, I'll be in touch." I threw the MB on the counter and it rolled off. "Get rid of that thing before it hurts somebody." I walked out without a new pen and was depressed about it.

MUHAMMAD VERSUS THE CHILD

I decided to take the subway back to the office being careful to avoid dog droppings, as well as cat, pig, cow, and horseshit along the way. It gave me an opportunity to think about SS and the future of our marriage.

In the beginning our relationship wasn't dissimilar in intensity or affection to our friends. We kissed in public, but not too passionately. We whispered sweet nothings in each other's ears, but not too often. We had sex regularly, but not enough to completely satisfy me. SS encouraged me to be successful because of the comforts she derived from my hard earned money rather than any great desire for me to be happy.

Then it suddenly dawned on me, SS doesn't get high grades relating to any single thing in our marriage. She was a mediocre mother, a lousy cook, a rotten lover, etc. I wanted an "A" wife. SS had the looks and the figure, but she was a selfish person, unwilling to share them with me. Bottom line, I wasn't happy. I felt I had the moral and legal grounds to split up with her. So regardless of what I ultimately decided to do, SS might agree, or she might tell me to shove it. But I had to have an opinion before this all heated up.

Another question was whether it's possible to climb up the slippery slope. SS and I were definitely on the slope, but did either of us really want to expend the effort to get back together? I take that back, did both of us want to make the effort? It takes two to tango. Considering that SS already hired an attorney, it might already be too late.

When sleazy marital attorneys get involved, they want to do a deal and earn a big fee. It's not in their interest to negotiate reconciliation. They make their reputation and money by screwing the opposition.

My deep thoughts were suddenly interrupted when several teenagers entered the subway car. They were yakking loudly with each other making everyone in the car feel as uncomfortable as possible. Their language was appalling ("fuck this and fuck that"). My fellow straphangers (a NYC word for subway riders) clearly were annoyed, but no one said a word or even looked at the kids.

A few boys didn't hold on when the train started to move and bumped into two construction workers. Some dirty looks passed between them and it looked like a fight might ensue. One of the boys said, "What's you lookin' at?" He was trying to sound as stupid as possible.

One worker was white and one was African American. It was the black man the young boy challenged. Why, I had no idea, as the man was over six feet tall and easily tipped the scales at 230 pounds. He responded, "You talkin' to me, boy?" You should know that the young boy was also black and when anyone calls a black male "boy" (even if it's another black person), there's going to be trouble and, maybe, bloodshed.

"Yeah fatso." The boy and his friends started to laugh mockingly at the worker. I'm still wondering why this young fellow, who might have weighed 140 pounds was messing with this monster. The construction worker and his buddy were dirty and obviously agitated about having worked like dogs for the previous eight hours and seemed poised to tear the boy's head off along with those of his pals.

"Listen here, little man. Unless you and your buddies are ready to go to war, you had better back off." The kid decided he might have bitten off more than he could chew and turned away.

My stop finally arrived and I needed to pass the noisy group to get off the train. I should have exited from another door, but the construction workers energized me. As I got into the middle of the crowd, I was jostled. I said, "Excuse me." Their response was more jostling as the door slid open. I finally got out and as the doors closed I yelled, "Fucking punks."

One of the boys got out before the door shut completely. He was surprised to find himself alone without his fellow juvenile delinquents. Most predators prefer to operate in packs, not by themselves. My heart was racing, as a confrontation was inevitable, a middle-aged man versus a skinny tenth or eleventh grade boy. "You kids are a real pain in my ass. What the hell are you trying to prove?" I made a feeble attempt to reason with the boy.

"Man, you some dumb mother fucker. I gonna kill your ass."

I'm thinking this kid has illusions of grandeur, as I outweighed him by 30 pounds, or he had a weapon. Before he had a chance to do anything, I slapped him as hard as I could with the back of my hand. He went flying into a garbage can. Fortunately, he didn't fall on the subway tracks.

On the ground, he began to sob as a trickle of blood leaked from his nose. Some people stood around and looked on approvingly. One guy told me I had better get out of the subway as quickly as possible.

I couldn't believe I actually struck a child, even though he deserved it. I risked getting arrested. I was sorry I got involved, and every passing second made me feel guiltier about confronting the boy.

Finally, back at the office, I had just a few minutes before I had to leave for the airport. I looked forward to some quiet time. As soon as I sat down the phone rang, and Liz was away from her desk. "Hello," I answered reluctantly. I knew it was going to be trouble.

"This is Don Elgin in Accounting. Can I have a few minutes of your time?"

"I'm leaving on a business trip. What can I do for you?" Nothing good can come from a phone call with a bean counter. This guy focused on expense reports, which were always being contested because Cohen thought every employee of GYP was trying to gyp the firm.

"Well, Rob Viand just submitted an expense report, which had some unauthorized charges on it."

"I really don't have time for this. Just approve the expense report on my authority."

"Sorry, Stoke, I can't do that. I have strict orders from Mr. Cohen that unauthorized charges must be paid by the employee."

"What are we talking about?"

"There are movie charges. We don't pay for employees to watch movies when they travel for the firm. And you should know two of them have pornographic titles."

I thought most hotels (the ones that don't have hourly rates) stopped using real titles on bills so a businessman could watch a dirty movie and put it on his expense report. "Are you serious? Just pay the fucking thing and drop it. How much did they cost?"

"Each movie is $15.00."

"You're wasting my time for $30.00 of charges, pornographic charges? Let me ask you something, Don. Do you ever travel for the firm?"

"Yes, occasionally I go on the road."

"Do you ever get horny?"

"What do you mean?"

"Do you ever want to get laid, but you're so busy that you don't have the time to find a nice girl or a hooker?"

"I'd never pick up strange women. I'm married"

"Come on, Don, we're guys. We get horny. We need sex. Right?"

"I'm telling you, I don't pick up women in bars or anything like that."

"That's the point. I don't have time to pick up women either," I lied. "Rather than have sex with a stranger, you can watch a heater flick and take care of your needs, right?"

"What do you mean, take care of my needs?"

"Don't bullshit me, Don. I'm talking about whacking off."

"I'm not going to talk about that with you. Viand has to pay for the movies. Period."

"What are the names of the movies?"

"You want to know the names of the movies? 'Asian Sex Kittens' and 'Fly Girls'. Why do you ask?"

"I'm going to tell Rob about our conversation and ask him whether the movies were any good. If he recommends them, I'm going to instruct him to buy a copy of each and send them to your home. If you're married... are you married? Oh yeah, you said you were. I want you to watch the movies with your wife." I slammed the phone down. I was running out of time for such foolishness.

I dialed up Rob. When he picked up, I pounced, "Rob, it's Stoke. I just got off the phone with Elgin in Accounting. He said you have to pay for the dirty movies you rented on a business trip and he wanted you to send copies of the films to his home." I hung up the phone.

The next call was to Cohen. I got his voicemail. "Norm, that dickhead Elgin in Accounting is harassing Rob Viand about renting porno movies on his last business trip. Tell him to get off my back and leave Rob alone. Rob told me he's quitting and this may dash any hopes I have of talking him into staying at GYP. It was nice talking to you today." I thought to myself, jerk off.

A BALL GRABBER AND A POT BELLY

With travel bag in hand, I proceeded to the street to find the car Liz ordered to take me to LaGuardia Airport. It was about 1 p.m. and the temperature was about 90 degrees with 100% humidity. I was perspiring profusely moments after reaching the curb on Park Avenue.

How the hell was I supposed to pick up women with Gil in a wrinkled and smelly suit? I hadn't brought another one with me. Big mistake. I hoped my charm would be stronger than my body odor. Thankfully, the car arrived quickly. I got in and it was hot inside.

After settling in, I said to the driver, "Turn on the air please."

"It's broken. Not working. Sorry."

"Shit. What's with you? It's the hottest fucking day of the year and your air doesn't work. Why did you take the call?"

"Just trying to make a living, pal."

"I'm not your pal. Let me out. I'm not paying."

"Like hell you're not paying. I took this call 30 minutes ago. You're paying."

I jumped out of the car and the driver got out and circled around to engage me. I think he wanted to beat the shit out of me. "You lay one hand on me and I'll have you arrested." I thought, two fights in one day. Great.

"Give me my money, you little creep." He called me little and I weigh 190 pounds. You could just imagine how big he was. A small crowd gathered around us anticipating an ass kicking (mine, that is).

Luckily, two cops passed by in their cruiser. They stopped. "What's going on here, fellows?"

I spoke up first. "This guy has no air conditioning in his car, so I'm not paying."

"He accepted the ride, so he has to pay."

"Okay, okay I get the picture. Listen buddy..." He was looking at me. "...you gotta pay the man. You got in the car."

"How the fuck was I supposed to know that the air wasn't working unless I got into the car?"

"You have two choices. You can pay or we all go to the stationhouse to talk this out. What'll it be?"

"I have to catch a plane. I can't go any place except to the airport."

"He owes me $25.00."

One of the cops looked at me. "You're obviously a rich businessman. Pay the man so we can move on."

I opened my wallet and threw the money on the ground in front of the driver. "Shove it up your ass." He started after me but was intercepted by the cops. I walked back to the street and hailed a taxi, an air-conditioned taxi.

I gave the call car driver the finger as we left, which served to infuriate him even more.

He jumped into his car and chased after us. Can you believe this guy? He stole my money and wouldn't allow me the pleasure of flipping him the bird.

I looked back and saw the police car chase after him. I was actually starting something of a riot. Shouldn't have been so free with the rude gesture, I suppose. The call car cut off my taxi and now the cabbie was pissed off. We stopped and my driver confronted the other guy.

They were nose to nose cursing each other in their respective foreign tongues. The cops caught up and I took the opportunity to make an escape. Finally, I found a taxi with air to take me safely to the airport. What a day.

The ramps that approached the check-in areas were jammed as usual. We sat without moving for five minutes and it was starting to get a little late, assuming that the security people were going to bust my balls like everybody else today.

Why is it that major cities never plan for the future, whether it's bridges, buses, roads, or airports? Even before the 9/11 tragedies, the airport situation in New York City was a disaster. You couldn't get into the airport, through the airport, or out of the airport without encountering lines and endless delays.

The baggage claim system was screwed up, as the union members took their sweet time after planes landed. Then, they demanded more money for less service and an even worse attitude. The counter people were under such stress that they always had a short fuse and no patience to be polite. Heaven forbid you push the call button after you board a plane. It's like an insult to the flight attendants. I don't know why the airlines even install them. If you press the button you get blackballed for the rest of the trip and very little service becomes no service. This is what I had to look forward to, as soon as I got out of the goddamn taxi.

We neared the American Airlines entrance and I started to get excited. I was so thankful. Maybe the day wouldn't end in total disaster after all. I really had to get to Chicago to speak with Gil about the SEC investigation. Finally, I freed myself from the taxi. I gave the cabbie a healthy tip and thanked him for his efforts. He smiled, as he probably didn't even know what the hell I was talking about. He only cared about the tip.

I walked past the porter. They were thankful I wasn't checking any bags. It was hot and they wanted to do as little work as possible. I didn't want to subject my bags to abuse by the handlers, and I needed to make a quick getaway at O'Hare Airport.

The terminal was very crowded. Revolution was in the air. When the lines get this long, I expect that somebody is going to draw an automatic weapon out of frustration and start shooting. It frightens me to be in this type of a charged environment. The way the day was going, I'd get the first bullet between the eyes.

Then I saw it, the dreaded security line. The security line is a 9/11 phenomenon. The bad guys got away with smuggling box cutters on the planes, which they then used to hijack airplanes that slammed into the World Trade Center. Then another guy put a bomb in the heel of his shoe. Other passengers overwhelmed him before he could do any harm. Now the security guards virtually had you strip down before you boarded a plane.

After waiting about ten minutes, I approached the entrance to the X-Ray machines. I took off my Rolex, my belt, emptied my pockets of coins and wallet, took off my shoes, declared that I had a laptop in my bag and held my pants up until I passed through the X-Ray device. No beeping, thank goodness. Nevertheless, a rent-a-cop asked me to step to the side. I told him that I didn't set off any alarms and I had a plane to catch. He said he needed to check me as part of the random inspection system. My number came up, too bad. It seemed to be coming up all day.

My pants were about to fall down, and now I was going to be subjected to an additional inspection. The guard said, "Raise your arms and spread your legs."

"My pants will fall down if I don't hold them up."

"Please mister, don't give me a hard time. I'm just doing my job."

"Doing my job." Now where have I heard that before? Security guards are really annoying. First, I had to put up with that moron at my building, now this guy. Most of these people never were in a position of legitimate authority. So, now they get to boss around rich folks, and they totally enjoy it. "I'm just letting you know in advance that my trousers will fall if I let go of them."

"Then just do it or I'll have you arrested."

Now I was really angry. "Who the fuck do you think you're talking to? I don't have to listen to your shit. Where's your boss?"

A female supervisor had already arrived on the scene. "What's the problem?"

The guard spoke before me. "This guy is refusing to cooperate. I asked him to raise his hands and he won't do it."

"That's a crock of shit. I told your buddy that my pants will fall down if I let go of them."

The supervisor was a very nasty looking large woman. She looked pretty tough, too. And she wasn't pleased about me upsetting her operation. "What's your name?"

"Stokley Spencer."

"That's a very athletic name. Mr. Spencer, our job is to prevent a reoccurrence of the events of 9/11. We search passengers when they have suspicious items on their person and when they have suspicious items in their luggage. Do you understand?"

"Listen lady, I really am not interested in hearing a speech. I have a plane to catch, and you and your gang of idiots are harassing me. If I really believed your people had the ability to actually catch a hijacker, I wouldn't mind going through this charade. But you're all a bunch of incompetents, capable of catching nobody."

"I understand," she said. "Please follow me." She pointed to an area with a curtain surrounding it.

I thought she was going to rough me up, so I hesitated. "I'm not going anywhere with you."

"If you don't comply, I'll call the police and you'll be arrested. I'm going to personally examine you and then you can go to your plane. I don't want you to be embarrassed by having your pants fall down."

I followed her behind the curtain and she told me to drop my trousers. I figured I better start going with the flow or I was going to get locked up. She proceeded to frisk me, across my back and down the back of my legs. Then she grabbed me in the crotch and smiled. "Yeow. What do you think your doing?"

"Just looking for weapons." She grabbed my balls. "Mr. Spencer, if you give any of my people any more shit, I'll personally kick your butt. Understand?" She squeezed the family jewels even tighter and I had the urge to scream, but restrained myself.

"I understand. Please let go." She did. I hiked up my pants, gathered my things and got the hell out of there. I heard her and the other dickheads laughing as I scurried down the corridor with my belt hanging down.

What else could possibly go wrong? I wondered. At least I didn't get locked up. I arrived at the gate about 30 minutes before the plane was scheduled to leave and rushed up to the attendant to check in. I didn't have an assigned seat and was hoping to get one on the aisle.

That cheap bastard Norm Cohen didn't even allow me to fly first class, so I had to suffer in the back of the plane with the common folk. And judging by the number of people in the waiting area, a lot of common folk were getting on this aircraft.

"I'd like an aisle seat please." If I were pleasant, maybe I'd get some service.

"I'm sorry Mr., ah, Mr. Spencer, but the plane is very full and we only have middle seats left."

"I suppose it doesn't matter that I have a full fare ticket and most of these other people are flying free or at a discount."

"You're right, it makes no difference."

"Why don't you assign aisle seats to business, full fare business travelers?" I emphasized the words "full fare."

"Because business travelers make reservations 24 hours before they leave and all these other people make reservations months in advance."

"What seat do I have?"

"The last row, 35E."

"Is that the toilet row?"

"It is. Sorry."

If there's anything worse than sitting in a middle seat, it's sitting near the toilets. The aroma from a bathroom, which 200+ people use during a two-hour flight, is enough to make you throw up. And the queue next to your seat is equally annoying.

"I'll be sure to fly a different airline the next time. Give me my ticket."

Airline employees are service people. But customers are no longer "always right." These people don't get into trouble no matter what they say because their unions protect them. They can tell a customer to go fuck himself without consequence.

Customers are victims of service people. I suppose my attitude only serves to inflame the conflict between airline employees and customers. But I'm sick of their act, which includes, bad manners, lousy service, whining about more money and better work rules, luggage that is ruined, and late planes. It's no wonder that every goddamn airline in the country is on the verge of bankruptcy.

I sauntered over to the one available seat in the waiting area. A young woman about 25 was gabbing on her cell phone, loud enough to disturb everyone in the immediate area. I guess that's why nobody was sitting next to her.

Within five minutes, I knew whom she went out with and slept with the night before (they were different men), how many pounds overweight she was, what bars she goes to in Chicago (I'd be sure to avoid them later this evening), and so on. To make matters worse, she had her luggage strewn all over the floor. I could barely get to the seat.

An announcement about our plane came over the PA system about boarding in five minutes. The woman dropped her phone from her ear and asked me what the announcement was about. I told her.

In a minute, another announcement was made about boarding procedures. You know the same old shit about boarding the last rows first and the first class passengers can board anytime and the weak and frail should board before anybody. The latter was impossible because the entrance to the gate was already so crowded that an impaired person couldn't possibly get through the crowd to the plane. She asked me what the second announcement was about.

"Why don't you put that stupid cell phone away and pay attention. If you aren't going to listen, I'm not telling you anything." She turned away thinking I might be the rudest person on earth. I really was acting that way. It was a bad day.

Since I was in coach, I boarded after the infirm and first class passengers. I wanted to tell everyone in first class that I hoped they came down with food poisoning from the airline meal.

In the back of the plane, you only get a drink and a cracker with processed cheese. Food poisoning on airlines has dropped dramatically since they stopped serving real meals. This was the airlines' plan to save themselves financially, cut out food service. The swill they used to serve couldn't have cost very much.

It was a long trip to the back of the plane. Since everybody disregarded the instructions to board according to their row number, I was had to squeeze past countless people to get to my seat. As I passed them, I intentionally bumped as many as possible with my carry-on and said excuse me each time.

As I neared my row an elderly lady had this big bag she was trying to force into the overhead compartment. A young guy was sitting right across the aisle ignoring the woman. I put my bag down and helped her, saying loudly, "I can't believe no one is helping you." I looked right at the aforementioned jerk. He gave me a fuck you look. I returned it. This was going to be a really pleasant flight.

Whenever a man gets on a plane he always hopes that a beautiful woman sits next to him. It's even better when the woman is talkative and finds him interesting. And the best thing is when the woman invites him into the bathroom for sex. I'm talking about membership in the "Mile High Club". On the other hand a fat slob (man or woman) with body odor could be seated next to you. Of course, a plane crash would be a worse thing to happen to you.

One time a flight attendant dropped hot coffee on me. In her desire to please the passengers even in turbulent conditions, this stewardess (it was in the days when you called the female attendants stewardesses) bumped into me on the aisle and burned me in the groin area. She started to wipe me down, stroking my crotch. If she hadn't rewarded me with an abbreviated hand job, I might have punched her out.

She was supposedly trained to balance coffee pots in difficult conditions. It was inexcusable. Later, I played the sympathy card and asked her out. She told me she wasn't allowed to date passengers. I said everybody took airplanes and were passengers, so whom did she date. She said no thanks, and gave me a fuck you look.

Another bad thing that can happen to you on a plane is for turbulence to occur while you're urinating I'm referring to those of us that stand up when we pee. It's hard enough maintaining your aim in those little bathrooms, but when the plane is shaking all over the place, it could be messy.

Sometimes people forget to lock the bathroom door. I've forgotten myself, but that's not what I want to talk about. One time I opened the bathroom door on a plane and a little old lady was sitting on the toilet with her underpants down around her ankles. I was so embarrassed I wanted to crawl into a hole. I closed the door quickly and dashed back to my seat. I kept my head down hoping she didn't see me and I didn't see her when she emerged.

One of the funniest things during a flight happened to a colleague. We were in first class. Actually, we were the only ones in first class besides the stewardesses. My traveling partner had to use the toilet shortly before landing. He had a bowel situation, which took longer than expected.

The plane was in final approach and he was still grunting away. The stewardess knocked on the door and told him to come out. He said he couldn't. More time passed and she knocked again. He said he still wasn't finished. Then she started to pound on the door like he was committing a crime.

This woman apparently never had a difficult bowel movement in her life. Boy, was he angry when he finally went back to his seat. Of course, I was laughing hysterically.

The following is a letter he sent to the President of the airline:

"Dear whatever his name was (I don't remember who was running the airline at that time),

Yesterday I was flying from Minneapolis to Omaha on your airline. I was in first class with my colleague. Towards the end of the flight, I had terrible gastric distress and had to move my bowels. Just so you know, I'm not crazy about doing this in an airline bathroom, but I had no choice.

In any case, the process was not going along smoothly, must've been the Mexican food I ate the previous evening. I suppose it was pretty stupid to order Mexican food in Minnesota, but I was in the mood. Well, one thing led to another and I was really suffering.

We were about ten minutes from Omaha and one of your rude stewardesses started banging on the door, ordering me to get out. Now what the hell did she expect me to do? I was in a bind and I was bound up.

I attempted to complete the activity as quickly as possible, but some things can't be rushed. The bottom line was that I finished up prematurely, and threw an incomplete pass, if you know what I mean.

Moreover, I soiled my underwear in my haste. Please understand I am an executive. I was on a business trip to speak with clients and now I had soiled draws.

You really should tell your flight attendants that they ought to be a little more flexible about such matters. What's the big deal? If the plane landed and I was still on the throne, no harm would have been done.

Regretfully,

My Colleague (I won't use his name because he would kill me if I did)"

I found my seat and my aisle-mates were already buckled in. An attractive woman had the window seat and a blue-collar type guy dressed in jeans and a Harley-Davidson t-shirt was on the aisle. Neither was obese so I'd have my seat to myself.

I took off my coat and threw it in the overhead compartment and kept my travel bag with me, which was serving as both an attaché case and a suitcase. I said excuse me and climbed over the motorcycle guy. He decided to not get out of his seat to make it easy for me.

The woman smiled at me, "It looks like a packed flight today."

"I'll say. I arrived at the gate in plenty of time and was assigned to a middle seat in the last row."

"The infamous toilet row with the smells, the line of people nearby and the non-reclining seats." The woman was obviously an experienced traveler.

"Yeah, I forgot about the uncomfortable seats. Fortunately, it's a short flight, if everything goes well."

"A cocktail will help us all get through the ordeal." She'd been in the toilet row before.

I liked this woman immediately. She was about 35 and I guessed she was unmarried as I saw nothing on her ring finger. She was wearing a basic beige suit with a starched white shirt. She had no jewelry except for a steel Rolex and pearl earrings.

But she wasn't wearing nylons, meaning she wasn't an investment banker. Yes, I looked at her legs. All investment-banking females wear nylons. But her legs were tanned and attractive and exposed with her skirt at about mid thigh.

I decided to keep the conversation going. I was carrying confidential material in my bag, and it wasn't smart to read in such close quarters. And besides, I already knew what I was going to talk to Gil about. "So what business are you in?" The biker gave me one of those looks, like what a line, you must be some kind of stud.

"I'm a commercial banker." She blew my nylons theory to bits. If the conversation progressed, I'd have to ask her about them. "I work for a large bank in New York City."

"Really, which one?"

"I'd rather not say. It doesn't make any difference, now does it?"

"Not really. I won't tell you where I work either. Can you tell me your name, or is that top secret as well?"

"You're embarrassing me. I don't have any secrets, but we just met and I don't think we should be trading too much personal information."

"I'm not hitting on you. I just met you 45 seconds ago."

"I know. But indulge me, or let's end the conversation. My name's Sasha."

"That's an exotic name." She didn't look like a Middle Eastern person. "What nationality are you?"

"American."

"Clever."

"What's your name?"

"Stoke."

Her eyes lit up when I said my name. It was possible she recognized me, but she tried not to let on. After all, I was very well known in the business. "What is you ethnic origin?"

"WASP. My ancestors came over on the Mayflower."

"Stoke is an unusual name. Is it short for something else?"

"Stokley. My father named me after Alexander Hamilton (this comment couldn't have made any sense to Sasha). But now you're getting personal." I teased her.

"Touché. Stoke's a very athletic name."

I told you woman thought I was an athlete because of my name. "I was quite a jock when I was a kid. Baseball and football."

"What do you do for a living?"

"I'm an investment banker." Now I was sure she knew me, but I let it slide. What difference did it make?

"I should have known by the suit you're wearing and your watch."

"I'm blushing." I wasn't really.

"You aren't. You have expensive tastes. What types of deals do you do?"

"General corporate stuff. I've been at it a long time. What about you?"

"I run a bank's loan syndication group. You know what we do, don't you?" She smiled when she asked me this.

"Of course. I negotiate with bank lenders in one way or another in almost every deal I do. I'm surprised I haven't met you before." The conversation slowed down and she picked up her *New York Times*.

I turned to the biker. "How're you doing?"

"I'm doing okay."

"Are you a New Yorker or were you visiting?"

"That's a personal question, and I thought we weren't talking personal in this row," he responded sarcastically.

"I guess you don't want to talk. It's your right. Have a nice flight." I wanted to add asshole to the end of my comment, but knew it would only lead to yet another confrontation. He turned away. I detected more than a trace of body odor, which blended well with the chemical and organic smells exuding from the toilet.

The plane took off on time and my row was fairly quiet. I was waiting to see if Sasha would resume our conversation. I glanced at her legs, and she caught me. I was embarrassed at first, but got over it.

If she was going to show 'em, I was going to look at 'em. Screw it. And besides, I was really sex-starved at this point. I asked her, "How long will you be in Chicago?"

"Just until tomorrow afternoon, then I go back to New York. And you?"

I felt like she was just counter-punching. Every time I asked her a question, she asked the same one. "I'm coming back to the City tomorrow as well, unless I get a better opportunity." What the hell, I gave it a shot.

"What do you mean?"

She called my bluff. Should I tell her I was getting separated from my wife, and ask her if she wanted to spend the night with me? Somehow I thought I'd probably strike out with that approach. "Well, it depends upon business. If things heat up on the deal I'm working on, I'll stay another day or two. If not, back home."

She smiled at me. I hate bad winners. I chickened out and she knew it. "What type of deal are you working on?"

I responded in a surprised manner, "I thought we weren't getting personal."

"You're right, forget I asked." She picked up her newspaper.

At that moment the grease monkey next to us started having words with the flight attendant. He wanted to go to the toilet, but the seatbelt sign light was still on. "Mister, you can't leave your seat until the seatbelt light is turned off by the captain. Please sit down."

"Look lady, I had a few beers in the airport and I gotta piss." Classy guy.

"I'm sorry, but you just have to wait." Actually, I was starting to feel sorry for the dirt ball. When you have to pee, you have to pee. What would be worse, the biker gets a little jostled in the toilet because we hit some turbulence, or he urinates in his pants and soils the seat. The latter would also be a huge inconvenience for Sasha and me.

"If that light doesn't go off in a few seconds, I'm gonna have a problem." At that moment, the light went off and two people raced by the biker into the toilets.

He was furious, and you wouldn't believe what this guy did. He unzipped and peed on the galley floor. At least he was courteous enough to turn his back and not expose himself. However, I'd say that the sanitary conditions in the galley had been breached, and I for one wouldn't eat or drink anything on the plane.

The flight attendant screamed and all the passengers turned towards the back of the aircraft. She picked up the intercom and made a call to someone on the plane.

The biker took his seat with a shit-eating grin, and settled in. In a moment, a pilot came charging toward the rear of the plane. The guy was visibly agitated. He was a big fella, and I suspected there was going to be violence.

I decided to stir the pot. "Hey buddy." I was talking to the biker. "The pilot is on his way back to kick your ass."

"Fuck him," the biker boldly responded.

"Where's the guy who urinated?" The pilot was speaking to the flight attendant.

She pointed at the grease ball. "What are you, some kind of pig?" The pilot initiated the confrontation. I was wondering whether there's a law that specifically prohibits pissing on the floor of an airplane. I guess most pilots take offense when somebody urinates any place on board, other than in the head.

The biker looked up, "Are you talking to me?" He had a fuck you look on his face.

He pointed to the urine on the galley floor, "If you're the one who did that, I'm talking to you."

The pilot was a big dude, maybe six three or four. It looks like he threw a few dumbbells around. If he had an attitude like most flyboys, the dirt bag was in for a beating.

The biker got up. He was less than six feet tall and had a potbelly. He had a few beers and even on a good day wouldn't be a match for the Red Baron. The biker shoved the pilot as he got up. Bad idea.

That was all the incentive that the Red Baron needed. He threw a left cross that landed flush on the biker's face. I thought I heard a crack. He came flying back onto Sasha and me. The pilot's fist was so large that he managed to break the dirt bag's nose and chin with one punch, the former being responsible for a significant amount of blood.

I jumped up trying to dodge the red stuff. My clothes were already a mess and I certainly didn't need this guy's bodily fluids on it.

"Get up." The Red Baron was dragging the biker out of the row, thus enabling me to avoid the blood. Sasha was in shock and didn't say anything.

He took him into the galley and threw him into his own urine pool. Then the pilot drew handcuffs from his back pocket and secured him to something in the galley. "If you make any more trouble, I'll come back here and rough you up again. Understand?"

The grease ball nodded and through his busted up mouth uttered, "She wouldn't let me use the toilet and I had to pee."

"Save it for the cops. You'll be arrested when we land in Chicago." The pilot then returned to the cockpit.

I said to the flight attendant, "I guess there will be no food service this afternoon?" She glared at me and walked away towards the front of the plane to get as far away as she could from the grease ball and his urine.

"What was that all about?" Sasha asked me.

"Simple, the biker urinated in the galley, and the Red Baron knocked him out."

"Where is the guy now? I couldn't see much after they moved towards the galley."

"It wasn't much of a fight. The pilot hit him once and handcuffed fatso in the galley. He won't be bothering us any more and now we have an extra seat in our row."

"Great. You're a heartless one, aren't you?" She smiled.

"The greaser got what he deserved." That seemingly ended my courtship of Sasha.

When the plane landed everyone had to remain seated as the police came on the plane and arrested the biker. They didn't even ask any questions. If they had asked me what happened, I'd have said the biker had no choice. When you gotta go, you gotta go.

We arrived early, but there were no gates available at O'Hare, so we parked on the tarmac and waited about 45 minutes.

Ever notice that the airlines are Indian-givers? On the rare occasions that you arrive on time, or heaven forbid early, the ground crews don't show up or no gates are available. It must be a requirement that you leave the airport unhappy.

When was the last time you said, "Oh, that trip was just delightful. It was fun going to the airport and hanging around going to all the neat stores. And the flight, it was a dream. I love the food and those really nice flight attendants." I'll tell you the last time that happened. Never, not once during my lifetime has that happened.

The airlines must have a squadron of people whose job it is to think of ways to fuck up your day, or to make you feel angry or sad.

I tried one last time to develop a rapport with Sasha. She continued to be aloof, circumspect, frigid, arrogant, and condescending. Also, she continued to just ask me the same questions I asked her. She did say that she was staying at the Ritz Carlton, the same hotel I was booked at.

I suggested we share a taxi (and check into the same room, only kidding), but she told me she was going to the Chicago office of her unnamed money center bank. I told her I hoped we'd meet again. She didn't respond. My athletic charm didn't work very well with this woman.

I hopped into a taxi at O'Hare and asked to be taken to the Ritz Carleton. It's one of the nicest hotels in Chicago. Most important, it is close to the nightlife on Rush Street. Another benefit is its proximity to Gil Richards' office, about two blocks away.

The weather in Chicago was rainy and humid, as opposed to sunny and humid in New York City. Somebody once told me that the most advanced races of people came from temperate zones around the globe. Most were very aggressive and interested in conquering others. Just think about it, the Huns, the Celts, the Romans, and a host of other successful groups of people lived in the cooler parts of the Earth.

Tropical places, on the other hand, were where civilization began, in places like Africa and the deserts of the Near East. And yet, the people in these areas and in most hot places are less developed from most every perspective, economically, socially and politically.

It just goes to show you why New Yorkers are such morons in the summer. No race of people can operate efficiently when it's hot as hell and their clothes are always drenched.

A ROOM FIT FOR A SHRIMP

I arrived at the hotel at about 5:15. Gil was expecting me at 5. Screw him. The guy got me into hot soup with the SEC, so he could wait.

The hotel receptionist was a knockout, a tall African American woman. She had mocha skin and was very well endowed. "Hi, my name is Spencer. I have a reservation," (and I'd like to spend the rest of my life with you, I just thought this).

"Alo. What is your family name please?" She thought Spencer was my first name. And she asked me for my family name, instead of my last name.

"Spencer is my last, I mean, my family name."

"I yam sooo sorry, Misser Spencer, tee hee." I guess she was either an airhead or some guy in human resources hired her hoping to get into her pants. She spoke like she arrived in America yesterday.

"No problem. Can I have my room key, please? I'm in a big hurry." This conversation was unlikely to result in a passionate encounter. Although, if I could tape her mouth shut, I might agree to break starch with her (bed sheets that is).

"Eer it ees. Av a nice stay. You're a pleasant man."

I smiled, grabbed the key and hurried over to the elevator. Thirteenth floor. What the hell was the matter with the owners of this hotel? Why would they have a 13th floor, for crying out loud? It's bad luck, and I certainly didn't need any more of that today. I looked at the package that came with the key and noticed that I was in room 1313. Vampires were probably lurking in the closet. I should've gone out and bought some garlic for protection.

And what's up with card keys? In the old days one used a real key to open doors. You know, those metal things with teeth on the end that fit into a lock. Now you get a piece of plastic that opens the door about 50% of the time. If you stay in your room one minute past checkout time, the card key stops working and you have to beg for forgiveness at the front desk.

Also, card keys don't have room numbers printed on them. You have to memorize your room number. Now, for somebody with an average IQ this shouldn't be too difficult. But remember, business travelers go out to dinner and usually drink too much. When drunk, your IQ drops temporarily, and remembering your room number becomes difficult as most have at least three digits. You may even have to sleep in the hall if can't find your way back to the lobby to ask what your room number is.

It would be terrible if you picked up a beautiful young thing and couldn't get in to the room. When entering a hotel with a companion, you have to act nonchalant and slip past the reception desk. Not that they would stop you or anything, but one must be discreet when on the wrong side of morality. Right?

Anyway, returning to the lobby to determine your room number could ruin the moment, especially if you told the bimbo that you were one of the smartest people on earth and a math major in college.

I finally got to my room and it was the smallest living space I had ever seen. I had to walk sideways to get past the bed and the wall. A credenza was nestled into the corner of the room. It had a TV set and a mini bar in it.

After the long ride from the airport in a quasi air-conditioned car in humid weather conditions, I was parched and attempted to open the mini bar. The door on the mini bar scraped the bed as I opened it. Incredible, you'd think the interior designers would've used their tape measures to ensure that this tacky and overpriced furniture fit in the room.

They just want the big money (20 or 30% of the price of the furniture), and didn't want to do any of the detail work. Everyone wants to be a "big picture person" and leave the grunt work for someone else. Designers have the biggest racket outside of investment banking.

SS and I bought a few apartments over the years and we had to retain design counsel (sounds like a law firm) because we're just too stupid to match a green chair with a green Oriental rug (SS's assumption, not mine). Anytime you pay a vendor a percentage of what they spend on your behalf, you'll be ripped off, guaranteed. It's simple, they'll always spend as much as they can to maximize their fees. It's human to do so.

I had a major battle with one of our decorators a few years ago about his fee for the antiques I wanted to buy. Here's the scenario, you judge. We went around to several antique dealers to look at things like Oriental rugs, lamps, and tables. I'd walk into the store with my "advisor" and would see something I liked. The item would have a sucker's price tag on it (for the walk-in trade), which was immediately reduced because my designer was a bona fide designer (I don't know how this was determined, but it happened automatically). The price was reduced by say 20% from the sucker's cost. So, if the tag indicated $1,000, my price would be $800 (By the way, I never bought anything that cost three figures, while decorating the apartment. I'm using these numbers to make the math simple for readers who don't have a calculator handy). Then, my designer would charge me 30% times the actual price, or $240. So, if I walked into the joint and bought the item myself, I'd have paid $1,000, but because he graced me with his 'expertise,' my price was $1,040.

This sounds like a reasonable arrangement until you recall that he only knew the address of the store and I selected the item. I could've looked up the addresses of antique stores in the Yellow Pages. To make matters worse, when I asked my designer whether the adjusted price (the semi-sucker price that I was supposed to pay, not the price that the walk-in traffic paid) was negotiable, he said absolutely not.

I refused to accept this and told him I was going to negotiate every single purchase. You may not believe this, but I never once paid his price. Not once. Every single purchase I made proceeded as follows: the sucker price was reduced by about 20%, I offered 80% of that price and we settled for 90%. Since I spent high six figures for the furniture, I saved a hell of a lot of money, no thanks to my designer.

Back to his fee. I told my wife that in the future I wasn't going to pay a 30% designer fee for antiques, only 10%. On items where he selected the fabric and coordinated the manufacture of a new piece of furniture, he deserved the full fee. When SS told him about our new arrangement, he went crazy and started to cry, literally. She came back to me and said I was being too aggressive. I said tough shit.

We happen to have a friend who's a high-end interior design consultant (I'm not sure what title she wants to attach to her name, so I might have just offend her. In any case, I'm not going to fall into another stewardess/flight attendant trap). Just to be sure I wasn't being a complete asshole, I asked her opinion of my proposed antique arrangement. You wouldn't believe the venomous response I received. She called me dirty names (affectionately, of course) and said she wouldn't do business with me under any circumstance and I was being a complete jerk.

I thought about her response and it dawned on me that maybe she wasn't the right person to ask. What the hell did I expect her to say: "Stoke, you're absolutely correct, my colleagues and I have been fucking rich people for years and we should earn substantially less money for our services."

Well, I felt a little guilty and told SS to tell our decorator that we'd pay him 15% for antiques, but only if he had his heart in it. I loved that part of the deal. Here I was tearing this guy's heart out and I wanted him to be happy and continue to work hard for me.

For a fleeting moment, I started to empathize with the poor bastard. My clients always screwed down my fees and they expected me to continue to work hard and be happy about the new arrangement. Bullshit. Fast forward ten years. SS and I lost our shirts when we sold the antiques that the decorator helped us purchase. There's justice in the world. I'm happy I chiseled him down and reduced his fee. We lost in the end because he didn't know what the hell he was talking about.

Back to the hotel room. I walked into the bathroom and was amazed to see that it was almost as large as the entire sleeping area. What idiot came up with this configuration? Maybe these were the type of rooms assigned to customers who got off on big bathrooms. Maybe some people preferred to sleep in the bathroom and not in bed. Maybe some couples wanted large showers to facilitate water sex. I'd preferred a larger sleeping area, and no bidet.

I couldn't walk around my bed without contorting my body, but I had a little bathtub to wash my rear end, in addition to a shower and a large bathtub to wash my whole body. There seems to be an emphasis on cleanliness at this place. Incidentally, I never met an American who ever used a bidet.

When an architect I once used recommended we install a bidet in our new bathroom, I told him to forget it and make the shower larger. The only person who knew the true value of a bidet was Crocodile Dundee. He cleaned his boots in it.

My final word on the hotel room relates to toilet paper. I don't understand why maids need to fold the end of it into a point. I won't use toilet paper handled by another person, so I always rip off the end that has been folded. If any hotel managers read this, I hope they tell their maids to stop touching the toilet paper unnecessarily.

The phone rang and I picked it up expecting to hear Gil's voice. But surprise, it was SS, the last person I wanted to talk to. "Stoke, it's me, Sharon."

"What do you want?"

"I'm sorry to disturb you. I got your number from Liz. Can you talk for a minute?" I'll bet Liz had a nice conversation with her. It wouldn't surprise me if Liz told SS that she was happy I was dumping her.

"I'm busy, I have to meet Gil in a few minutes. I thought you spoke your mind earlier today."

"Maybe I'm being to aggressive. I decided I want to save our marriage. Don't you?"

"I'm not sure anymore, Sharon. I've had enough of your attitude."

"What about the kids?"

"I'm not living with you or anybody for the sake of my children. It's not healthy for them or us, unless we can patch things up."

"You're right. I don't want to fight anymore. Really, I just want to be happy with you, like the old days."

"Sharon, we were never happy. You just wanted a rich husband, and you found one. You're a gold digger. You don't care about our relationship. You only want the good life."

"But I love you, Stoke. You've always been good to the kids and me."

"Keep the boys out of it. This is between you and me. For our entire married life you acted like you were doing me a favor every time we made love. Shit, I could've had any woman I wanted, and here I am begging you for sex. It's been a degrading experience sleeping in the same bed with you. You're a cold fish and nothing more than a high priced, a very high priced, prostitute. Sex for money, but not too much sex and certainly no passion." That should get her goat.

"That was a terrible fucking thing to say to me." Usually when a woman uses the 'f' word, you've really made her angry.

"The truth hurts, doesn't it? You never enjoyed being with me. I might as well have purchased a blow up doll and slept with it. At least she (or it) wouldn't complain and I wouldn't have to buy her (or it) a piece of jewelry every time I got laid."

"Sounds like you've made up your mind, Stoke."

"After you told me you were conspiring with an attorney, I was sure you had already made up your mind."

"I just said that to make you angry. We only met once. It was no big deal."

"Bullshit. It's a big deal. I gotta go. Good-bye. We'll talk when I get home tomorrow."

"Don't hang up, Stoke. You really don't mean what you're saying. I know you don't."

"Sharon you don't know me. You're a selfish bitch. You never tried to make me happy. Every time I touch you, you freeze up. You despise me. Why don't you just admit it? I want to find somebody who will love me in every way, not just because I have money."

"After I get finished with you won't have any money."

I slammed the phone down on the receiver. "Bitch," I mumbled to myself. I noticed the message light was illuminated. I called the automated message center and found out that Gil had just called.

Someday you'll arrive at a hotel and will never speak with a human being during the entire time of your stay. The whole place will be automated. The receptionists already act like robots (and airheads). The fancy hotel chains teach them to be impersonal. In the future, you'll walk in, state your name and present a big brother ID card. A robot will then spit out a room key. If you don't like the room, tough shit.

A "non-service" hotel would drive SS crazy. She never accepted the first room assigned to her. She always wanted to change rooms as a matter of principal. On our honeymoon, we checked into the Hassler Hotel in Rome. The manager of the hotel was literally waiting for us at the front door. We had a suite, not just any suite. It was the one you see in the background on postcards of the Spanish Steps.

We were escorted to our room, which to be fair was old and a little dark. SS immediately said she wanted another room and we'd be happy to pay more for better accommodations. I thought the hotel manager was going to have a stroke. He was mortified and started speaking very quickly, half in English and half in Italian. The gist of his comments was that we had the best accommodations in the city and we couldn't possibly pay more than we were already paying. I wanted to get on a plane at that moment and leave Rome. From that point on, I began to think that I had probably made a mistake marrying this woman.

SS wasn't very pleasant in restaurants, either. We also visited Paris, and had reservations at

Tour d'Agent near L'Cite. The dining room has a beautiful view of Notre Dame. We entered and were asked to wait for a moment.

At the bar, SS started busting my balls about getting a table by the window so we we'd have an unrestricted view of the cathedral. I told her to relax and that we shouldn't be too pushy. But she'd have no part of it, and told me to give the captain some money. Like a dope I went over to the headman and slid a $100 bill into his hand. He looked at it, sneered at me and slid the bill back into my hand. Truthfully, I didn't know whether the tip was too small, if he didn't accept bribes (unlikely, he's French), if he hated Americans, or if he was insulted I gave him US dollars rather than French Francs. The guy was a snooty, arrogant prick and put us at a rotten table, at which the sommelier abused us as we considered our choice of wine. SS was so obnoxious during our trip, that I didn't think we'd ever be welcome back to Europe again.

Hotel automation is a bad idea, so if any hotel big wigs are reading this, I recommend the following services be provided to businessmen. The receptionists should be beautiful babes from every corner of the globe. They should include every nationality, just none from France. When you walk through the front door, the lobby should have the feel of a high priced brothel. Other beautiful women should escort you to your room. They should tease you by suggesting they would like to stay with you overnight.

The maids should be long-legged and dressed in short little dresses with frills at the hem and low cut necklines. Push-up bras should be mandatory for all domestics. Actually, French maids are a good idea, and they should wear a lot of perfume and be available as bed partners. You know I'm only kidding, but all men think of this stuff every time they go to a nice hotel. Seriously, personal service is important and appreciated. Ugly people with nasty attitudes don't cut it.

I called Gil's private line and a woman answered. "Hello, Gil's Escort Service. How may I help you?"

"Who is this?"

"Why, I'm Sophie. Who the heck are you?"

"I'm Stoke. Please put Gil on the phone."

"Why, of course." The woman answered in a huff.

"Hello." It was Gil, thank goodness.

"Do you have prostitutes working in your office? Who is Sophie?"

"You asshole, Sophie's my daughter."

"Oh shit. Sorry Gil."

"Don't sweat it. You'll get to appreciate her sense of humor this evening. She's a little different. Where the fuck've you been. I'm sitting here like a schmuck waiting for you."

"I just got off the phone with my wife. We're having some problems."

"What kind of problems?"

"Marital."

"Oh, boy. Are you finally going to trade her in?"

"Come on Gil. Don't talk about her like that."

"We've been out together with Sharon lots of times. I told you on many occasions she's a liability and you should get rid of her before your net worth gets any larger."

"Well, I just might make a break. She's driving me crazy. I can't stand her anymore. And she's already consulting with an attorney,"

"Beat you to the punch, huh? Are you still fucking her? I'll bet you aren't."

"That's personal."

"Are you having sex with her or not?"

"Not for a few months."

"Hell, I'd have a nervous breakdown if I didn't have sex for a month. My heart would give out. Unexpended bull juice clogs up your arteries."

"What are you talking about?"

"Are you getting any on the side?"

"No, but I'd like to."

"Well tonight's the night. You and I are going to do some tom-catting later this evening."

"We need to talk about the SEC problem first."

"Don't sweat it, we will. Come over to my office."

"See you in about 20 minutes." We hung up.

BOARD SEX

I decided to leave the hotel immediately to avoid any more attempts by SS to contact me. My marriage was in the crapper and anything I said at that moment wouldn't improve the situation.

Although I attempted to freshen up, I was still rumpled after an exhausting day in the hot sun, in taxis, and in airports. The stress relating to all of the things happening to me only served to increase my perspiration rate. I figured Gil wouldn't give a shit if my suit wasn't pressed and my shirt was slightly washed out.

The walk over to Crucible would take only fifteen minutes. I wasn't in a hurry because our meeting wasn't one I looked forward to having.

Just outside the hotel door, an attractive woman walked up to me. "Hello. How are you tonight?"

The prostitute light went off in my head. I was so hard up that I considered pursuing this lady of the night, but Gil was waiting. Too bad, this gal was stunning and dressed in a very sexy miniskirt. It was drizzling outside and she wore an unbuttoned light raincoat so buyers could inspect her wares. I'll bet she would've been an expensive date. I proceeded past her without saying anything and didn't acknowledge her advances.

"You don't have to be rude. I just said hello. If you aren't interested in talking to me (or having sex with me), you should be polite and say you're busy." The woman was actually insulted, a prostitute with thin skin. I guess she was the sensitive type.

I almost said something nasty, which would've been consistent with my behavior all day, but resisted. The prostitute was polite to me and I should be polite to her. What's fair is fair. "I'm sorry, you're absolutely correct. I'm not interested, but thank you anyway. Have a nice evening (having sex with strange men)." What a day, apologizing to a hooker.

Crucible occupied two floors of the Sears Tower. After the World Trade Center attack, security at the building was on high alert. The powers that be figured that Osama's wackos would be looking for another target and why not the tallest building in one of America's largest cities?

Getting into and out of the building was reminiscent of the World Trade Center before 9/11, a lot of good all the security did for the poor people who lost their lives that day. It was easier to pass security at an airport than it was to enter the Tower as a guest. Can you imagine?

So much time had passed since that tragic day and we were still being inconvenienced. Like every American, I despised the people who attacked us on that fateful day. I lost friends, as did many other New Yorkers, but you have to hand it to the terrorists. With box cutters, they hijacked four airplanes and made direct hits on the two World Trade Center buildings and the Pentagon. They should be inducted into the "Terrorist Hall of Fame."

When inducted, you will rot in hell and be tormented by Satan for eternity. What warped mind fabricated the story that you will have sex with virgins in Paradise if you killed innocent non-combatants? It's an amazing concept. Strap on explosives, walk into a pizzeria, and slaughter women and children having a slice. Upon your death, the orgasms begin.

I'll bet the person who dreamt up this crock of shit was a radical and crazed cleric. I'd like to see the section of their holy book that contained this promise. Killing for religious reasons is barbaric and brings to mind the crimes of the Crusades when men murdered others in the name of God.

My theory about all this is that Muslims are so poor that they depend on their clergymen to give them strength to deal with the hardships of life. Most holy people do an amazing job giving people hope through faith in their God. But when fanatical clerics call for their followers to cleanse the world of every person who worships another god, it's wrong and sparks increased terrorism.

Our forefathers made a brilliant move separating church and state. They knew that government could not compete with religion. It's much easier to be unfaithful to your government than to your God. Government is temporal, and irrelevant after you die. Religion is eternal. A mistake relating to the latter will have eternal consequences.

Throughout the world, the clergy have a huge impact on political affairs. They oppose any type of government that diminishes the power of their church, mosque, or synagogue. Our forefathers overcame this opposition and it resulted in the greatest government in history.

The question I always ask myself is why people from around the world hate Americans? As I see it, there are multiple answers to the question. Generally speaking, have-nots hate (or at least are jealous of) the haves. If you're dirt poor, you assume those who live in fancy houses and drive expensive cars are cheaters. A class struggle is under way in America, based upon this premise, as certain politicians try to garner votes by criticizing wealthy people.

Secondly, Americans aren't the most modest people and our middle class is far more prosperous than 99% of the rest of the world. Our materialism, arrogance, and tendency to be bad winners are resented universally. In most places outside of the United States, people work to survive. Here we work to buy a bigger house, a larger car and fancier clothes. And we're free. We can say what we want and go where we choose. We can worship however we like without persecution. The world is jealous of us, period, end of story.

Now, I have no idea how this relates to blowing up the World Trade Center. Some warped minds must have decided that American infidels needed to be taught a lesson, so they recruited 20 or so fanatics for a kamikaze mission and several thousand Americans died. What the hell kind of world do we live in?

Because some crazies in the Middle East hate us and want to kill us, I'm going to be inconvenienced for the rest of my life. I remember the days when I'd get to the airport 10 minutes before departure and have plenty of time to board the plane. Now I must arrive two hours early. The same holds true for entering a building. I have to be at a building 30 minutes early to arrive on time for a meeting. Every visitor is considered a potential terrorist with a briefcase full of TNT. It really pisses me off.

There are, maybe, 1,000 fanatics in the world that orchestrate terror on a global basis, and all four billion of the rest of us have to suffer. Well, you know where I'm going with this. I walk into the Tower through a metal detector and it's déjà vu with the security people. Just like at my own building and the airport, I get my balls broken. What a drag. Fifteen minutes to get on the elevator.

At last, I reached Crucible's offices. The secretary at the reception desk recognized me and told me to go right back to the Board Room where Gil and some other people were waiting for me. I knew the way having made many presentations to the company's Board of Directors on numerous occasions. I decided to make a quick pit stop. Who knew how long we'd be tied up in the meeting? When you're on the road, never walk past a bathroom.

The facilities were immaculate. The lavatory at GYP was also very clean, as compared to those at the investment bank mentioned earlier.

Some guy walked in after me and took his place at a urinal next to me. It's bad form to stand next to another man while taking a piss if there are other open holes, so I immediately disliked him. I'm sure he peaked over the separation at some point.

I finished first and proceeded to the sink to wash up. While I was soaping up, the guy walks right past me and out the door without stopping. I've seen this many times before, and it grosses me out. The man was just handling his penis and likely splashing urine on himself. It can be a sloppy process if you're not careful, and here he was returning to the general population with contaminated hands.

I don't touch door handles in bathrooms because if I did, I'd be (for all intents and purposes) touching that man's and every other non-washer's private parts. And if I touched my mouth after I touched the door contaminated by non-washers it would be the equivalent of doing you know what. I know I'm obsessed with cleanliness, kind of like Howard Hughes, but I really think it's justifiable in our society with all the unsanitary people we come into contact with. At any given moment, there are thousands of men shaking hands with others who just finishing shaking their penises.

I entered the Board Room and Gil was delighted to see me. What the hell, we'd probably be sharing a prison cell together soon. Two men and one woman were also present, including the guy who didn't wash his hands.

First, I was introduced to the woman, Sophie Richards, Gil's daughter. She had a sexy voice over the phone and a body to go along with it. Sophie wore a very short skirt and a sweater that exposed a lot of breast and just a little bare midriff. Her tummy was flat and ripped. She was about 26 or so and spent hours in the gym.

The two men were attorneys from the company's General Counsel Office. I nodded at them and avoided contact with the non-washer for obvious reasons. Neither of these men said a word the whole time I was in the room. From the get go, it was difficult not to stare at Sophie whose melon sized breasts and exposed legs were a sight for sore eyes.

"Stoke, how are you?" Gil asked me.

"Just terrific, although it's been a trying day. I feel like the whole world is out to get me today."

"Fear not, after we finish talking business, Sophie and I are taking you to dinner and then to a club where you can get yourself into trouble. I hope you're well rested because things don't start happening until after midnight." Gil ignored the two lawyers. I wanted to tell him that one of them had contaminated hands and should be kept away from all food and drink.

I looked at Sophie, "So what do you do at Crucible (besides looking fabulous)?"

"I just graduated from Northwestern where I received my MBA." The woman should be working the telephones at 555-SEXY having phone sex with strangers. What a voice. I suppose an MBA would make her just a little over qualified for a position where you encouraged men to masturbate.

"Is you father grooming you to take over Crucible?" I asked her with a wry smile. Physically she needed no grooming. She was just about perfect.

"If he can talk the Board into accepting a woman into senior management, it's a possibility."

At least she knew that there was a Board, and that it was supposed to have some control over her father. I'm not sure Gil cared about his obligations to the Board.

"Well, I sure as hell would vote for you if I was on the Board. I'm so sick of having to look at your old man's face after all these years. Gil, why don't you pass the baton to your daughter now? You know she's the right person to take over."

Gil jumped in. "If you're finished insulting me, I'd like to move on, unless you want me to leave you alone with my daughter." He smiled as he said this.

I thought that was an excellent suggestion, but responded, "OK, let's get into the SEC inquiry."

Gil obviously had been revving himself up about this whole situation all day and opened the conversation. "I'm so sick of the overreaction by the SEC to the scandals at all those other companies. I've been running this fucking company for 20 years and never had a problem. All of a sudden I got these government weenies trying to get into my pants."

"Your right, if you didn't do anything illegal." Now I knew why the lawyers were present. Gil wanted this whole conversation to be privileged so he could speak freely. Good idea actually. "Also, I really don't appreciate getting my ass reamed by my boss without a heads up from you."

"You're right. I should've called you. Sorry about that. But it's not a big deal."

"What are the charges? I ran out of the office as soon as I could when my boss told me about this, so I really don't know very much."

"The SEC said I misled the new investors. Since we sold bonds publicly as part of the leveraged buyout, the SEC reviewed the projections after the fact."

"Because you missed the numbers by such a large margin?"

"I guess so. We fell short of the estimates provided in the offering documents and I suppose some of the bondholders started bitching to the SEC."

"I didn't have a chance to go back and compare the projections to your results this year. How bad is the variance?"

"The projections had us earning $750 million before depreciation, interest, and taxes. This was supposed to come from revenues of $3.5 billion."

"What will the actual results be for the year?"

"400 on 2.7."

Holy shit. Why didn't you tell me about this earlier? Maybe we could've managed the expectations of the bondholders. What was the reason for the shortfall?"

"Well, to be honest, I used the most optimistic numbers I received from my operations people, which accounts for about $150 million of the earnings shortfall. The rest comes from problems relating to the radar transaction."

"Is there anything else I should know about, as if that isn't enough?"

"Yeah, there's another issue." Gil responded in a very quiet voice.

"What else could possibly be wrong?" I responded.

"I've had a stormy relationship with my former Board, which came to a head while we were negotiating the buyout. For Christ's sake, I put all these people on the Board. I thought they were my friends, but times are changing and directors are becoming more independent these days." Gil seemed saddened about this. He must miss the days when he did anything he wanted to and they just acted as his rubber stamp.

"Did you lie to them about something?"

"Not really. The problem actually relates to one specific director."

"Which one?"

"Marion."

"Marion Denning?"

"Yeah."

"She's an educator, isn't she?"

"Marion's a dean at Northwestern. She was helpful getting Sophie into the business school."

Sophie jumped in. "Marion is a terrific person. I really like her a lot, so I can't believe she'd turn on my father."

"Sophie, please, let me finish. There are some things that happened that you don't know about. The fact is Marion and I started dating after she joined the Board. We tried to be very discreet. Only a few people actually knew, and I hoped it would remain under the covers, so to speak." He smiled.

Marion Denning is purported to be one of the great academic minds in the country. She's also one of the most beautiful African American women on the planet. In spite of her age, about 44, very few younger women can hold a candle to her in the looks department. She'd compete quite effectively in the Miss America contest. And she has a 160+ IQ to go along with her physical attributes. It's no wonder Gil was attracted to her. "So, what's the problem?" I figured they're both single, why not have a good time?

"Well, everything was going along fine. She knew I fooled around regularly, but she didn't care. Marion is an independent and confident person, and we weren't going to get married or anything like that. I saw her once or twice a week, schedules permitting, and we had a great time. We even vacationed together last spring."

I queried, "You have a platonic relationship with her? That would be a first."

"Are you serious? The woman is a knockout. She's wild in bed. We screwed until neither of us could walk. It was great."

The others in the room had embarrassed looks on their faces. I think they would've preferred not to know all this. I was a little surprised Gil would get into all the gory details in front of everyone, especially his daughter. I'm sure he felt safe because of the attorney privilege thing. "I can't wait to find out where this is all heading."

"Marion has a 25 year old daughter. Marion got pregnant in college and the child's father married her. Their marriage didn't last very long, and thereafter, she dedicated herself to the child and academic achievement."

I responded. "Uh oh."

"Marion's ex husband is a former professional basketball player. The guy's name is Jay Olsen. Maybe you heard of him? He's a real good-looking guy and their daughter Sylvia is magnificent. The ex is white and together Marion and Jay created a thing of beauty, six feet tall, and now a professional model."

"Gil, what did you do?"

"We vacationed in St. Bart's with Sylvia. Mother and daughter are totally uninhibited and were constantly parading around our villa and beach area without any clothes. Marion and I were going at it around the clock. We weren't very discreet and the daughter must have gotten turned on. St. Bart's has that effect on you. One morning, Marion went shopping in town and left Sylvia and me alone. We talked for a while, and she started asking me personal questions about my relationship with her mother. One thing led to the next, and to make a long story short, Marion came home early and found us in bed together."

"Oh my God. Did Marion go crazy?"

"No. She quietly packed up her things and left that afternoon. Sylvia and I stayed for another couple of days. What the hell, the damage had already been done. Mother and daughter aren't on speaking terms. Marion stopped communicating with me, except at Board meetings."

"So what does this have to do with Crucible?" I could probably piece together about 20 or 30 problems, but figured I'd let Gil tell me.

"Marion chaired the Compensation Committee of the former Board."

"Great, you were having sex with the person responsible for you compensation. That'll play well with the press."

"It better not get into the papers."

"Stop teasing me. Get to the point." I was starting to get impatient.

"Marion approved an addition to my compensation last year that never got reported to the whole committee."

"What are we talking about? I hate to ask."

"Five million."

"Oh shit. Why didn't you get approval in the normal way? You wouldn't have had any problems."

"We were negotiating the buyout. Marion and I thought that extra comp would look bad, especially since my total comp in the previous year was slightly off the charts."

"Is she threatening to reveal this to the buyers?"

"Actually she already told the original Board in a conference call a few days ago. Marion said she approved the payment with the understanding that I'd disclose it to the Board and to the buyers during the due diligence process."

"Marion is doing this for revenge?"

"I guess so. Either that or she's afraid it would've come out in the wash sometime after the buyout. By controlling the flow and spin of the information she can protect herself."

"Does Applegate know yet?"

"There's an emergency Board meeting on Friday with the new owners, at which time everything will be put on the table, the radar deal and the previously undisclosed bonus. He will find out immediately after that meeting is adjourned."

"How do you plan to defend yourself at the meeting?"

"Not sure yet. My dick has gotten me into trouble once again."

"Gil, you may be indicted for embezzling money from the company,"

"Not likely, I already returned it. But it sure as hell ain't going to endear me to my new stakeholders, especially Applegate."

"Returning the bonus was a smart thing to do. But you didn't follow the rules and the new Board may feel obligated to hang you."

"I know, and Marion's gonna help them."

Sophie sat up and spoke. "Dad, you really messed up this time. How could you do that to Marion? She's so beautiful and you had to seduce her daughter?"

"Look honey, I'm not perfect. I admit that I have self control problems when it comes to women."

While father and daughter had a father and daughter talk, I had a flashback to the good old 1980s, when anything was permissible. Gil would've just been one of the many players then. It's hard for me to believe what actually went on during those days. Everybody on the Street was fooling around. Compensation was terrific and the champagne was flowing.

BBQers were all over the young professional men, and senior partners were all over the young professional women. Everybody was getting laid. I never could understand how people could date, mate, and then resume a business relationship the next day at the office. We all worked very hard, and I suppose the rules of the road were that there were no rules.

Senior men used their power to get their way with women, and were never held accountable. The only way a woman could be safe at the time was to go steady (or get married), or find a mentor. It was kind of like being in jail. You needed protection.

Having said all this, the 1980s could not have been more fun. We had a lot of disposable income and everybody had a live-for-today mentality. I loved telling and hearing stories from the night before. But those days are gone forever. If you fuck around today, you get fired. If you talk dirty, you get fired.

"While you two chat, I'd like to make some phone calls and check my email."

"You can use my office. Give us about 20 minutes. OK?"

"See you in 20." I was sure that Gil could convince his daughter that he was innocent of just being a normal man with a healthy sexual appetite. It wouldn't surprise me if he'd had this conversation with her before. I'm sure Sophie's girlfriends were very attractive and that Gil would have liked to date some of them as well. Some guys workout to eat. Some guys make money to buy cars and other toys. Gil Richards directed all of his energies to being with beautiful women. And the more dangerous the situation, the more fun it was for him.

I've had friends who behaved like him over the years, men who would take any chance to have sex with women. Conquest was what made their lives worth living. Unfortunately, one can't have morals or be empathetic in any way to be successful in this lifestyle. Every woman is fair game, married or not.

I believe seducing a married woman, even if she wants to be seduced is a crime against humanity. It's also a way to get your head blown off by an irate husband. Why target women already involved with men, when there are so many others available?

Getting older has its benefits, as the universe of women who can reasonably be your partner increases every year. When a man is 20, he's attracted to females between 18 (legal reasons) and 25. When a man is 30, the range increases from 18 to 35. When a man is 50, he might be interested in woman from 20 to 50. I like to stay at the younger end of the range, but I've noticed that really powerful men have affairs with women around their own age. Here they are with several hundred million dollar net worths and they cheat on their wives for another frumpy 50 year old. Go for the gold, gentlemen. Go young.

I knew the way to Gil's office. As I walked through the halls of Crucible, I admired the art on its walls and the beautiful furniture that decorated this place of business. Ever notice that many companies buy expensive, museum grade art for their offices. It's almost as if CEOs want the world to believe that they're connoisseurs of the arts, which they think camouflages the fact that they're despicable and underhanded corporate marauders.

Interestingly, they use resources belonging to the stockholders to execute this strategy. If you invest in a company that manufactures widgets, do you really want the company to buy Monet paintings? No, you want the company to manufacture better widgets than the competition and earn greater profits.

To make matters worse, the CEOs act as if they personally own the goddamn art. So, here I was wandering among priceless pieces of art owned by a company that makes radar equipment for the military. That makes sense, right?

I wondered what the new owners were going to do about all this stuff. If it were up to me,

I'd tell Gil to sell everything immediately. He'd probably say that all the beauty inspires the employees to make more money for Crucible. Bullshit, sell the stuff, and if the company loses money it should come out of Gil's pocket.

I entered the CEO's office, the most opulent of all the opulent offices on the executive floor. Gil never scrimped when it came to his luxury. His office was huge. It had a monstrous desk, from which a long conference table jutted out. With this configuration, Gil could conduct a large meeting of up to 12 people. On the other side of the room, was a complete living room.

I could just imagine how many women had sex with him on the couch. It had to have DNA samples from scores of conquests. No woman was safe from Gil. He'd seduce secretaries, executives, bankers, vendors, and probably cleaning people.

Behind his desk he had a headshot of Sophie. What an angel. On the other side of the desk was a picture of Bill Clinton with his arm around Gil at a fundraiser.

Gil would support any politician who was in a position to assist Crucible. And he'd do whatever was necessary to market his company to the military. Gil and Bill (sounds like an act) must have had a great time telling dirty stories. I wondered if they ever went out together. I'd have to ask Gil later about it that evening. My money was on Gil for the most outrageous office sex, although the former president hit new heights during his administration. Gil's escapades would blow away (no pun intended) the antics of most other sex crazed men.

Gil had a huge IBM desktop computer. I had used it before, so I knew how to get online. Bankers are totally dependent on email and voice mail these days.

When away from the office, emails were usually sent and received with gadgets known as blackberries. They're a vile innovation that everyone in our business constantly fiddles with. While meeting with clients, bankers will use their blackberries under the table so the client doesn't notice. But you know, they always notice, and it's a rude thing to do. In fact, when somebody uses a blackberry while I'm speaking, I'm tempted to grab the device and smash it on the floor.

I see professionals tapping away on the stupid little machines in restaurants, at soccer games, at parent/teacher conferences, and even while their kids are trying to talk to them. I really don't need to be that online (or rude and inconsiderate), so I don't use one myself.

I connected to the GYP system and typed in my password. All major companies have elaborate sign-on procedures to protect their systems from hackers. These people enter other user computer systems and try to fuck them up. I'm no expert on this stuff, but from what I understand a hacker's only objective is to create havoc.

Many of these delinquents do it for sport resulting in millions of dollars of damage. It's some kind of honor to destroy corporate property in the sinister world that these creeps live in. Every time one of them is caught, the book on them is that they're lonely, unhappy people. That makes sense.

A new terrorist objective is to cause disruption in cyberspace. Most terrorists just aren't smart enough to pull it off, though. I pray they're never successful recruiting any of the more intelligent hackers. It would be a real problem if they did. In our day and age, we must be diligent every waking moment, because somebody wants to make our lives miserable.

The screen lit up as I momentarily made contact with GYP and then it disappeared. I'm one of those people who always have trouble with high-tech equipment. Nothing ever works right for me. My computer is always crashing (I think gremlins live inside of it) and my access to the Internet is always being cut off. I don't really believe any of these internet communication companies know what they're doing. Technical problems are surfacing faster than they're solving them as new features are introduced.

The same is true for cell phones. You'd think that money spent on this technology would afford us uninterrupted access from virtually anywhere on the planet. Nope. You can't even get good service in New York City. When using my office or home computers, I'm always on the verge of throwing them out the window. Finally, I gave up trying to connect to my computer at GYP.

I called into email. I had 26 voice messages. Can you imagine it? I must be some popular guy. Slowly, I worked my way through each message taking notes and recording phone numbers.

Included was a hate message from SS. She figured that talking with me live was too painful and it was impossible to make her points. Voicemail enables one to deliver a speech on any subject without interruption. Her tack was to be venomous in this message. It was a vintage SS strategy. Usually, it bothered me, but not anymore. I just erased her message after listening to it for just a few seconds.

I also had a message from Cohen. He gloated about my growing problem with the SEC and Crucible. Cohen never let an hour pass without checking his messages. I tried to respond in a way that would ruin his evening. I told him that the SEC and/or the Justice Department were investigating an embezzlement accusation at Crucible, and GYP might be implicated. I went into little detail so that Cohen would spend hours worrying about its impact on GYP.

I made my way back to the conference room after about 30 minutes where I saw Gil and Sophie continuing their father/daughter conversation. The contaminated attorney was gone. I didn't want to have anything to do with this conversation, as it was strictly family business. I saw Sophie really going at her father through the glass door, and suspected Sophie was one of very few people who could speak to Gil Richards in such an aggressive fashion. I opened the door and said, "Excuse me. May I come in?"

Gil turned and saw me. "Sure, you can, Stoke. Sophie and I were just clearing the air." He leaned over and kissed his daughter on the forehead. She smiled. I guess she still loved her father even though he was sex crazed.

I wished SS and I had been able to communicate. Maybe we wouldn't be on the verge of divorce if we had been able to talk things out over the years. I really believe that married people must work constantly to stay happy.

One element of this process is to confront problems immediately and not let them fester. If something is pissing you off, you should talk to your spouse and settle it. If you're nice and explain your position calmly, you have about a 50/50 chance of successfully resolving the problem quickly. Sometimes one party will dig his or her heels in and a calm conversation can get heated. But this is healthy as well.

Don't keep bad feelings to yourself, as they'll eventually surface anyway. I was jealous of Gil and Sophie's ability to hammer things out. I assumed they did this many times over the years.

"I can go back to my hotel and stay busy if you want more time to talk."

"Stoke, I really appreciate your sensitivity. Would you mind it if we just delayed our dinner by an hour or so? We'll pick you up at the hotel at 10. OK?

"Sure, call me and I'll be waiting at the front door of the hotel for you." I left the room and headed towards the elevator. On the way I bumped into the contaminated attorney. Just my luck.

He spoke. "Mr. Spencer, I suspect we'll be seeing a lot of each other in the coming weeks as the SEC investigation proceeds."

There was something about this guy that really turned me off, in addition to his unclean habits. "I can't wait."

"No need to be too concerned. It'll be difficult to prove that Mr. Richards wasn't forthcoming during the buyout negotiations. Business conditions change rapidly these days and the radar situation could not have been anticipated."

"You sure about that? By the way, what's your name?"

"My name's Al Nash. I'm Assistant General Counsel at Crucible. And yes, I'm sure the SEC will have a difficult time proving anything detrimental to Richards."

"I see. You're the General Counsel's assistant. I'd have thought that this situation would've warranted the top guy." This was an obnoxious thing to say and I knew it would infuriate the man.

"Don't worry about my legal skills, Mr. Spencer. I can assure you Mr. Richards and Crucible will be well represented."

"Are you going to look out for my firm's interests in this process?"

"Well, you know how it works. We have to take care of our own first and foremost."

"There's something else you should keep in mind, Mr. Dash." I mispronounced his name on purpose. I figured I might as well keep this conversation as confrontational as possible.

"My name's Nash, not Dash."

"Sorry." I wasn't. "Not being able to prove anything isn't good enough for me."

"What do you mean?"

"I prefer to do business with people who have integrity and don't cheat even if they can get away with it. Just because the SEC has an elevated burden of proof, doesn't get Gil or Crucible off the hook as far as I'm concerned."

"I'll be sure to tell Mr. Richards you feel that way. And remember, you were sitting by his side throughout the whole process. If Richards or Crucible is implicated you and your firm will be held accountable."

"Are you threatening me?"

"No, just giving you the lay of the land from a legal perspective. You're going to be working with us whether you like it or not."

"I'm going to tell the truth, Al. I don't lie. And one more thing, wash your hands after you take a piss. It's unhealthy not to. And don't ever try to shake my hand."

"Fuck you."

"Likewise, I'm sure."

I walked back to the hotel, which enabled me to reflect on the conversation I had with Nash. I sensed he was a mean and diabolical man. I'll remember to be very careful when speaking to him.

Attorneys are running this country. Many are sneaky bastards who will do anything to win a case. The only problem is that while they're elevating their egos and lining their pockets, our lives, livelihoods, and integrity are on the line. I hope Nash was giving Gil good advice, as I wouldn't hesitate to confront him if I believed he was manipulating his client.

As I approached the hotel, I saw my favorite prostitute. In my most friendly tone I said, "Good evening. How's business?"

"Not too bad. It should pick up later when all you handsome businessmen come back to the hotel after drinking too much."

"Well, I really don't need any liquor to see that you're a lovely lady of the evening. If I wasn't so busy I might even partake in you charms."

"Why thank you, sir. If you do, I'd be happy to extend a 20% discount. Good night."
Everything is a business transaction, even for hookers.

FULLY EXPOSED AND ON THE SHEETS

I walked into the hotel and realized I had nearly two hours before Gil was scheduled to pick me up. Sitting in my room alone didn't seem like such a good idea, so I made my way to the bar.

As I walked in, whom do I see but Sasha, the anonymous banker from my plane ride earlier in the day? She was chatting with three men. I should have turned around and walked away, but I needed a drink. The men were fairly young and I could see that they were kissing up to her. She must be their boss. They were dressed in khakis and sport coats, 21st Century business attire for men. Sasha had on different clothes than what she wore earlier. A short skirt, a sleeveless cotton sweater and high heels all accentuated her physical assets. They seemed to be having a good time, as far as I could tell. Sasha was in the middle of it all. I sat at the bar and sipped on gin watching CNN on one of the two TVs at either end of the long bar.

Same old crap was happening in the world. The Republicans and Democrats were calling each other names as the presidential election drew near. The Democrats selected their man to run against George Bush, John Kerry, senator from Massachusetts. Kerry is more liberal than most of the people in his home state. He speaks against every single thing that the incumbent president said and did. The evening's news was chock full of Kerry criticisms and responses from the Bush campaign.

About ten minutes passed and Sasha either didn't see me or chose to ignore me. I was trying not to feel hurt (only kidding, I could care less). I have to admit that she looked terrific in casual clothes. Her group was sitting at the other end of the bar and I could see a lot of leg as Sasha perched herself on the edge of a barstool (her male colleagues were also taking it all in). I thought it was a little strange that she'd dress down for a business meeting, but I was wrong about female bankers wearing nylons.

I couldn't resist making my presence known and told the bartender I wanted to buy her a drink. Since I didn't know whom she was with, I might create an uncomfortable scene. What the hell, you had to take chances in life, right?

When the bartender made my offer to her, she smiled and nodded at me in thanks. I could see Sasha referring to me over the next few minutes trying to explain why some strange guy in the bar was buying her a drink, and no doubt telling them about our plane ride. The group cracked up a few times. Finally, she left her associates and walked over to me. "Thanks for the drink. Can I get you one?"

She was still counterpunching. "Nice to see you, Sasha. Do you always dress so chic for business meetings?"

"Sometimes I do. It depends upon whom I'm meeting with."

"You look great, by the way. I hope I'm not interrupting an important meeting."

"Thanks, and not at all. They're three guys I hired last year out of business school. I asked them to meet me for drinks. I wanted to see how they were doing."

"And how are they doing?"

"They're very happy. It's tough because I spend most of my time in New York, so we communicate mostly by phone and email. Young professionals like to see their boss in the flesh, if you know what I mean." I'd like to see Sasha in the flesh too?

"I know a lot about ass-kissing. By the way, this is the second time we've seen each other. I think you should tell me your name and with which company you're affiliated."

"Stop it. Sure I'll tell you. My name is Sasha Schwartz and I run the loan syndication group at National Metropolitan Bank."

"I can't believe we've never met before."

"Actually, I transferred from another area of the bank six months ago and was put into this new position. My former job wouldn't have brought us into contact. Anyway, I haven't been in the market very long. I'm sure we'll run into each other from time to time."

"I hope so. Please don't be too tough on me."

"Well I know who you are and I know your reputation, Mr. Stoke Spencer. You and the GYP partners don't take any prisoners, so I'm the one who better be careful."

"I'm flattered. Are you doing a deal in Chicago, or just meeting with the troops?" I could tell Sasha was starting to feel more relaxed because of my charm or the drinks, or a combination of both. I really didn't care why it was happening. She was attractive and nice and that's what mattered.

Sometimes it's difficult to judge how good-looking a woman is when she's sitting. Sasha was standing next to me giving me an opportunity to check out her assets and liabilities. I didn't know whether she was just friendly or sending me a sign, and I saw no liabilities.

Guys are always looking for a sign, but get very few of them in most large cities. You could be the best looking man in New York City walking down Fifth Avenue at high noon. Ninety percent of the women would walk past you and not even give you a look. I guess they think that if they smile at you they're obligated to have sex with you. It's really kind of stupid, but the concept is fine with me.

"I'm assessing my people in Chicago. It's a large group of 20 professionals. My predecessor was a nice man who just didn't have the stomach to terminate the non-performers. That's the primary reason I was asked to replace him."

"So, you're a tough one, huh? The grim reaper."

"I like to think I'm a good business person. We have to maintain a consistent level of performance in our syndication group."

"What do you mean? I'm not an expert on selling bank loans. Maybe you could give me some pointers, so I can take advantage of the banks when I deal with them in the future."

"Very funny. Are you really interested?"

"Sure I am." Can you tell I was turning on the charm? I'm not interested in loan syndication at all. I do business with the banks all the time to get my deals completed with their money, so I'm polite to them. But very few bank syndication types look like Sasha.

"Our syndication business consists of two parts, the people who evaluate them and price them to the market, and the ones who sell them to institutional buyers. The former is a small group I control tightly. Pricing a deal correctly is how we make or lose money on a transaction. All pricing takes place in New York."

"I'm with you." This wasn't exactly rocket science, but I tried to look like I was really engrossed. I was very engrossed by her body.

"Good. After a loan is priced and we're ready to go to market, the sales people must spend time to understand the company and the investment considerations and be able to sell to third party investors. When we review deals with the sales force, we have to accommodate our weakest personnel, or as I describe it, we dumb down. In a nutshell, I want to fire those with the poorest credit skills, so we spend less time educating our own people and more time marketing to buyers."

"Very good strategy. Is this your brain child?" Actually, her strategy made sense. I couldn't understand why everybody in the business wasn't already doing the same thing.

"Actually, no. As a matter of fact the same thing happens to our children at school. Teachers have to educate the child with the least ability in the class. The result is that better students work at less than full capacity because they're always waiting for the slower children to catch up. Efficiency decreases."

"Isn't it difficult to separate the fast learners from the slower ones in your area, as most graduated from excellent colleges and are purported to be very intelligent?"

"Yes, but as you know, intelligence doesn't automatically make a person a good banker or a good sales person. Management must take the time to observe so we don't unnecessarily penalize people and ruin their lives."

"I'm impressed. By the way, it's killing your colleagues that you're spending so much time with me."

"You're right. Why don't you come over and have a drink with the boys. They'll get a kick out of meeting a famous guy like you."

We walked to the other end of the bar. "Gentlemen, I want to introduce you to the infamous Stoke Spencer of GYP. Everybody shook my hand enthusiastically. I hoped they all washed their hands after they pissed. I'm now obsessed with this issue.

"As I mentioned to you before, Stoke and I flew to Chicago earlier today and had a remarkable experience with a motorcycle gangster who sat next to us." Sasha proceeded to tell the boys about the sleaze ball who urinated on the plane. We were all laughing. Sasha was a good storyteller, and not afraid to use descriptive words.

One of them asked, "Did he get arrested when you landed?"

I responded. "The pilots wouldn't let us deplane until after the police took him off in handcuffs. I actually felt sorry for the guy even though he was a slob. When you gotta, you gotta go." Everyone laughed in agreement.

We chatted for a while about business conditions and other boring subjects like the Chicago Cubs, who blew the National League playoffs the summer before against the Florida Marlins, who then defeated my beloved Yankees in six games. I gave them all kinds of shit about the plight of the Cubs.

They correctly pegged me as an obnoxious New York fan and a bad winner. I took the time to remind them that the Yankees have won 27 World Championships and lost another 13 World Series contests. I decided to back off before they dragged me outside and kicked me around. We had a good time and drank a little too much. Sasha appreciated me entertaining her boys.

One of the men said, "Sasha, we have to get going. Sorry we can't have dinner with you. There's a party I'm taking my buddies to. I hope you understand. The females await us."

She smiled. "No problem. I'm exhausted anyway. I'll see you in the office tomorrow morning. Don't drink too much or get into any trouble." She smiled lovingly at them. It looked like Sasha developed close personal relationships with her subordinates.

We were left alone and some decisions had to be made, like what the hell were we going to do now that we were alone. I spoke up, "I'd take you to dinner myself, but my client is picking me up in about an hour or so."

"Thanks anyway. Why don't you keep me company for a while."

I could read a lot into that, but decided not to get too crazy. "I'd like that. We sat down at an open table and ordered another round. I think Sasha was starting to get just a little tipsy.

She kicked off the conversation, "Are you married? Actually, I know the answer because you're wearing a wedding band."

"Sort of."

"What's that mean?"

"Like every investment banker in the world, I'm having marital problems. My wife is a total pain." I almost called her the "c" word, but that might have short-circuited our little chat.

"That's not a good thing. Do you have children?"

"Two boys."

"What kind of problems are you having?"

I thought it was pretty bold of her to ask. The alcohol was making her more courageous by the minute. "We've certainly come a long way since the plane ride. You wouldn't even tell me your last name, now you're diving into my personal life."

"You're right. Sorry, I shouldn't pry."

"It's OK. But if I answer your questions, you have to answer mine. Deal?"

"Of course. It's only fair."

Sasha looked better with each passing moment. She was becoming less restrained. Her face was more relaxed, as compared to earlier in the day. And she seemed comfortable with me. I was feeling very attracted to this woman, and I knew that was a potential problem.

"My relationship with my wife has been on a downward slope for some time."

"Really? Since when?"

"Since we got married. I should've never married her in the first place. Everything was fine until our wedding night, then everything turned to shit."

"Sounds pretty serious."

"What about you? What's your story?"

"I got married right after undergraduate school to my high school sweetheart, but it only lasted for two years."

"How come?"

"He's a really nice guy, but a creative type who couldn't appreciate my career aspirations."

"Must be tough for a sane guy to be married to a female deal junkie."

"Really. Ego issues developed and he continued to use my job as a reason to criticize me about being too aggressive. I have trouble leaving it in the office."

"You'd think investment banking types would be better off marrying creative people. At least then their marriages would have some variety in them. The flip side is that the life of a banker requires so much dedication that personal relationships often get strained, regardless of what the spouse does for a living. So what happened after you dumped him?"

"Thanks for that, but he dumped me. I focused on my career and dated from time to time after we split. I was a pretty lonely person and began to worry about my biological clock."

"You mean you want to have babies?"

"That's part of it. I need to have a real relationship with a man. I need somebody to come home to every night. You understand, don't you?"

"Absolutely. Did you find someone?"

"I started to accept more introductions from friends and met a man three years ago, whom I see regularly."

"Are you going to get married?"

"No. I don't want to marry him."

"How come?"

"I don't want to appear arrogant, but he isn't well educated. Our best moments are in bed, not discussing philosophy."

"What's wrong with that? Can't be so bad if you're both gratified sexually."

"Sex isn't everything. He just isn't right for me long term."

"What the hell does that mean?" I thought sex was everything. That was probably because I wasn't getting any.

"It means he looks great, makes a good living running a construction company, but he reads the *New York Post*."

"So you're not going to marry any man who doesn't read the *New York Times* and the *Wall Street Journal*?"

"Correct. I wouldn't have said it quite that way, but that's exactly what I mean. And he must read the editorial section, not just the sports section of the paper."

"Do you love him?"

"Sometimes."

"Uh oh. Other than being a palooka what else is wrong?"

"He gets a little rough with me on occasion."

"He hits you?" I was shocked that a woman of this caliber would put up with physical abuse. But story after story is popping up in the press about the horrors that some women are subjected to by abusive men. It's easy to say, just leave when you're living in fear every day for yourself and your children. But it's difficult to do.

"Not exactly. He gets a little frisky during sex and when he gets really angry with me. I can't believe I'm telling you this." Sasha was starting to get upset.

Going home to someone night after night who isn't interesting must be difficult for an intelligent person. Picture it. Sasha walks in at 8:30 or 9 and the palooka is sitting in his boxer shorts watching the New York Knicks on the boob tube. She walks up to him expecting a hug and a kiss and he says the Knicks are behind by four and burps. She really doesn't give a shit about the Knicks and resents the expulsion of air in her face.

Having not eaten anything since lunch, Sasha is famished. She asks the palooka what he wants to do for dinner, and he tells her that he's already had some Campbell's Soup and chips. Sasha goes into the bedroom to change, puts her head down on the pillow and dozes off on an empty stomach.

All of a sudden the palooka shows up with beer on his breath and wants some action (the Knicks won). She says she's too tired to make love. He tells her to roll over, or else. What a shit life.

"Don't sweat it," I said. "It's our secret."

Sasha was starting to tear up. The woman was really sad about her current life. This happens to a lot of professional women. They have a hard time keeping a man interested while reaching for the brass ring.

"I appreciate your listening to my problems. I have to use the powder room."

"No problem. I'll wait for you."

"I'm going up to my room. I don't like to use public toilets. Why don't you come up and we can break into the minibar. I'm not trying to seduce you or anything like that. We both have enough problems, so I doubt an affair would be mutually beneficial."

This woman sure was brazen, horny, and/or drunk. "Okay, I'm game."

I paid the tab and we proceeded to the elevator. There were other people who were going up to their rooms, and no one gave us a second look. I always feel guilty about riding up a hotel elevator with a woman who isn't my wife.

I said to Sasha, "Nice weather in Chicago."

She cracked up and said, "It's wet and humid, what are you talking about?"

Sasha got off on the 14th floor and I followed. Silently and discreetly we walked down the hall to her room. She slipped the card key into the slot and a red light came on. I told you about those stupid card keys. They don't work most of the time.

Here a woman is taking me to her hotel room and the key backfires. It was ruining the moment I was about to experience, not. "Shit, what the hell is wrong with this key?" She was furious. I didn't know whether she was angry about being locked out or because she had to pee badly. "I have to go downstairs and get another key."

"Let's just go to my room. I'm on lucky thirteen. I don't want you to have an accident or anything."

"Girls aren't like that. We can hold it indefinitely. Okay, let's go and not test my bladder strength."

My key worked, thank goodness. "Help yourself to the bathroom. It's clean because I haven't used it yet."

She giggled, but knew there was some truth to the statement. "Yeah, guys are such slobs." She walked into the bathroom and shut the door.

The woman sounded like a racehorse as she urinated. I was kind of embarrassed that I heard her. Now, what are you supposed to do in this situation? I'm totally confused about the correct etiquette.

I should write to Abby:

"Dear Abby, I have been blessed with an excellent bladder so when I urinate I sound like Sea Biscuit. I get funny looks from people when I come out of the bathroom. Can you give me some guidance? Should I turn on the faucet and attempt to drown out the noise? Signed: Really Pissed."

"Dear Really Pissed, Your letter is gross. What the hell kind of operation do you think we have here? Do you really expect me to give you advice about how and when to urinate? I don't think so. Maybe you should use your backyard, then no one inside will hear a thing. Signed: Abby."

"Dear Abby, I don't own a house. I live in the city. Do you have any other suggestions? Signed: Really Pissed."

"Dear Really Pissed, Just piss on your building. Signed: Abby."

When Sasha emerged from the bathroom, she looked relieved but had a confused look as she scanned my room. "This is the tiniest hotel room I've ever seen. Are you able to fit past the bed and the wall?"

"Very funny. I was going to complain when I saw this room, but I thought I'd just be sleeping here. I didn't expect to have company."

She blushed. "Hey, I came to your room to use the bathroom and have a drink, remember?"

"So, let's drink. Make yourself comfortable." I noticed Sasha was a bit tipsy. She let her shoes fall off and hopped on the bed. Her skirt hiked up to the top of her thighs, but she pulled it down lest something be exposed. She was a real lady even after a few drinks. "What'll ya have?"

"I feel like having something feminine. How about some chardonnay."

"You got it." I unlocked the mini bar and grabbed a screw cap bottle of chardonnay for Sasha (Can you believe nine bucks for screw cap wine?) and a beer for myself. I thought I should avoid the hard stuff and save myself for Gil.

I served the drinks and sat at the desk, which was about four inches from the bed. Sasha looked comfortable lying back on my pillow. If we didn't have sex, at least I'd be able to smell her later on the pillow. "So what are you going to do about the guy that knocks you around?"

"Well, it's not as bad as you think. You know, we've come a long way in a few hours. Here I am in your hotel room on your bed talking about my personal life."

"We're just having a dialogue. Think of me as your psychiatrist."

"Right. My boyfriend's a big guy and not gentle physically or mentally. He's a typical sports fan, a tailgater, if you know what I mean."

"I think I do, but physical abuse is unacceptable, no excuses. If he roughs you up, you should not see him." I was dead serious.

"It's not always horrible."

"Are you saying you like to get shoved around?"

"Not really. So what about you, Stoke? What's your endgame?" She wanted to change the subject and I complied.

"My wife has not made me happy in a long time. She's a self-centered bitch in the first degree. She lives like a queen because of all the dough I bring home. Over the years, I have more and more dinners with clients and try to stay away from her."

"Sounds like a disaster waiting to happen."

"No shit. Ironically, it came to a head today. I've been lonely for a long time."

"You know we have a lot in common. Two unloved people meet on an airplane and commiserate. I appreciate your talking with me and telling me about your issues."

"Ditto. You're very nice. I didn't think so on the plane. First impressions aren't always correct." I was starting to get just a little mushy.

"Mind if I pour myself another glass of wine?"

"I'll get it for you." Wow, she finished the first glass in record time. Maybe she thought she was in a drinking contest.

"No, relax. I can help myself." She hopped off the bed and edged her way past me. As Sasha slipped by, she kissed me on the cheek and stroked my head (I was now happy the room was so small). She had such a gentle touch, and I was very aroused.

She poured her drink and we continued to look at each other lovingly. As she went by again, she put the glass down on the desk and sat on my lap. We kissed passionately. Her tongue probed my mouth, and my hands were all over her. She moaned when I gently touched the places she wanted me to touch. I picked her up and carried her to the bed where our kissing and groping became even more intense.

Then, the phone rang.

"Godammit."

"Don't pick it up the phone. Just hold me."

"There's nothing I'd like more, but it may be my client. Hello." I answered the phone a little out of breadth and regretted it.

"Stoke, it's me Sharon. Can we talk?"

"Absolutely not. We can't talk. I have to leave my room in a minute. This isn't a good time to talk." Sasha gave me a funny look and went into the bathroom. "Sharon, I'm getting off the phone. We're finished. I've thought about everything and I hate you. Goodbye."

"Don't hang up, Stoke. I've been thinking about us all day, and I still love you. Come home to us. Let's be a happy family again."

"We've never been a happy family. I have to go. Goodbye." I hung up.

"Sasha, please come out. I'm finished." She walked out in her bra and panties. She had a fantastic figure. Her bra pushed up her breasts and they were beautiful. I didn't realize it because she hid them with the clothes she wore. Her legs were long and muscular but very feminine and graceful like a ballet dancer.

"I thought you might need some diversion from your marital problems."

She walked towards me and fell on her face, likely a function of the booze she consumed. I could see the new glass of wine she poured herself was already empty. Sasha got up and tried to regain her composure. I wasn't even tempted to laugh because I was so focused on her long blonde hair, sexy underclothes and fantastic figure.

This was starting to get really serious and there I was at the top of yet another slippery slope. Who the hell was this woman? Was she another crazy broad who wanted to make my life even more confusing than it already was? Did I want to have sex with her? Actually, the answer to that question was yes. Would she accuse me of raping her? Visions of Kobe Bryant flashed in my mind. Kobe's the LA Laker accused of raping a domestic in a hotel room.

"Sasha, are sure you know what you're doing? You had a lot to drink. Maybe we could just talk (and I can stare at your body)."

"Stoke, that rhymes with poke. Get it?"

"Yeah, pretty funny. Why don't you sit down and relax?" I didn't want her to trip again and hurt herself.

"Are you trying to talk me out of making love to you? Are you gay?"

Oh, brother. I was being so honorable that she thought I was a homosexual. Now I know how Rob Viand felt when his family questioned his masculinity. "No, I'm really attracted to you." That's what I get for being a good guy.

"Then why don't you get undressed and make love to me."

The phone rang again. What bad luck. Here I was on the doorstep of entering the Palace of Sasha, and I get interrupted once more. "I gotta pick this up."

"Don't do it, Stoke. You're going to regret it." She sang the last part of her comment.

"Sorry." I picked up the receiver and did regret it. "Hello."

"Stoke, it's Norm Cohen. I need to speak with you about the voicemail you left me."

"This isn't a good time, Norm. I have to get back to you."

"No, you have to talk to me right now. What about the voicemail you left me?"

Sasha could've been a dancer at a gentleman's club because she had all the moves. After turning on the radio to a local rock station, she gyrated to an old favorite, "Knocking on Heaven's Door," sung by Guns and Roses. I liked this song a lot, as it reminded me of my youth. Sasha seemed to be inspired by this rendition of the song, originally sung by Bob Dylan. The music turned her on as she bumped and grinded to the beat.

"I wanted to forewarn you about another problem at Crucible."

"Gil Richards is creating a lot of problems for our firm. After you called, the SEC contacted Antun again and gave him a heads up about an illegal payment made to Richards. Is that what you were referring to in your message?"

"Yes." Sasha was so hot. She was spinning around, but she seemed to be a little wobbly.

"Did you have any involvement in the illegal payment?"

Finally, Sasha fell on the bed and started touching herself and making love to an imaginary person. The booze was really starting to hit her and I wanted to join her party.

"Stoke, come to me and kiss me all over." I covered the mouthpiece of the phone.

"Who's that? Are you with someone?"

"No. It's the television. The payment wasn't illegal. Marion Denning, a director and head of the Compensation Committee of the old Board approved it." Sasha was starting to doze off.

"The SEC told us that the Board didn't approve the payment, and Richards may have embezzled the funds. "

"It was a misunderstanding between Marion Denning and Gil, that's all. He paid the money back to the company. It's a non-issue. I have to go."

"Wait, Stoke. I need to …"

I hung up the phone and stared at the woman on my bed.

"Sasha, are you awake?"

"Yes, make love to me Shmoke." She said this with a very groggy voice.

"My name's Stoke." She was really crocked. I considered my options. One, take my clothes off and have sex with a woman in an alcohol-induced coma. Two, don't have sex with her. It's not often that opportunity knocks in this manner and it was going to take a lot of self-control to walk away.

Morally, it was a fielder's choice. Sasha was a mature woman, who had been around the block a few times and so I could live with a decision to make it with her. She came to my room willingly and said she wanted me. She didn't say no, not yet anyway. But she was drunk and not in total control of herself. I decided to do the honorable thing, nothing. The phone rang again.

"Hello." I wanted to rip the goddam thing out of the wall.

"Stoke, it's Gil. We'll pick you up in 15 minutes. OK?"

"I'll see you at the front of the hotel."

I turned off the radio and then quietly straightened myself out trying not to disturb Sasha. I wrote the following note.

'Dear Sasha, I really enjoyed meeting you. You're an attractive woman and I'd like to get to know you better. No, we didn't do anything! Leave your phone number and I'll call you. Stay as long as you want. It would be great if you were still here when I returned. Be back late. Stoke.'

I left the room with mixed feelings. On one hand, I passed up an opportunity to get it on with a very attractive, albeit totally intoxicated woman. From what she told me she wasn't naïve about men, after all; she'd been married before and was now living with a palooka (I love that name). Therefore, I didn't think anyone could ever accuse me of taking advantage of the situation.

But she was drunk, so a case could be made that I assaulted her because she wasn't able to make a consensual (or sober) decision. Frankly, I missed a rare opportunity to get laid, but I shouldn't dwell on it. I wasn't going to leave SS for Sasha, but I was going to leave SS.

I was sure she would thank me for not doing what most men would've done without a second thought. Drunken sex is probably not a good way to start a new relationship any way. Then again, maybe Sasha wanted to make love to me (she said she did) and would be disappointed that I wasn't by her side when she came to. Maybe she would think I'm gay and uninterested in women. Maybe she would tell people that I'm a homosexual. That's bullshit. Not a word of this non-encounter will ever be uttered by her lips. The bottom line is, I was probably better off that nothing happened, but I hoped I'd have another opportunity with Sasha.

It's amazing how much territory your mind can cover in such a short period of time. I hadn't even gotten to the lobby and I analyzed my encounter with Sasha and the morality of what I did and didn't do.

Unfortunately, my clothes were even more wrinkled because of my limited (albeit fully clothed) intimacy with Sasha. The mirror in the elevator didn't lie. There was nothing I could do about my appearance, so I decided not to worry about it. And besides, Gil wouldn't give a damn, and Sophie hadn't yet acknowledged my existence.

I had a thought. Wouldn't it be interesting if I brought Sophie back to my room later while Sasha was still there? It's doubtful Sasha would participate in a threesome, but you never know. If Sophie were anything like her old man, she'd be all over it.

Threesomes are a guy's ultimate fantasy because the chances of it actually occurring are virtually zero. But there are many things that must come together for it to become a reality. The man has to be attracted to both females, as he may be called upon to do certain things that he wouldn't do with a strange woman. The women have to like the man for the same reason. The women have to like each other and not be threatened by the other's physical attributes. For instance, you couldn't have a successful threesome encounter between a handsome man, a beautiful woman and an ugly woman. Everybody has to be really fresh and clean, so threesomes will seldom happen on the spur of the moment.

You have to find a comfortable place for the meeting to convene, and you have to be able to get them there without attracting any attention. Say you were using a hotel room. Other guests and hotel employees would know what you were up to if you were in an elevator with two good-looking females and had a stupid grin on your face.

I've never been with two women, but I have a friend who has. He told me that important decisions have to be made so that nobody's feelings are hurt. After all, you don't want any of the three to feel left out or resentful when it's over. It's important to carefully orchestrate specific acts so each person is fulfilled. As I indicated, I'm a novice at this, but I've thought about it many times. I want to be ready if I ever get lucky.

I arrived at the hotel's front entrance five minutes early, and went out into the humidity, which was unbearable. Chicago's proximity to Lake Michigan increased the moisture in the air. When it was warm in Chicago, it was wet and warm.

Some guy drove up to the hotel and lifted a golf bag from his trunk. Golf has been my nemesis for many years. It's a game that I've tried to master, but I've always fallen short. As I mentioned earlier, I was an average athlete as a kid. In baseball I'd be the fifth kid chosen out of ten. I wasn't great, just a solid weak B player.

Golf is another story, however. The Spencer's have a long history of golfing achievement. My father was a scratch golfer when he was in his prime, meaning that he scored around par every time he played. I had some uncles and cousins who were also good players, and everybody expected me to be a competent golfer because of my genetics.

My father belonged to an established country club located in Westchester, where I ultimately became a member. I really worked at my game when I was growing up spending hours practicing and thousands of dollars taking lessons with a professional (it was so important to my father that I be a good golfer that he paid for the lessons).

I really don't know why I have so much trouble with the game, but I am not consistent. Sometimes I hook the ball, and sometimes I slice the ball. One pro told me that I had so many things wrong with my swing that it would be impossible to fix. We actually spoke about my becoming a lefty and starting over. Can you imagine being that bad at anything?

I had my moments, but pars would be followed by double bogeys and bogeys would be followed by triple bogeys. I never made many birdies, so I can't remember what followed them.

Golf is a very technical sport. Don't believe anybody who says all you have to do is step up to the ball and whack it. Or, any decent athlete can be a good golfer after a few lessons. That's nonsense. Every golf shot is different, except for the drive, where you're able to give yourself a perfect lie every time.

Unfortunately, the driver is the longest club in the bag and the most difficult to hit straight. The height of the rough and whether the ball is on flat ground impacts your shots. If your feet are above or below the ball, it requires you to make an adjustment in the way you strike the ball. The ball can be on an uphill or downhill slope. It can be in a sand trap or in the woods. Then you have the greens. Some are fast, and some are slow, depending upon how closely they're mowed. You may be putting uphill, downhill, or cross-hill. Trying to hit the ball on the right line at the proper speed are two things that I can't seem to do simultaneously.

The physics of the game are so precise that a microscopic error will cause your club to strike the ball improperly resulting in a rotten shot. Trust me, the game is impossible, except for those unemotional machines on the Professional Golfers Tour.

Golf is the worst thing I do in life. My relationship with SS is even better than my golf game. That's saying a lot. But I'd rather be miserable on the course than spend time with her.

In any case, my temperament makes it impossible for me to deal with the rigors of the game. When I make a bad shot, my next shot is likely to suck as well. I am incapable of forgetting a bad shot that happened moments earlier. It's just not human to forget about bad things so quickly. Humans like to brood and be angry. I like to brood after I make a crappy shot.

So, I'm often puzzled why my pro and caddy can't understand why I behave the way I do. I've probably thrown and broken more golf clubs than anybody I know. Correspondingly, this has resulted in my purchasing more clubs than anybody I know.

I have a caddy with whom I play most of the time. His nickname is Chopper. I'm not sure why people call him this, but it may have something to do with his teeth, which remind me of one of the villains in a James Bond movie, a guy named Jaws. He was about six feet six inches and had all this metal in his mouth, which he used to bite and kill people. Chopper has that kind of mouth. I'm worried that if I make a bad shot he will sneak up on me and bite me on the neck.

Most caddies are destitute, and barely have enough money to survive. They caddy because they love golf or they're too dumb to do anything else. Some are intelligent, like the Chopper. Some of them are terrific reading greens, like Chopper. Reading greens means trying to predict which way the ball is going to roll and how fast you have to hit it to get it near the hole. Chopper tries to help me with every aspect of the game.

But most important for me is a caddy that can serve as my therapist. I need psychiatric support when I play. I'm dangerous to others, and myself, as I'm always on the verge of throwing a club. Often a bad shot hurtles me into a severe fit of rage or depression, and sometimes I even feel suicidal. When I play poorly, my problems in life seem that much deeper. I might hook a ball out of bounds and start to talk about how much I hate SS, or that GYP isn't paying me enough.

Chopper keeps telling me that I'm a good player, capable of shooting pars. It's total bullshit. I don't have the ability to string two good shots together during a round of golf. But caddies like

Chopper say this crap to duffers like me all the time so we come back, play again, and give them large tips.

Caddies also want you to tell them about your personal problems. They love to hear about how tough your life is, misery likes company, I guess. Chopper really got excited when I told him how much I hate SS. He's been encouraging me to get some action on the side ever since. I think that was good advice. I think it's stupid to tell a caddy about your problems, when he can barely get by.

Or, even worse, a money issue. I spent $100,000 joining the club and I told him that I couldn't afford to pay cash for a new Ferrari until I received my bonus. How does that make the guy feel? Like shit, I'll bet.

To sum up my golf experience, I'm dumbfounded why men play the game at all. Regardless of your skill level, every golfer is in a continuous state of agitation. It's not fun to play golf, and yet most men love it.

By the way, every golfer tries to play as fast as possible. We wait all week to play on the weekend and get pissed off if a round of golf takes too long. If the game is so much fun, why the hell is every golfer trying to get home as soon as possible? They must be married to women much nicer than SS.

SALUTE TO MURDER

Gil preferred to drive himself, unlike many other big time executives. He once told me he had ten cars. I can't remember all of the makes, but they included Porsche, Rolls Royce, Bentley, two Mercedes (one of which had just pulled up) and several other types.

He was about ten minutes late, but finally arrived at the hotel. "Get your ass in the car, Stoke. We're gonna have some fun tonight."

"Yes, sir." The doorman opened up the back door, as Sophie was sitting in the shotgun seat. She seemed uninterested in me. I was interested in her, as her skirt was riding high exposing her long, tanned legs. What a knockout. I shouldn't be thinking about my client's daughter this way, should I?

"Sophie and I worked out our differences and now we're ready for dinner and dancing. How 'bout you, Stoke?" I didn't hear any enthusiastic acknowledgement from Sophie.

I'll bet Gil would've loved to hear about my encounter with Sasha. After all, he's always telling me about his latest conquests. But I don't think the encounter would "count" in Gil's mind without penetration, so I kept it to myself.

"I'm ready to roll," I said. "I had a few cocktails before you arrived, and it helped me forget about our SEC problem for a while."

Gil raced down the street just as the back door of the car slammed shut. "Shit. I don't want you to worry about those SEC dicks. They're just harassing me. You and I did the LBO together. You were with me the whole time and know that I didn't make up any numbers. Right?" It sounded like he had been coached by that asshole Nash.

"I don't know that, Gil. You didn't give me the straight story about the radar deal. If the deal had stayed on track, the numbers in the prospectus would've been accurate. You didn't tell me the radar deal was in trouble. You also neglected to tell me about your secret bonus."

"Let's not get into the bonus thing again. I told you I gave the money back. It'll go away."

"The SEC called GYP's counsel and said otherwise." I dramatized this comment for effect. I wanted to engage Gil on the subject.

"What are you talking about? Why would the SEC call your counsel?"

"He has a good relationship with one of the guys at the SEC. He used to work there. They wanted to give him some advance notice."

The Mercedes was speeding through the streets, and I wondered if Gil had a few cocktails before he picked me up.

"Those fucking snakes. They told me they were going to drop the whole thing after I told them I repaid the money. You just can't trust government bureaucrats."

"Gil, they're going to try to get us. I know it. And another thing, you better keep Nash away from me. He approached me after I left you. I don't like him, and I don't trust him. I just hope he's giving you good advice about this whole affair."

"Nash has saved my ass many times over the years. Do me a favor and try to work with him. OK?"

I didn't respond but wasn't optimistic about establishing a relationship with his attorney.

Suddenly, Gil was leaning on his horn screaming at some guy driving an old Honda. Apparently, Gil suffered from road rage.

Road rage occurs when I'm driving my car and I get pissed off at every other person driving within one hundred miles of my car. Road rage makes nice people turn into raving lunatics. Generally, people would say I'm a fairly even-tempered person ready to turn the other cheek to avoid conflict, but not while I'm driving a car.

A car empowers me. Several thousand pounds of steel strapped to my body transforms me into a deadly missile. I'm invincible when I'm in my car. So, when some shit head has the audacity to cut me off, I want to kill him, curse him out, or at least give him the finger. Nobody cuts off Stoke Spencer.

Although many people experience road rage, only a few would actually get out of the car and start a fight. Once detached from my killing machine, I revert to being the same coward I was before I got into the car. If I confront someone, I might be unfortunate to encounter the one in a thousand crazy that wants to shoot me or smash me over the head with a tire iron. So, the smart thing to do is stay in my car. But when some asshole drives right up to my bumper and starts blinking his bright lights and honking his horn, I want to tear his head off.

Gil was screaming profanities at this guy and driving right behind him. "Daddy, calm down, the guy's not even doing anything. Why are you driving this way?"

"Sophie, this moron is driving too slow and won't let me pass."

It was a two lane street. But that didn't make any difference because Gil was in road rage.

Finally, Gil tapped the other driver's bumper with the Mercedes. Both cars stopped and Gil and the other driver got out to have a chat. By the way, Gil was one of those maniacs who would welcome hand-to-hand combat. Of course, I got out as well. I had to back up my client.

The other man said, "What do you think you're doing? You bumped into me. Is there something wrong with you?" He was a short and dumpy fellow, not well dressed and about 40 something. He reminded me of the "Colombo" character on television.

Gil obviously wanted to establish his dominance right out of the box. "You little twerp. You should've gotten out of the way and let me pass."

"Believe me, I wanted to let you pass, but I couldn't find a place to pull over. You know, you can get arrested for what you did."

"What are you a lawyer or something?"

"No, I'm a cop." Oops. Gil was in big trouble.

"Let me see you're driver's license." The twerp pulled out his badge.

I jumped in. "Officer, my friend and I are having a horrible day. We're totally burnt out. Won't you please drop this whole thing?"

"I really should arrest you, Mister ..."

"Gil Richards. I apologize, officer."

"Well, take it easy and give people in crappy cars a break." He returned Gil's license.

Gil said, "Will do, and thanks." We sheepishly got back into the Mercedes and drove off, way ahead of the cop's Honda.

"Damn, that was a near disaster." Gil was energized and relieved. He had dodged a bullet. "I didn't know Chicago P.D. had dwarves on the force." Sophie and I laughed at the comment.

"Daddy, you must calm down. You get upset over such senseless things."

"I know honey. I can't always control myself. Thanks for standing beside me, Stoke. I'm really starving. I hope you guys are hungry. Our reservation is at an Italian place called Salute. It's very old and supposedly frequented by mobsters."

I said, "Great. I hope you behave yourself. Sounds like we could get whacked if you're disrespectful."

"Don't sweat it. I go there all the time. The owners know me. It's one of the most difficult places in the universe to get a reservation. Every table is reserved every night, so the only way you get in is for a regular to lend you his table."

Sophie asked, "What kind of people have reservations?"

"If I told who they are, I'd have to kill you." Gil laughed at his own comment. Sophie and I didn't.

I queried, "I suppose this is a famous joint?"

"Right. They say Al Capone was an original owner. He was always hungry after murdering somebody. The restaurant has some interesting photographs of Chicago gangsters dining in Salute's back room. There's a lot of history associated with the place."

"Did anybody ever get murdered in Salute?"

"Stoke, I knew you'd ask that. Yes, several people, but nobody recently."

I asked, "In what kind of neighborhood is it located?"

"That's an interesting question. Actually, the place is in a terrible part of town. To be specific, it's in a ghetto. There's been a long-standing arrangement between the owners and the gangs that control the area. In a nutshell, the mobsters threatened to kill anyone who fucks with Salute or its patrons."

Gil was driving like a maniac once again, going through red lights and looking to get into more trouble with the law. My life was in jeopardy just being in the car with him now, and after a few bottles of wine at dinner, the probability of being in a car accident would be exponentially greater. Thankfully, we arrived at Salute.

Gil wasn't exaggerating. The restaurant was in a two-story building, which stood amid tall housing projects. Every wall in the area had graffiti on it except those near Salute. Kids were roaming around, but none of them approached this protected building. Outside were limousines and many fancy cars. If you parked one of these vehicles on a street one block from the restaurant, it would be on milk crates by the time you returned.

Several boys passed and turned away. I guess they weren't allowed to look at the place either. There was a man (an understatement, he was six foot and nearly 300 pounds) who served as the valet parking attendant. Basically, he took your keys and double or triple parked your car outside the restaurant. This is one man you wouldn't want to cross. Gil handed his keys to the parking attendant and gave him a C-note. I'll bet the attendant makes $1,000 in tips every night.

We entered Salute. It was like taking a trip back in time. There were celebrities mingling with real life wise guys. The mobsters were real characters, dressed in sharkskin suits with their shirt collars over their jackets. Their shirts were unbuttoned and every man had a hairy chest and gold chain. It was like they were in uniform.

Each man's hair was similar, greased and combed straight back. As they spoke with each other, arms and hands flailed about (typical Italian-speak) and you could see the pearl handles of their handguns under their coats. What the hell am I doing in this place? I wondered.

There were only ten or twelve tables, each with six or eight seats. Almost everybody was smoking. If a diner didn't the like smoke, they should go eat elsewhere. I recognized a few people including a U.S. Senator and a few athletes. In fact, a Chicago Cub was present. The losers.

Screaming was the way you communicated at Salute. Laughing hysterically, belly-type laughing, was happening throughout the place. Everyone was friendly. There were several women in the room, classy babes, who might've been hookers. I could just feel the illicit business going on all around me.

The owner came over to greet Gil, who obviously was a regular. "Bona Sera, Signore Richards. And welcome to the beautiful Sophie." The owner seemed like a real charmer.

"Torre, how are you? Thanks for arranging a reservation for us. Please thank Aldo for me next time you see him." Who the hell is Aldo? Maybe he meant Waldo. You know, Where's Waldo tonight?

"We're always happy to have you as a guest at Salute, and I'll thank Aldo on your behalf."

"I want to introduce you to a very good friend of mine, Stoke Spencer. He's a true connoisseur of Italian food, even though he's a WASP. Stoke meet Torre Botto, owner and slave driver here at Salute."

Torre snickered.

I said, "It's a pleasure to meet you Torre."

He was dressed like all the wise guys in the place, suit, open shirt, chains, along with a monstrous gold Rolex watch.

"Welcome to my restaurant, Stoke. Have you been here before?"

"No. But I'm from the home of many excellent Italian restaurants, New York City. I look forward to your cuisine (and observing how the Chicago Mafia does business while stuffing their faces with pasta)."

"Please, come with me. I'll show you to your table. You'll be sitting next to some of my regular customers. They're very nice, but a little crazy and quite noisy. You'll have fun, I think."

I said to myself, why am I here? I feel like I'm in a time warp. Any minute, I expected Al Capone and Frank Nitti to walk through the door with machine guns ablaze. I wondered what role these men played in the criminality of the area. On one hand, most people underestimated how much influence organized crime really had. Then again, it's not like the old days when organized crime had its fingers in liquor, gambling, prostitution and the like.

Today, most of these industries have been institutionalized and are controlled by legitimate companies (except for prostitution, of course). Rumors abound that the bad guys still "dip their beaks" into these activities (that's Italian-speak for sharing in the profits). Mostly, the "organization" is involved in strip clubs and narcotics, but only as a distributor of the latter. Day to day street sales are managed by local gangs and leaders in the minority neighborhoods. I couldn't wait to talk to the gumbas at the next table to find out what they did for a living.

Unlike many restaurants in New York, we didn't have to wait around at Salute to be seated. There was only one seating each night at each table. If we wanted to stand or sit at the bar for half the evening it was perfectly all right. When a customer wanted to eat, he just had to let Torre know. Torre never overbooked. An important person would be insulted from such a frivolous act.

In my city, it was like the restaurants were doing me a favor at $75 per head (before wine). To add insult to injury, I'm required to drink cocktails at the bar for 30 minutes before I'm seated. To be honest, I don't think the owners of the restaurants were doing this to increase their revenues, although it probably had a significant impact on profits. Rather, overbooking was a defensive tactic against the ubiquitous last minute cancellation by New Yorkers. Empty tables are the bane of the restaurant business, and result in losses. So, the owners overbooked and the hopeful diners just waited around. It's exactly the same thing airlines do to ensure high capacity.

A couple of months before, I went to a popular restaurant in New York (I won't use the name, even though they deserve to be exposed) and had an unbelievable experience. A client and I checked in with the maitre 'd and were told to wait in the bar area. To make matters worse, most of the people who greeted us were rude and condescending and couldn't afford to eat in the place themselves.

The maitre 'd was an anorexic young woman who might have been attractive if she gained 20 pounds. She was clearly over her head (her organizational and interpersonal skills sucked). I knew the former to be true because there were just too many people waiting around and getting pissed off. Her defense when somebody complained was to respond with attitude and without exactly saying it, indicating that if we didn't like the service we could get a hot dog.

I wanted to knock over her sissy reservation table, but just retreated to the bar like all the other dumb asses where my client and I had two drinks. After 25 minutes, I left the bartender a handsome tip for being polite and filling our glasses to the brim with alcohol. I usually won't wait this long to eat. If I wanted to stand in line before I ate, I'd join the Army. But I knew this restaurant was notoriously late (not fashionably, but rudely).

I asked the skinny bitch how much longer we had to wait and she said, "your table is being cleared right now," as opposed to "the people at your table are paying the check," or "we're very busy tonight, so our reservations are a little backed up." What she meant was "fuck you, we'll seat you when we're good and ready."

After being treated like vermin the previous two times I went there, I swore I'd never return. It was a Monday night, so I hoped it wouldn't be too crowded (wrong). I told Twiggy to cancel our reservation (which didn't mean a goddam thing anyway) and that we were going to have hot dogs. Not really, I just told her to cancel because we had waited too long. I spoke to her calmly, but loudly enough so that all the people who were waiting to be seated could hear. I hoped to start a riot, or at least a mass exodus from the restaurant, but disappointingly nothing happened. I suppose everybody was hungry and felt they had already made an investment in eating at this place.

Would you believe someone from the restaurant called me the next day to apologize and to offer me free dinner for two? I said, "Thank you, but I'm sure that if I accepted your offer, you'd make me wait again. I really don't want your free meal. And one more thing, tell the skinny maitre 'd to be more polite to the clientele."

Back to Salute. In about three seconds a waiter came to take our drink order. I asked for a wine list and was told there was no wine list. He said we could have red or white and we'd enjoy whichever we chose. I asked what the names of the wines were. He said they didn't have names. I asked how much each bottle cost. He said I should talk to Torre about that. I gave up and ordered a bottle of red. It arrived 30 seconds later. After all, they didn't need to look around their wine cellar for a particular brand. They only had two brands, red and white.

I have to admit it tasted great, but all I could think of was a bunch of fat Italian women dressed in black squashing the grapes with their bare feet in the cellar. I think feet are a disgusting part of the body, so my question is, do they wash their feet before the "squashing of the grapes?"

Torre arrived five minutes later. Gil, Sophie, and I were talking current events, Iraq, sports, business, etc. "So, what would you like to eat tonight?" Torre asked in his heavy Italian accent.

The guy was probably born in America or came here as a young boy, but he still sounded like he just stepped off the boat. It was good for business to be ethnic at Salute (that's Italian ethnic).

"Can I see a menu? I'm not sure what I want." Gil and Sophie started to giggle.

"Signore, we have no menus. You just tell us what you want to eat. If it's Italian food, we make it for you. Everything is fresh."

What a joint. All drinking and eating decisions were based on trust. There are no wine lists or menus. You don't know how much anything costs. I might be paying and was worried about the expense report, which I'd have to submit to Cohen. "OK. I understand. Sophie, you order first."

Torre talked us into a four-course meal (not counting dessert), consisting of antipasto, pasta, meat dishes and light salads. Gil said, "You're going to love this food, Stoke. These people know how to cook."

"Torre didn't write down anything," I said. "I'll bet he screws up our order."

Gil said, "You're on. One thousand says the order comes to us without a hitch."

Wow, a thousand dollars. Gil would think I was a pussy if I backed off. "Ok, a grand, but I have one condition. Sophie is the judge, not you. Her decision is final." I was hoping that she'd side with me. Maybe she was still angry with her father.

"Good idea. Hopefully, we won't be so drunk that a decision can't be made." I couldn't wait for the next ride in Gil's car (not).

The place was incredibly noisy. The loudest people were the ones sitting next to us. They were telling stories and roaring after each one ended. To make matters worse, the guy next to me was a big fat load, who kept sliding his chair into mine every time he went into a laughing fit.

The cigar smoke was making me sick. These guys hadn't even started dinner and they were sucking on those vile things filling the air with pollutants.

After getting bumped for the twentieth time, I turned to fatso and said, "Excuse me, but you keep bumping into me."

Fatso looked me right in the eyes and said, "You got a fucking problem?"

Whoa. Those were fighting words. "You don't have to be any more rude than you've already been. Your friends are screaming at the top of their lungs and smoking those disgusting cigars. That's my problem. "

"Hey Jimmy. This guy says your cigars smell like shit and we're being rude. Whatdaya think about that?"

"Tell him to fuck off, Bobo."

"You heard Jimmy, fuck off."

Bobo? The guy's name is Bobo? And they said fuck every other word. Where did these cockroaches come from?

Gil intervened us before things got out of hand, and I ended up with a fist in my face. "Take it easy, Stoke. We're guests here. These gentlemen are regulars at Salute." He yelled over to the other table, "How you doin Bobo?"

"Ay, Gil, how's it hanging?" Bobo and Liz must have taken English together in school.

"Sorry about my friend. Stoke, meet Bobo." We shook hands. He almost crushed my hand with his vice-like grip.

Gil actually knew these people? I said, "I'm sorry I mouthed off to you. Can I buy you and your friends a round of drinks?"

"Don't sweat it." The six men at the table responded happily to the offer of a round. "Of course we accept your kind proposal."

They went back to their screaming and smoking and I turned back to Gil. "I can't believe you know these people."

"I know a lot of people, Stoke. To build a successful company you have to call on the services of all types."

"What the hell could somebody like fatso do for you?"

"Let's put it this way. If I decided to have John Applegate at United American knocked off, I would probably ask Bobo to do it."

I gulped. "I understand." I didn't and was wondering whether I really knew Gil after all these years.

The door of the restaurant opened and three men and one woman walked into the place. One was an older gentleman, impeccably dressed. He wore an expensive suit that I recognized to be English made. He had silver hair combed straight back with just a touch of oil in it. He looked about sixty and strutted in like a nobleman.

The other man was much younger and looked like he could be related to the older one. Unlike the senior man, the younger one wasn't wearing a tie and looked like the other wise guys at Salute.

The third man was a Bobo look-alike. He was monstrous, six-three and 250 pounds, a typical bodyguard type. He wore a sport coat and a black t-shirt underneath (he probably couldn't find a dress shirt that fit).

The woman was a bimbo, good-looking and very made up. She had on a really short skirt and silk blouse that hung off of her large breasts. She was about six feet tall with her stiletto heels and towered over her escort.

Everyone in the restaurant stopped what he or she was doing (talking loudly, smoking, or stuffing their faces) when the foursome walked in. Torre ran over to the man and kissed his ring, then kissed both of his cheeks as the old man stood impassively scanning the room. If he had been wearing a white robe, he could've been a pope.

Then the crowd erupted in applause and kept yelling bono fortuna, Don Vitello (I think that's good luck in Italian). I know a little Italian (in particular food items as I go to a lot of Italian restaurants), and vitello translates to veal, Don Veal. What a stupid name for somebody trying to act like Marlon Brando in the Godfather. I must admit that, notwithstanding his name, this guy looked the part, and everybody in the place knew and respected him.

The Don raised a hand in response to the welcome and they all went back to whatever they were doing. Torre escorted the Don and his small entourage to the corner table at the far end of the restaurant. And you guessed it. The Don sat in the seat that faced the door. If there was a hit tonight, we were in the line of fire. Then I saw something interesting. The Don looked at Gil and acknowledged him with a slight movement of his head. Gil did the same and saw me watching.

Gil explained, "That's Don Vitello, the most powerful man in this part of Chicago." Gil told me this as a matter of fact.

"You know him?"

"For many years."

"Are you kidding me? Isn't he a criminal?" I said it in a very low voice.

"Stoke, show the man some respect. He's done more for this neighborhood than the state and local governments combined."

"Does Crucible do business with the Don?" I was wondering what the hell Don Vitello actually did, but was afraid to ask. Maybe he was the President of Mafia, Inc., which specialized in murder, extortion, bribery, and prostitution. I hoped Crucible didn't need any of these services.

"The Don has helped me with some political problems in the past."

"Like what?"

"The unions act up, and he settles them down. The authorities get too frisky about how we operate our factories, and he defuses their concerns. He's very well connected in many places."

"Do you pay him for his assistance, like a consultant?"

"Yes, like a consultant." Gil was dead serious and I was really uncomfortable. I was worried about what I had gotten myself involved with, doing business with Crucible all these years.

"Does the Board know that you do business with the Don?"

"I don't tell them about every bit of minutiae that occurs at Crucible. So, the honest answer is that they don't know about Don Vitello."

"Is it a coincidence that he's here tonight and you're here tonight?"

"No. We have some things to discuss."

"Please tell me it has nothing to do with the SEC."

"Actually, it does. Let's change the subject." At that moment, Sophie's cell phone rang and she answered it. The ring didn't disturb the other diners because the din drowned it out.

Cell phones are one of the most useful tools in our new society and one of the most intrusive and annoying devices known to man. I already discussed my feelings about blackberry gadgets, and this is a convenient moment to give you my take on mobile phones. The benefits are obvious and most importantly include portability. The negatives are controversial. For one, many restaurants have already banned them because they're disruptive to patrons. The phones have silly ring options that include "God Bless America," "God Bless the Queen," and the "Notre Dame Fight Song."

While eating, I get so aggravated when I hear a cell phones ring. But even worse are the conversations that take place in public areas. Usually, reception isn't perfect, especially in New York City, and the user is screaming to be heard. Everyone in the immediate vicinity can hear the conversation, because most cell phone users don't take the time to move to a private place to talk.

One of the most outrageous scenes I've ever witnessed was just a few months ago. Five women were having lunch and each one of them was on her cell phone talking. Why the hell did they agree to meet, if they wanted to talk to somebody other than a person at lunch?

Another time in the same restaurant, two men were having lunch and one of them was on the phone for most of the time they spent together. Imagine how terrible and unimportant a person would feel sitting there like a dummy while the other was gabbing away.

It's illegal to talk on a cell using you hands while driving in New York State. The reason is perfectly clear, the odds of having a car accident increase if you're doing things other than driving when you're behind the wheel. But the law doesn't deter very many motorists in my town. A $100 fine isn't severe enough for these offenders. They should lose their license for a year. That'll put an end to this unsafe activity. If you must talk while driving, use a headset.

I see caregivers talking on their cells and ignoring the children they're responsible for. I'm always tempted to find out who they work for and let the parents know how their money is being spent.

In this regard, I have a good idea for a new business. I call it "Parent Alert." Every stroller should have an emergency phone number on it. If you see a care provider abuse a child in any way, you call us at the number and we then would inform the parents. I believe talking on a cell while you're supposed to be caring for a child is a form of neglect. This reminds me of the signs on trucks, which say "How am I driving?" They have a number to call if you see the driver doing something illegal or stupid.

Many people yak on their cells walking on the streets of New York City. You must be alert when strolling down our avenues, or a driver in road rage may run you down.

Finally, I want to remind all of the habitual cell phone users that antennae may cause brain tumors. Do you really need any more incentive to stop using cells?

Sophie finished talking and smiled at me. What a fox. I said, "Important call?"

"No, just a friend who wanted to get together tonight. But I can't because I'm supposed to entertain you." Her response was sarcastic. I wanted to tell her to get lost if she was unhappy being with me, but Gil might have objected.

Gil snickered. I guess he thought it was funny when his daughter insulted others. "I'm sorry you feel that way. Why don't you run along and meet your friend. Your father and I will find something to keep us busy."

"Sorry, I didn't mean for it to come out that way. So tell me, Stoke, are you married?" She tried to rally from her rude comment.

What a retarded question. "Yeah, I'm married. But I hate my wife." My response was just as retarded.

"Are you going to divorce her?"

That was a pretty forward question. "Maybe." Untrue, there was no doubt about it.

"When you're not working, how do you keep busy?"

I try to seduce young women like yourself. I really said, "I play golf."

"Are you a good golfer?"

"No. I suck."

"You should take some lessons."

"I've been taking lessons for years, and I still don't play very well. Do you play?" I tried to get off the witness stand.

"Sure. I'm pretty good too."

"Really. Do you have a handicap?"

"Of course I do."

"Are you going to tell me what it is?"

"I'm a two. I used to be a scratch player, but haven't been on the course very often in the past few years."

"Get the hell out of here. You're a two?"

"Yup."

"You're a real player. But you play from the ladies tees." I teased her.

"I play from the men's tees. I did at college as well."

"You played in college?"

"I was an All-American at Duke."

I was so depressed. Every time I play golf or talk about it I feel terrible. "What do you do at Crucible?" Gil had gotten up and walked away, obviously bored with our conversation. I didn't see him in the restaurant. I looked towards the Don and he wasn't at his seat either.

"I'm in the marketing department. My father wants me to work in all of the important areas of the company. He wants me to take over some day." She laughed, but I think she really meant it.

"You're being groomed to become CEO."

"That's what he says."

"Where did your father go?"

"He went to the back room."

I saw an innocuous door leading to the back rooms. I decided to explore. "Excuse me, I have to use the facilities."

"Sure. Don't be too long." She didn't want to sit alone in this crowd being the only woman who wasn't a hooker.

I went through the door exiting the restaurant area and saw the toilets. Down the hall I passed another door, which was half open. Someone yelled out, "Stoke, come in here, please. I want to introduce you to somebody." It was Gil.

As I entered, I recognized the Don sitting in an easy chair. He looked like a king sitting on his throne. "I don't mean to interrupt you. I was looking for the bathroom." I lied.

Gil replied. "Not at all. This is Don Philippi Vitello. This is my good friend Stoke Spencer."

"You have a very athletic name, Mr. Spencer. Do you play sports?"

I wish the ladies were as interested in my name as Don Veal. "It's nice to meet you. How should I address you, sir?"

"You may call me Don Vitello. Don is a title of respect I have earned over many years. I hope you're comfortable with this."

"No problem, Don Vitello." If I said no, he probably would've shot me. I wanted to ask him how much veal was per pound. What an absolutely foolish name for a man of such high status (not as far as I'm concerned, but among his criminal friends). But he really had a great presence and clearly he was not one to piss off.

Gil stepped into the conversation. "Stoke is my financial advisor. He's worked with Crucible for many years. His firm has been very supportive providing investment banking services."

"I see. Is Mr. Spencer aware of your problems with the SEC?"

"Yes, he is. In fact, his firm is mentioned in the inquiry."

Oh shit. I'm discussing an SEC problem with a Mafioso boss. "Unfortunately, my firm and I are deeply involved."

"Not to worry, Mr. Spencer. I have some friends who have friends at the SEC. Maybe we can arrange for this situation to go away." He smiled broadly.

Double shit. This is unbelievable. I'm here doing business with the mob. I've got to get out of here, before they tell me something I don't want to know. "I left Sophie alone, I should get back to her. It was a pleasure."

Gil said, "I'll be finished in a few minutes."

When I got back to the table, Sophie was on her cell phone again. In the past, when you were bored, you lit up a cigarette. Today, you dial up a friend.

She hung up. "Where've you been, Stoke?"

"I bumped into your father and Don Vitello in the rear of the restaurant. Does you father do a lot of business with that man?"

"I'm not involved in any of that. So, let's get personal. Are you in the market?"

"What do you mean?"

"Are you dating?"

"I'm married. I don't date. I cheat on my wife."

Sophie cracked up. "Well at least you're truthful. Do you cheat with many women?"

"As many beautiful women as I can seduce." This was true only in my dreams.

"That really turns me on. Brutal honesty. I suppose your sex life at home is non-existent."

"Right. A woman's first line of defense is her body. It becomes unavailable to her husband when there are marital problems."

"Stoke, I know that. I can't sleep with a man if I'm angry with him."

"Well I can have sex with a woman, even if I'm angry with her."

"That's the difference between the sexes. Guys are only interested in getting laid, and gals want some affection and commitment." Sophie uncrossed and crossed her legs. The act took my breath away. She had a fabulous figure, and I felt a surge of testosterone shoot through my body.

"Look, everything men do is directed towards sex. We earn money, become powerful and all that stuff so we can attract women for sex. Women are drawn to successful men, so I have many relationships. It's really that simple." What a load of bullshit. I wish I were half as good with women as I was portraying myself. But I figure the best defense is a good offense.

"You're very confidant, Mr. Stokley Spencer. I like that in a man. It's incredibly sexy. Maybe you and I should go out on a date sometime."

Like father like daughter. "Your father is my client. I don't think he'd approve of me going out with his daughter."

"He doesn't have to know. I'm an adult. I can do whatever I want."

"Yeah, but he pays me huge fees each year. You'd have to be really something for me to risk all of that. "

"I am Stoke. I am." She smiled beautifully.

I was starting to wonder who was conning whom. At that moment, daddy returned. And I could see the veal man returning to his seat.

"Are you having fun?" He smiled at both of us. I wondered whether he was actually trying to set me up with his daughter.

I answered. "This place is amazing. I got to meet the boss of bosses. Every wise guy in Chicago is in the house. What else could I ask for?"

"Are you being sarcastic? Just wait, the food is out of this world."

"Gil, seriously, I shouldn't be in a place like this. I could lose my job. Norm Cohen is looking for an excuse to hang me considering all of the other problems I have. Can we eat and get the hell out of here, please?"

"Relax, Stoke. Nobody in Salute is going to squeal on you."

"And what is the Don going to do about the SEC? I hope he's not going to whack a government official."

"You're reading too many gangster novels. He has some friends that may be helpful, that's all. You don't want to know anything else. Just trust me." He was right. I didn't want to know anything else.

The food finally arrived. It was a feast fit for a king, I mean a Don. Fried zucchini, clams casino and steamed mussels to start. Then, we ate eggplant, pasta with pesto and linguini with tomato and basil. The main courses consisted of steak in a spicy tomato sauce, sausage with peppers and onions and veal chops (in honor of the Don). All this was followed by a plain light salad. Garlic permeated the whole restaurant. It was an epicurean's dream.

After dinner, not one of us could eat another thing, so we ordered some espresso and Italian cookies. It was midnight and the night was still young, at least from Gil's perspective. I declined grappa and any other after dinner drink.

Suddenly, a young man started belting out a song in Italian. I thought I was at the opera. I hate opera, but this guy could sing. The whole place was mesmerized. The waiters stopped moving among the tables and the cooks stopped cooking and every soul listened to the man with the beautiful voice. When he finished, every person in the restaurant gave him a standing ovation. The singer started to cry in appreciation. Italians are very emotional.

The night was going to get crazier. I felt it in my bones. I hoped the feds weren't taking pictures of the customers tonight. I'd hate to be associated with these people. Gil picked up the tab, thank goodness. Actually, he just signed a chit. I suppose if you don't pay the bill someone will pay you a visit and break your kneecaps, but being denied access to this food might be a worse penalty. It was too bad that I had to eat the food with a bunch of felons.

As we exited, Torre kissed Gil. Gil nodded at the Don who nodded back. A deal of some sort had been struck. I prayed nobody would be killed to rectify the SEC problem.

I heard some screaming and looked to my right. Two thugs were viciously beating a man. The victim was trying to run away but couldn't escape. He was subjected to a barrage of fists and feet meant to maim and cripple him. The Don's bodyguard appeared at the door of the restaurant and said something in Italian to the two attackers, who immediately backed off. The huge man approached the victim, bent over and whispered something in his ear, and kissed him on the lips. Very strange things were happening. Then one of the attackers walked behind the man, drew a pistol from his belt and shot him in the head. Blood and chunks of his skull were spewed all over the street. I was in disbelief. I couldn't speak. I couldn't move.

The bodyguard walked past us, winked and put his fingers on his lips as if to say you better not tell anybody what you saw. Sophie was crying hysterically. It was the most horrible thing I had ever seen. Gil hustled us into the car.

"Gil, that man was executed. We should call the police."

"If you have a death wish, call the police. If you want to live, forget what you saw."

Sophie spoke up. "Dad, we have to report this. The man was murdered."

"I said drop it. We don't know what it was about." Gil drove away at high speed. "Let's go and have some fun."

"How am I going to have fun?" I said. "I just witnessed a Mafia assassination."

"Stoke, you're getting on my nerves. You keep worrying about things you have no control over. I told you the SEC problem will go away. Now, I'm telling you, just forget what you saw outside that restaurant. You'll live longer if you do,"

Holy shit. How bad can a day get? "Would you take me back to my hotel. I think I've had enough."

Sophie said, "I'm tired, Dad. I want to go home too."

"I'll take you back to the hotel. Sophie, you can get a taxi from there. I have some things I need to take care of. Stoke, you owe me a thousand. The service was impeccable." I didn't respond. We drove in silence and Sophie and I got out of the car at the hotel.

NOT EVEN FIVE SECONDS

The situation was very strained. A man was murdered in front of our eyes, and I wanted to call the police to report the crime. Gil was dead set against contacting the police and became so upset with Sophie and me when we insisted. It was almost as if he was somehow involved in the assassination. I said to Sophie, "What do you make of what just went on?"

"My father reacted in a strange way."

"You can say that again. Is everything OK with him?"

"Lately he's been more irritable than normal, snapping at people in the office. I just assumed it had to do with the SEC investigation."

"Also, the new Board has been putting a lot of pressure on him since the buyout was completed. He no longer has his buddies at the meetings. They've all resigned and been replaced with people close to the new owners."

"Now he's accountable to strangers who've invested millions in Crucible. Word has it that they're not happy about Crucible's operating results. Maybe they just don't trust my father."

"I wouldn't be too happy either if my deal started to crater immediately after it was completed. What about the military?"

"What do you mean?"

"Are the military procurers putting pressure on Crucible relating to the radar business?"

"As a matter of fact, my father has had several meetings with military types over the past few weeks. They were contentious, based upon his mood after they ended."

"Did you ask him about any of the details?"

"I tried, but he didn't want to talk about it. From what I understand there's a middleman between Crucible and the military who's causing some problems."

"What kind of problems?"

"He was the person who originally put the radar deal together. Supposedly, he was a former army officer who was involved with the development of the new radar system. After he left the service, he approached us and offered to consult on our behalf. He told us several branches of the military wanted to buy a new generation of sophisticated equipment. I don't really know the details. Anyway, he said he might be able to help us land the contract. He was paid a large retainer fee."

"Do you know the man?"

"No. I never met him and don't even know his name."

"Would you like to go inside and have a drink? No sense standing in the humidity."

"Sure."

We went to the same bar where Sasha and I met earlier. The place had been converted into a club of sorts since then, and it was packed. The place was filled with a lot of young people dancing to a live band. The female talent in the place was amazing, although Sophie more than held her own. Some guys stared at me as I escorted her into the room. They were wondering what a fox like Sophie was doing with a middle aged, slightly overweight man in a wrinkled suit. They probably thought that I was loaded (had money, not necessarily drunk) or Sophie was a hooker. We found a place in the corner that was somewhat shielded from the loud music.

I started the conversation. "Salute sure has great food. That was quite a spread Torre laid out for us."

"I love that place, although the people I can do without. A lot of creeps are in the place every time I go there."

"You only go to Salute with your father?"

"Mostly. I could call Torre and get a table when I want, but I usually stay away."

The bar was really jumping. The crowd was getting wilder by the second, especially on the dance floor. It appeared that this was the hot spot for young Chicago businessmen and women. They go to dinner, get smashed, and then come here at about midnight, at which time the place shifts into high gear.

What struck me was that there were as many women as men, and that nearly everyone was dressed in business attire. Many of the women had suits on, and they were dancing up a storm, grinding with their partners and making out in every part of the room. I wished there was a place like this in New York. Come to think of it, I'd be hard pressed to enjoy myself because I'd probably know so many of the customers.

I had the urge to urinate, and couldn't remember the last time I relieved myself. I'm surprised I didn't piss in my pants when I saw that man get murdered. "Sophie, I have to leave you alone for a minute, gotta use the facilities." I screamed to be heard over the blasting beat of the music.

"I need to use the ladies' room, so I'll go with you." We gave the waitress our drink orders and made our way to the toilets.

Other conversions were made for the nighttime clientele. One was that the men's and women's bathrooms became the same bathroom. I've been in places like this before and don't get it. I could understand if the owners wanted to save money and build only one rest room. But that was never the case. I guess it's really cool to get drunk and pee in the same place with the opposite sex.

Sophie and I smiled at each other when we figured out that we were going to the same place. On one side of the cavernous room was a waterfall that served as a gigantic urinal. There were no individual stations. You just squeezed in shoulder to shoulder and did your business. If you were shy, the splashing water inspired you to go.

One fellow was so drunk that he fell into the waterfall and got soaked. No one cared, except for those who got splashed. The other side of the room had the toilets, and guess what? No doors! So the ladies had to take a seat and anyone could watch, including the men wandering around the room. What a stupid set up.

Nevertheless, each stall was filled and it didn't seem to bother the women. When I turned away from the waterfall I saw Sophie on the toilet. She smiled and raised her hands indicating, when you gotta go, you gotta go.

On the walls separating the urinal and toilets were many sinks and mirrors. Men and women were milling about talking, making out and snorting cocaine. The users didn't seem to be concerned about who saw them using drugs.

I'm a drinker not a drug user. In college, I dabbled a little just to be sociable, but never got into the drug scene. Paranoia about the long-term effect of drugs and the penalties for being caught made me avoid it. Granted, you can get pretty sick from drinking too much, but the risks associated with drug use are far worse.

If I found out that any of my junior people at work were users, I'd fire them on the spot. The regulators in the securities industry don't test for alcohol, but they test for drugs. There must be a good reason for increased diligence in this area.

Thankfully, we finally exited the uni-bathroom. I couldn't stand the smoke (cigarettes and marijuana) or the lack of privacy. Going to the bathroom isn't a team sport, so I don't want to be with men or women when I do my thing. I said to Sophie, "That was really gross."

"I'm speechless. It's the first time I've urinated to a crowd and in front of a date."

"Sorry about that. I turned around and there you were. I should have anticipated it and kept my head down."

"It's OK. We all urinate. It's not a secret, but I'd prefer to do it by myself."

"You're a good sport, Sophie. And you're so gorgeous. I wish you weren't my biggest client's daughter."

"Why are you obsessing over that? Let's have some fun. What ever happens, happens."

That sounded like an invitation to me. I was so aroused that I could scream. I wondered whether Sasha was still in my room. My life was falling apart, so I might as well go double or nothing and try my luck with Sophie. Oh boy, another slippery slope.

We got back to the table and our drinks were waiting. "Stoke, will you dance with me?"

"Sure." We made our way onto the crowded dance floor and started doing our thing. After enough alcohol, I lose my inhibitions. I don't know what I'm doing, and I don't care.

Liquor was a great thing for the dancing business. I bet 50% of all people who dance wouldn't without having had a few drinks first. I include myself in that group.

Sophie, on the other hand, knows what she's doing. She had her arms in the air, swinging her hips back and forth and really getting into the music.

Every so often she'd approach me and push her pelvis or breasts against me, just to make sure I remembered with whom I was dancing. After the first song, she put her arms over my shoulders and started to grind against me. Boy, was she sexy. She smiled when she felt my excitement.

"I really like you, Stoke. You're a good guy, not an asshole like most of the men I go out with."

"Sophie, this may all be very innocent and that would be OK. But I don't feel innocent, and you're turning me on."

"Relax. This is the way young people dance today. You used to call it dirty dancing, like in that old movie."

I looked around the floor and she was right. Dancing was a sex act with your clothes on. All the girls were pushing their asses and breasts into their partners (male and female). If I had a daughter, I'd forbid her from coming to a place like this.

"I see somebody I know. Do you mind if I go say hello?" Sophie walked away from me before I responded.

I sat down at our table and took a sip of my gin and tonic. I needed some refreshment as the club was filled to the rafters and the air conditioning was unable to cool the place adequately.

I looked for Sophie in the crowd and saw her with a man. They were standing close to each other as they spoke. The words seemed to be heated, so it was probably some sort of lover's spat, but who knows? My expectations about Sophie fell to a more realistic level.

On the dance floor, I had illusions of grandeur. You know, up to the room and hot sex until the sun came up. That wasn't going to happen. I had too much to lose and Sophie was just a cock teaser.

A woman, a stout woman, sat down next to me an asked if the seat was taken. I said, "Yes, you're in it." She smiled.

"How are you doing tonight?" She asked.

"Just great. It's hot as hell in here, but my drink is refreshing. You want something?"

"Sure. I'll have the same as you." I gave the appropriate signal to our waiter, indicating that I needed another drink for the lady. "So what do you do for a living?"

"I'm a banker. You probably knew because we're required to dress like dorks."

"Most of the men in the club are dressed like you. You look just fine." She had a deep voice.

"What business are you in?"

"I'm a cop."

"No shit. What kind of work do you do?"

"I'm a detective. I investigate horrible crimes in this crime ridden city."

"Really? Any exciting things happen to you lately?"

"Before I came over here tonight there was a murder at a restaurant called Salute. A man was shot in the back of the head right on the street."

I couldn't believe the cop was talking about a crime that I witnessed. "Do you know who was involved?"

"Probably the mob."

"Sounds pretty horrible." I wondered whether I should tell this cop I was there, but didn't think it would be a good idea.

"I'd like to put a cap into the head of every one of those fucking punks." She crossed her legs as she said this, and I could see they were really muscular. Sex with this babe would be hazardous to your health. If you made a false move she might put a cap in your head or squeeze you to death with her boa constrictor legs.

"I'm sure that would be unacceptable to the defenders of our civil liberties."

"Yeah. They're so worried about the rights of the fucking criminals that they forget about the rights of the victims."

This woman seemed very passionate about law and order. "I agree with you. You look like you work out quite a bit."

"I do a lot of weight training. Never know when you're gonna need some muscle to apprehend a perp."

Sophie was standing over us. "Am I interrupting anything?"

"Ah, no. This is ..."

"Raymond."

"Raymond, allow me to introduce you to Sophie. How did you end up with the name Raymond?"

Raymond got up. "See you around." She seemed a little disappointed. She sashayed away.

Sophie started laughing aloud and was nearly in tears. "What are you laughing about?"

"That was a man. You didn't know, did you?"

"Get the fuck out of here."

"Trust me. If you went into the bathroom and saw Raymond, he would've had his skirt hiked up peeing against the wall just like you."

"He's also a cop. A cop in drag."

"He's a cop?" Sophie seemed concerned.

"Yep, and he told me about a shooting outside of Salute tonight."

"Come on. How the hell did he know about that?"

"Maybe he was on the scene before he got dressed up to come out tonight."

"What did he say about it?"

"He speculated that it was a mob hit. Boy, I feel like a real schmuck."

"You would've been really surprised if you put a hand up Raymond's skirt."

"You got that right. So, who were you talking with?"

"An ex-boyfriend. He still hasn't gotten over me."

"Then why did you go over to him?"

"He keeps leaving messages on my machine. Some of them are obnoxious. I told him he better end it immediately or I was going to call the cops."

"You could tell Raymond."

"Right."

"Do you have trouble ending relationships?"

"I don't, but the guys I go out with seem to."

"You must be unforgettable."

"I am." She winked.

I suddenly had that feeling again. She just reiterated her interest in me. My spirits were on the rise. However, the thought of the murdered man lingered in my mind. It's not easy pondering sex and a bullet in the back of someone's head at the same time.

Sophie would be the perfect elixir to the horrible experience we had. She got my mind off the dead man's body and onto hers. "Are there many transvestites in this place?"

"Everybody does whatever they want in this club."

I scanned the dance floor and noticed girls dancing with girls and guys dancing with guys. I hadn't been in many places like this. It's a free country, but I find it hard to take it in stride. My question is, were all the same sex dancers homosexuals, or were they just experimenting?

When I was young, homosexuals stayed in the proverbial closet and went to places where they wouldn't be harassed. Today, it's all in your face. Political correctness has overwhelmed our society. Public displays of affections by all types are commonplace. Personally, I don't care what people do in their bedrooms. But to see intimate activity by anybody in public is annoying and not appropriate for youngsters. "So do you disapprove?" I asked her.

"I really could care less." I was sure she was being truthful. Young people today are as tolerant as they have ever been, especially in big cities.

"Have you ever had a relationship with a woman?" I couldn't believe these words came out of my mouth. Must've been the alcohol.

"That's a very personal question."

"Don't answer if you're not comfortable."

"It's OK. Yes, I've made out with a few women when I was in college."

Now this conversation was really getting me worked up. In case you didn't know it, most guys are turned on by the prospect of seeing two women have sex. "Were they enjoyable experiences?"

"Sure, they were a real turn on. To be honest, I found the absence of a penis to be an issue. I guess I'm programmed that a sexual encounter must end with intercourse. It must mean that I'm heterosexual."

"I'm really interested in your feelings about the experience. Were you more at ease with a woman? Was the encounter less stressful than with a man?"

"In a way, it wasn't as pressure packed. With men, you know what they want and you have to decide whether you want to comply. With a woman it was a more natural activity, if you know what I mean. By the way, I've only slept with men since college."

"It sounds like you've learned to accept the stress of heterosexual lovemaking because the ultimate sex act is only possible with a man."

"I think that's right. Have you ever been with a man?"

"Fair question. The answer is absolutely, no fucking way. Let's change the subject. I'm still pretty shaken up about what we saw today. Are you?"

"Of course. I just hope my father isn't involved."

I added some philosophical perspective to the conversation. "Me too. Sometimes financial problems drive people to do extreme things. But murder is on the far end of any spectrum."

"Do you think the murdered man knew he was going to die tonight?"

"I have no idea. He probably wasn't optimistic about living another day while those two thugs beat the shit out of him. The expectation that your life will be over in a moment has got to be a surreal experience."

Sophie responded with great concern. "It's kind of like being on an airplane that you know is about to crash."

"Right. What the hell are you supposed to think about at that moment? Do you ask God to forgive your sins? Do you think about your family? Do you just cry like a baby?"

"I just hope I'm never in that situation and my demise comes suddenly and painlessly."

"I agree. But what should we do about the murder? Should we call the police? How can we *not* call the police?"

"I'll talk to my father tomorrow and discuss it with him. We weren't involved in anything, so I don't know why he'd object to making a call."

"Get in touch with me after you speak to him. If the police find out we were there and we didn't step forward, they might think we played a part in the murder."

"I definitely will. What happens next with us?" She certainly was confident. I thought I was supposed to ask that question.

"What do you want to do?"

"Why don't we go to your room, have a drink, and have a quiet chat?"

"OK. Let's get out of here." My heart started to pound furiously in anticipation. But then I thought of Sasha.

We went up to my room and the bed had been turned down. Fortunately (I guess), Sasha was gone. There was a note on the dresser, which I quickly slipped into my pocket, to be read later.

Sophie turned to me and kissed me passionately. I kissed her back, hard. She tasted fantastic and smelled just as good, even after a long day. I was really aroused and she knew it when she pressed her body against mine.

Our foreplay didn't last very long, and I'll spare you the details. Truthfully, it'd been a while since I was with a woman, notwithstanding all of my bluster to the contrary, and I got too excited too quickly. I could tell Sophie was an expert by the way she handled herself and handled the relevant parts of my body.

We didn't shower beforehand, and so our preliminaries included nothing that should've resulted in an orgasm. We kissed, touched, and moaned for about three minutes. To be frank, I ejaculated just as we began to have intercourse. I finally had my chance with a beautiful woman and it was over in one stroke. I discharged like a sex starved teenager getting laid for the first time.

I guess Sophie was looking forward to a mature and exciting experience with an older man, slow lovemaking ending in simultaneous gratification (not just mine). She was visibly pissed off. "Stoke, when was the last time you had sex?"

"It's been a while. Sorry I came so soon. I couldn't control myself because you're so unbelievable." I tried a diversionary tactic. Blame my sexual incompetence on her good looks.

"You know, I have needs too. You were so selfish. You seduced me and left me totally unsatisfied."

"Do you think I did it on purpose? I want to make you happy, Sophie."

"I'm really disappointed. That whole thing was pathetic. You're a grown man. Don't you know how to make love to a woman?"

I felt like an idiot. "Listen, Sophie, the night is still young. Let's have a drink, relax and start all over again. I'll do anything you want."

"You're the worst lay I've had since I was thirteen years old. My first experience lasted about ten seconds, which was five seconds longer than what happened tonight. I can't believe I trusted you."

"You're really being cruel, Sophie. Guys have issues sometimes. I've never suffered from premature ejaculation. I'm sorry. It'll never happen again. Come here and let me hold you."

"No thanks. I'm leaving. Maybe you drank too much. You better get some practice or see a sex therapist."

I was crushed. I stepped over the line on to a slippery slope and was a dismal failure. The inability to please a woman is something all men worry about. To ejaculate before you even get started is an unmitigated disaster. I was devastated.

Here I'm having sex with my largest client's daughter and she thinks I'm a lousy lay. What if she tells her father? Gil would be more angry with me because I was a terrible lover than because I had sex with his daughter.

What a fucking day. I hope my plane doesn't crash going back to New York. If it does, Sophie might tell everybody at my funeral that I came prematurely. My friends would know that all my success in business was a cover for my inadequacies in bed. SS could add her perspective as well.

We had an adequate sexual relationship, but I'm sure she could tell a few stories that would confirm Sophie's observations. Maybe it was my prostate that was causing all this. I'm ruined. I made a mental note to discuss this with my urologist. I hope he doesn't start laughing when I tell him what happened.

"Please stay. Why don't you sleep with me and we can make love in the morning. The booze will have worn off and I'll ravage you to your satisfaction."

"If I believed that would happen I'd stay, but I don't. I'm out of here." Sophie dressed and walked out leaving me alone with my thoughts.

A tremendous feeling of inadequacy overwhelmed me. To be frank, my sexual experiences wouldn't put me in the top quartile of lovers, maybe not even in the second quartile. But my performance tonight wouldn't even get rated because it was a non-event. It was non-sex.

In fairness, a lot of sexual frustration had been building up inside of me for quite a while. I hadn't been sexually active for several months. I tried to think of the last time SS and I had intercourse and to my astonishment, I recalled that it was two and a half months earlier. In my last encounter with SS, we got into bed at about 10:00 to watch television. After a brief spat about what program we should watch, I popped the question, "Sharon, we haven't been close in long time. Could I make love to you?" She said, "Only if you click onto my program." I controlled the remote in my family, as men should, but I had to yield to her television demands if I wanted to get laid.

Everything is a deal with SS. I traded material things for sex. Our relationship was tantamount to prostitution. So, I clicked to her channel and turned towards her to kiss her. She said, "Make it fast, Stoke, I don't want to miss anything." I can't really remember how long we made love (and I use the term loosely), but it must have been longer than the time it takes to complete one stroke.

SS laid on her back like a dead fish, wishing it were over before it started and thinking of more pleasant things. I managed to remain semi-aroused in spite of her TV demands and orders to finish quickly. It was strictly physical, devoid of love and tenderness. She wanted to watch her program, and I wanted to relieve myself. I didn't even say thanks. I just rolled over and went to sleep. The deal was completed and there was nothing more we needed to talk about.

I hope you can understand how I found myself with strange women this evening. What is a man supposed to do if his woman deprives him of sex? Should a man be faithful if his spouse has no interest in him physically? Can a relationship exist between a man and a woman without sex? Should it be acceptable for a married man to pursue other women for sexual purposes if he doesn't want to end his marriage? Is a man unfaithful if he has sex with another woman because his wife won't? Can a wife impose celibacy on her husband?

I was in a conundrum. For sure, there's no universal answer to this question. I decided I wasn't going to worry about the morality of extramarital sexual activity. SS deserved unfaithful behavior on my part, so fuck it.

Back to Sophie. Picture it. Beautiful woman wants to make love. Horny guy. In a hotel room after many drinks. One stroke. Woman unsatisfied. Woman really unhappy. Shit, what a disaster. I wondered whether I should even call her to discuss what happened and beg for another chance.

I now knew how fragile my ego is about issues relating to virility. I wondered what would've happened if I had made love to Sasha. It probably would've been a wham, bam, thank you ma'am moment. I didn't have a chance to read her note until now. I reached for my pants and pulled out the envelope. It was written on stationary from the desk in the room. I opened it and read the following:

'Dear Stoke,

The events of this day are very confusing. You indicated nothing happened between us, which is a relief. Is it really true? You swear you didn't take advantage of me? A gentleman wouldn't, of course, but I need to be positive.

I'm unsure what to write next. You're a married man, so it's inappropriate for me to encourage you to call. But you said you were breaking up with your wife. Famous last words.

In any case, I enjoyed spending time with you. I'm terribly embarrassed that I drank too much and passed out. I tried to straighten the room before I left. Why don't you call me? My business card is enclosed. We can discuss whether it makes sense to get together again.

Sasha'

It was a nice letter. Maybe I should have made love to her. I felt positive about what I did. It was now 3:30, so I decided to end this crazy day.

LEAVE ME ALONE ALREADY

The telephone rang and at first I didn't know where I was. After a moment, I remembered I was in a hotel and looked at the clock. It was 11:30. Oh shit, I missed my plane. I didn't even think to ask for a wake up call before I went to bed. The phone continued to ring. I picked it up. "Hello."

"Stoke, it's me, Norm. Why aren't you back here? I thought you were taking the early flight."

"I had a long night. I couldn't get up. What the hell is the rush?"

"More Crucible problems. Have you been watching CNBC?"

"What happened now?"

"The US Attorney is indicting Gil Richards for securities fraud and for stealing millions from Crucible."

"Great."

"That's not all. Some guy who was consulting for Crucible was murdered yesterday in Chicago."

I just wanted to go back to sleep. This all had to be a bad dream. "What did the papers say about the consultant?"

"He was helping Crucible with the radar deal."

"Oh shit."

"You don't know anything about that do you?"

"No, Norm. I'll get back to the office as quickly as I can."

"You have a lot of explaining to do, Stoke. This situation is spiraling out of control."

Right. "Bye." I hung up the phone.

I called Gil's office. "This is Stoke Spencer, may I speak to Mr. Richards, please?"

"I'm sorry Mr. Spencer, he's in a meeting. Can he get back to you?"

"Would you tell him I'm on the line? It's important."

"I'll let him know you're holding."

The phone came to life after about two minutes. "Hello, Stoke, it's Al Nash. Can I help you with something?"

"Yeah, put Gil on the line."

"He's busy. What do you want?"

"You better watch you mouth or I might come to your office and kick your ass."

"Save the histrionics, pal. We have some serious legal issues brewing and we're trying to work through them. I'll tell him you called."

"Wait a second. Has Gil been indicted yet?"

"I can't talk about that."

"Don't give me that shit. I'm on the hot seat as well."

"We expect papers to be delivered any moment. You should expect a lot of conversation with the US Attorney. You better be careful what you tell them, Stoke."

"If you threaten me one more time I'm going to punch your lights out."

"You're a violent man, Spencer. Why don't you give us all a fucking break and get the hell out of town. We'll call you if we need you."

"I decided to play my wildcard. "What's with the guy who was murdered outside of Salute?"

"Hold on."

The silence was overbearing. Finally, "Stoke, it's me Gil. What do you know?"

"I know you're ruining my life. I heard that man who was killed was working for Crucible. Is that true?"

"Yes. I hired him to help me with the radar deal."

"Why the fuck was he murdered last night just after you spoke with the Don?"

"We shouldn't be talking on the phone. I have to go. Don't mention that we were at Salute last night to anyone. That could be a really dangerous thing to do."

"What are you talking about? Is my life in danger?"

"Yes. Keep your mouth shut. Goodbye." He hung up.

I called my number at work. "Mr. Spencer's office."

"Liz, it's me."

"Where the hell are you? Did you miss your plane?"

"Chicago, and yes."

"Don't be a wise ass. This place is jumping with all sorts of rumors and legal activity. I think it has to do with Crucible. Antun Smith and Norm are interrogating everyone who's worked on the Crucible account. I think they're setting you up."

"Is Josh Aaron around?"

"Yes. I saw him this morning."

"Get him on the phone for me."

"Stoke, it's Josh. What the fuck is going on? Are you in some kind of trouble?"

"I think I am and it's much more important than financial impropriety at Crucible. I need your help."

"You got it. What can I do for you?"

"You told me one time that you went to school with a guy who's a District Attorney. Is that right?"

"Yeah, my buddy Stan Forman. We went to Columbia undergraduate school together. Great lawyer. He wants to stick a needle in the arm of every felon in America. He's a real crusader. He could've made a lot of money, but doesn't give a shit about material things. He just wants to prosecute felons."

"Can you arrange for me to meet with him?"

"Of course. Should I tell him about Crucible?"

"Sure, but the Crucible problem is only part of a much bigger situation. This is life and death stuff, Josh."

"When do you want to see him?"

"Ask him if he can have a drink with me tonight at Andersons by our office."

"Seven, OK?"

"Perfect. I have to get on a plane. Thanks."

"No problem."

JOY TO THE WORLD

I showered and put on clean underwear, a clean shirt and my suit, which was crumpled on a chair. I forgot to hang it up in my rush to have sex with Sophie for five seconds. I packed my bag and dashed off to O'Hare Airport.

The traffic was moderately heavy, even at midday in Chicago. The planes left for La Guardia every hour, so I figured I could easily get on the next flight. After spending 20 minutes trying to figure out the automated ticketing machine, I made my way through security uneventfully. I guess the security assholes in New York didn't tell the security people in Chicago I was in town. The airport was packed. O'Hare is always busy. I had 45 minutes before the plane left. I booked a first class seat. What the hell, I'd probably be behind bars soon, so I decided I might as well live it up.

I had so much on my mind I didn't even think about meeting another attractive woman on the plane. It's difficult to focus on sex and related things when you're being investigated and witnessing murders.

While waiting in the lounge to board, I recapped the issues I had to deal with upon arriving in New York. I had to have a serious conversation with Cohen. Surely, he'd have Antun Smith with him for support. They'd ask me over and over whether I was involved in any crimes relating to Crucible. We'll talk about Gil and the nature of his impending indictments. And we'd discuss the murder of a man who was supposedly a consultant to Crucible in Chicago.

I'd have to call SS to discuss the tenuous status of our marriage. She'd beg me to not leave her, and I'd ask her how it felt to beg. I've been begging her for sex for most of our married live. She'd use every psychological tactic to get me to reconsider my decision. SS would cry, scream at me, threaten me, and call me names. None of this would be successful as they had been so often in the past. I was finally in the driver's seat. I earned all the money in our family that enabled her to live the way she did. She'd have to take money from me, and that wouldn't be easy. I'm no fool, and I know what she's entitled to by law, but SS was going to have to work very hard with a divorce lawyer to get one red cent.

I'm not a vindictive guy, but I was actually beginning to look forward to making her life as miserable as she had made mine. The boys would stay with their mother and I expected a real struggle, as they tried to understand the significance of our marital problems. But they'd grow out of it, and would likely find an SS to make their lives miserable someday.

My relationship with Gil was probably at an end. He was dead meat as far as I could tell. Once the feds are on your case, it's unlikely you can get away unscathed. The big issue is that my revenues at work would decline materially if Crucible got flushed down the toilet. But I always knew Crucible was a risky situation based upon Gil's volatile personality, so I'd been establishing new relationships with a number of other companies over the past two years. Everything should be OK unless I'm implicated, which is unlikely because I didn't do anything illegal.

However, the murder of that man made me nervous. I wasn't worried about the fact that

I didn't report the crime. Rather, I was worried that the Don would try to have me killed if I cooperated with the authorities. My meeting with Stan Forman would be the first step in sorting that out.

And finally, I had all these women to deal with. Should I call Sasha? Should I call Sophie? Should I go to a sex therapist to find out whether I'm a chronic pre-ejaculator? Ugh.

An announcement was made about my flight. The attendant called for children, the infirm, and first class to get on the plane. I boarded and took my first class seat, which had plenty of legroom. I was on the aisle and didn't buckle up because my seatmate hadn't yet arrived.

Then a stunning woman came into view. She had to be about 50 years old, but was the most beautiful and sophisticated female I'd seen in a long time. She had a knee length pleated skirt, a kilt type garment colored in tartan. Her blouse was white silk and I could see the faintest outline of her breasts through it. The blouse was a huge turn on. Guess where she stopped? Not by me, but in the row ahead of me. I was really bummed out.

I pulled the airline magazine out from the pocket in the seat in front of me and surveyed the crossword puzzle and the other brainteasers. Does anybody read these magazines? They're total crap, and chock full of advertisements by the airlines.

Suddenly, a man approached the middle-aged goddess and indicated she was in his seat. And would you believe it, she came back a row and asked to pass by. I stood up and ascertained that she was tall, maybe 5 feet 10 inches, so we were nose to nose when I got up. She gracefully slid past me and her breast touched my chest very lightly. I was immediately stirred. The good news was that I was able to control myself and didn't discharge. This problem was going to haunt me until I determined that I was capable of having sex like a normal man for three or four minutes, or whatever the average copulation target was these days. And I don't mean the times you read about in the pornographic magazines. I'd settle for much less.

She sat down and crossed her legs. Her skirt went up her thigh just far enough to make me nuts. "How are you today?" What a line. I'm such a stud.

"I'm fine, and you?" She answered me. I took the first step.

"It's been a few tough days, but I'm on my way home." I omitted many relevant facts that included getting divorced and being investigated by the SEC.

"Always helps to be home. I live in New York as well."

"Where about?"

"Upper eastside."

"Me too."

She opened her "Wall Street Journal" and put on these cute reading glasses that sat on the end of her nose. "Well the business world's a mess. So many executives are getting themselves into trouble these days."

"I know. Believe me, I know."

"Are you a lawyer?" She asked.

"Banker. We get sucked into trouble when our clients misbehave."

"A new problem in today's news."

"Which company," I asked.

"Crucible and its CEO are being investigated."

"Is that right?" I could see the story was the first one on the front page. "I met the CEO at a fundraiser last year. He's a charming man."

"I know Gil Richards myself."

"He's a friend of yours?"

"Sort of." I had five-second sex with his daughter.

The plane took off and I asked, "Mind if I read your Journal."

"Help yourself. I bet you want to read about your friend, Mr. Richards."

I smiled and took the paper. "Thanks." The story read as follows:

'Gilbert Richards, Chairman and Chief Executive Officer of Crucible Corporation was expected to be indicted by the US Attorney's Office today on 25 counts of fraud relating to the leveraged buyout of Crucible. An investor group led by Swarthmore Partners acquired Crucible for nearly $10 billion three months ago. The indictment alleges that Mr. Richards falsified Crucible's results leading up to the buyout enabling him to obtain a higher price for the company. He personally received $1 billion for his ownership in Crucible.

"The US Attorney's Office will also indict Mr. Richards on a single count of grand larceny relating to an alleged $5 million unauthorized payment he received before the buyout closed. The indictment indicates that Marion Denning, a Board member of Crucible before the buyout, had brought the situation to the attention of the authorities. She was also Chairwoman of the Compensation Committee of the company.

"In a related story, James Digon was found murdered in a back alley in a Chicago suburb. Mr. Digon was an advisor to Crucible and a former Army procurement officer. He was assisting Crucible in a multi billion-dollar radar transaction, which the military was negotiating with the company. The police have stated that Mr. Digon was killed outside a nearby restaurant called Salute, often frequented by Chicago crime figures.'

I whispered to myself, "Oh my God."

"Pretty bad, huh," my seatmate responded.

"Yes. I've actually done a lot of business with Richards, so this is all quite disturbing." That was the understatement of the year.

"What's your name?"

"Sorry, I should have introduced myself to you. I'm Stoke Spencer. And you are?"

"Joy Adamson."

"I've heard of you. You're a judge, aren't you?"

"Yes. I'm flattered you know me."

"How can I not know you? You presided over a number of precedent setting securities cases in the past few years. All of us in the business are petrified about appearing before your court."

"Oh stop it. I'm only mean to felons. To everybody else I'm just a kind old lady."

"You must be kidding. You're beautiful."

"Stoke, how nice of you. Are you somehow involved with Crucible, if you don't mind me asking?"

"Afraid so. I did the buyout for Gil. I suppose I shouldn't talk about it."

"You're absolutely correct. Who knows I might actually try the case. Only kidding, I'm a state judge, not a federal judge. It seems the US attorney has this situation firmly in control."

All of a sudden the plane started to shake and rock back and forth. "I guess we found some turbulence." I don't know what I'm talking about, but it really felt like something more serious than rough weather. And when I looked out of the plane, I saw sunny skies.

The pilot came on the intercom. "Ladies and gentlemen, we have encountered a mechanical problem. It seems that our landing gear hasn't fully retracted into the body of the aircraft. I don't think it's serious and will keep you informed. I'm going to intentionally shake the plane around to try to make the landing apparatus move up into the fuselage, so you'll experience turbulence type movement of the aircraft. I'd like everybody to be seated and to keep your belts fastened. When we fix this problem, I'll let you know. Don't get upset, we're trained to deal with this type of situation."

Joy spoke first. "I think maybe this might be a little more serious than the pilot has indicated."

"I think you're right. When the wheels don't retract it creates a drag on the plane, and landing is always a bitch without wheels."

"I'm very frightened. Are you?"

"Excuse my French, but I'm scared shitless."

"May I hold your hand, Stoke?"

The beautiful judge asked to make contact with me, as we were about to be in an air crash of some sort. "Of course you may."

Being on the verge of the end of my life, it's ridiculous to be thinking about sex, but the pilot did say the plane would be all right. She gripped my hand and the back of my arm was against her breast. For weeks, I'd been trying to score unsuccessfully and now all these women couldn't seem to stay away from me. Unfortunately, my sexual opportunities were accompanied by numerous complications and bad landing gear.

I snuggled closer to Joy and she responded. I think it was because she was nervous, but you never know. The plane jerked violently left and right, and a few people started to scream. Here I was, just as I dreaded. I got to think about crashing in an airplane for an hour or so before it actually happened. Everybody on the plane would be going ape shit and I'd have to figure out what I should be doing during my last minutes on earth. I said a little prayer to myself and asked God to take care of my family. Maybe I was overreacting at this point. This whole thing might work out.

Then, a woman in the forward part of the coach section, which was near us, jumped out of her seat and started to scream. She spoke of dying and was literally out of her mind. The flight attendants tried to settle her down, but she was delirious, talking about heaven and hell and repentance. As an aside, I hope you realize I'm telling you a story about things that happened to me several weeks ago. I'm going to survive, so don't get all choked up. Back to the story.

Joy said to me, "I can't believe my life is going to end this way. I have so many things to do before I die."

"You're not going to die, Joy. I'm sure this is something the pilot's can take care of."

At that moment the plane shook again and more people started screaming. The shaking was followed by a quick descent, which was followed by even more screaming.

"You're sure about that? This isn't looking good, Stoke. I'm happy I'm spending my last moments with you though."

She leaned over and kissed me on the lips. I think it was a goodbye kiss, but I got turned on anyway. The insanity of hitting on this woman at this particular moment knocks me for a loop as I think back. I can't believe I wasn't thinking about the things you're supposed to think about when you're going down in a plane. Maybe it was a blessing in disguise. I probably would've been screaming like all the other sissies in the plane if I hadn't been so preoccupied with Joy.

"I feel the same way, darling." She kind of gave me a blank stare. Like what the hell are you talking about? We're about to die and you're whispering sweet nothings in my ear.

But then we moved on. "What things will you do the minute we walk off this plane?" I figured this line of thought would keep her mind off the impending crisis facing us, and me as well.

"I've been in love with a man for several years. He's married and unwilling to leave his wife.

I've never been married myself because of my career. Anyway, if I survive I'm going to convince him to take the plunge and start a life with me. I refuse to go to the grave without the happiness made possible only with a family."

Damn. I'm trying to put the moves on this woman and she's thinking about another man. Suddenly another violent tremor. More screaming. I have to admit that I refocused on the landing gear problem, since sex, or a conversation about it wasn't in the cards. "That was pretty bad. I wish the pilot would give us an update. It would be nice to hear that some progress was being made. Don't you think?"

"Stoke, you should be directing your thoughts towards your life and what you accomplished as a man, husband, and father."

"I'm more accomplished at business than I am as a family man. In fact, the first thing I'm going to do if I survive this flight is to get divorced from the horrible bitch I'm married to." At this point, I didn't see any need to mince words, as I wasn't going to get laid, and I was probably going to die in a few minutes.

"That's terrible. You shouldn't speak of your wife that way."

"She's an impossible person to live with, and I can't believe I stayed with her this long. I'm unhappy and need to find somebody to be a real companion. Say, I have an idea. If we walk off this plane today, why don't we get married? I need to get a divorce, but we could move in together. It'll take your mind off that jerk that won't leave his wife, and you can help me though my situation. Our relationship could be platonic, unless we find that we're compatible. What do you say?"

"That is the dumbest thing I ever heard in my life. You expect me to move in with you, a strange man, if we survive? You're trying to take advantage of this dire situation. I need to think about it. I never did anything crazy in my whole life. I could make up for lost time by doing something so insane." She was totally confused by my suggestion.

You never know when your efforts will be rewarded, do you? Picture it. Plane going down. I propose to a strange, beautiful, successful woman. She accepts, maybe. Sometimes I can't believe myself. I actually had a chance. "Kiss me. Let's lock up the deal. You want to do it, right?"

She leaned over and kissed me passionately. I gladly accepted her darting tongue. This was unbelievable. I hoped we survived the flight. I wanted to ask her to go into the bathroom, so we could really consummate the deal. I didn't want a platonic relationship, and I don't think she did either.

The pilot came on. "Good news everybody. The landing gear has retracted. Everything is fine. The rest of our trip will be uneventful. I promise." A loud roar ensued. The seat belt sign was turned off and drinks were offered free to all of legal age.

I looked at Joy, who had a relieved look in her eyes. "Are we still on, or were you just saying all that because you thought you were going to die?"

"Stoke, you're an amazing man. I'm fifty years old and that's the first time I've ever done or said anything like that. I'm a little embarrassed, to be honest with you. If we died you'd have been the last person I kissed and spoken to. Isn't that romantic?"

"Actually, I really meant what I said." I smiled at her but I knew what she was about to say.

Joy leaned over again, kissed me even more passionately and pushed her breasts into my chest. "I guess we now know what people think about before they die. I said I'd do things with you that aren't possible. I hope you'll forgive me."

"No problem. Could we go on a date sometime? Maybe you'll really like me when our lives aren't in danger." I'd also have an opportunity to find out whether I have a chronic sexual performance problem. It would be a bummer to have two trysts where intercourse lasted less than ten seconds in total.

"Sure, I'd love to. Here's my card."

We spent the rest of the flight chatting about living, not dying. Joy was a fabulous person and I decided I'd definitely call her.

The landing was uneventful as the pilot promised. As I deplaned, I thanked the flight crew for bringing the aircraft home safely. I wanted to say that I could've used about 15 minutes of more suspense to make my move on Joy.

We strolled through the airport together. It was a pleasure to be with such an attractive woman. Men stared at her as we passed. Imagine, 50 years old and still turning heads.

It was about 2:30 and I had to decide whether I wanted to reenter the lion's den known as GYP. Cohen would be waiting for me at the door. I decided instead that I needed some exercise and would go to my health club to relax for an hour.

When we passed through security (thank goodness the morons don't check you on the way out), we spotted a driver who held a sign with Joy's name on it. "I guess this is it. You're carriage awaits."

"Duty calls. I hope I can calm myself down from the experience of the past two hours."

"You can do it. We weren't in any grave danger or anything like that." I lied.

"Well, I don't know about that. But something else of great significance occurred."

"What was that?" As if I didn't know what she meant.

"I think I was starting to fall in love with you. When you think you only have a few minutes to live, decisions must be made spontaneously and your life goes into fast forward. A woman doesn't want to feel alone seconds before she dies."

"You got that right. I wish we could do more together on the falling in love stuff. I'll call. OK?"

"You better." She kissed me lightly on the lips and set off with her driver.

IF LOOKS COULD KILL

I went to the taxi stand, where about 50 people were waiting on line, even though it was midday. While I was waiting calmly, this man turns to me and says, "If dimwits weren't running this operation, we wouldn't be standing here like fools."

Just what I needed. I survived a near fatal plane ride and now this bozo was going to make me crazy about waiting in a line for a few minutes. "Take it easy pal. It's one of the minor inconveniences of New York."

"Well, I'm from New York, and I don't like having to wait around because the taxi commission, or whomever is in charge doesn't have a clue about what they're doing."

"It's not going to get better, so maybe you should just move to a different city." Maybe I could convince him to leave town so he never would bother any New Yorker or me ever again.

I asked myself why I was encouraging a colloquy with this dumbbell. He was dressed like a businessman, a suit and all the accoutrements. His clothes were ill fitting and must have been purchased when he was 20 pounds lighter. And he was lugging around two large bags, a sign that he was either an inexperienced traveler or he liked to keep the baggage claim personnel busy. "I'll bet this attendant doesn't make $10/hour. What do you expect, a rocket scientist? And besides, he has no control over how many cabbies come to the airport."

"I know all that, but look at him. He's a slob."

Look who's talking, I said to myself. "He doesn't earn enough money to buy suits. Give 'em a break."

The man was sweating profusely. "You're right. I'm just in a hurry."

"Never assume transportation in this city will be timely." I consider myself an expert on New York City transportation issues.

"You want to share a taxi? I'm going to midtown."

"No thanks."

"Come on, we can save a few bucks."

"I don't care. I need to make some phone calls and don't want any company. Sorry."

"You're pretty obnoxious. What's your problem?"

"You. You're my problem. Stop fucking whining and don't talk to me anymore. I've got a lot of things on my mind, and they're more important than waiting in a taxi line."

"Have a nice day. I hope your taxi crashes and you get killed."

"Thanks. Same to you jerk." I turned away. Another successful encounter.

After 15 minutes, I finally got into a taxi, alone. A Middle Eastern man was in the driver's seat (what else is new). He had all sorts of communication equipment. Great. New York taxi drivers can't drive for shit, and yet they try to do it while talking on the phone.

I had a sense that this was going to be a rough ride. "46th and Park, please." My health club is in the MetLife building. I struggled to fit my feet into the area between the seat and the taxi Berlin Wall.

"OK."

We didn't move 100 yards and the driver was yakking away on his phone. It might not have been too bad but he was screaming into the device in a foreign language. "Excuse me. Would you please shut the window?"

Taxis have a Plexiglas barrier above the front seat. It can be closed, but you must ask. I asked. He complied, but gave me a dirty look.

Suddenly the radio was on and some man was speaking in French, I think. I knocked on the closed window and yelled, "Please shut the radio." He complied, but gave me another dirty look. "Are you deliberately trying to make this trip unpleasant?" He probably didn't know what deliberately meant. I got no answer, just one more dirty look.

The traffic was a mess as we approached the Tri Borough Bridge. I'd been working and traveling for a quarter of a century and there's been roadwork and construction on or around this bridge the entire time. The construction companies must be making gigantic profits from this never-ending project. Lanes were closed, and workers were standing around doing nothing. It's all a huge scam. And these guys made big bucks relatively speaking.

I've always been tempted to scream out the window and tell the assholes to stop standing around and finish the job already. But they'd probably throw a wrench at the car.

Amazingly, many of the workers did so without proper protection. Their eyes were exposed as they jack hammered away, and their ears subjected to a continuous din. It's no wonder health costs are skyrocketing in the country. You'd think the unions would insist that their members protect themselves. Construction workers think it's a joke to be safe, because they're such tough guys.

Anyway, four lanes shifted into two. It was hot as hell outside, sunny and humid, and the air conditioning in the car sucked. Recently, the taxi companies had installed air conditioning controls for the passengers. Of course, they never work properly.

"Would you please turn up the air, thank you?" The driver turned around and gave me another dirty look.

If looks could kill I would've been dead before we exited the airport. "Did you hear me? Turn up the air. It's too hot back here." The driver snarled at me and raised his hand as if to say OK. At least that's what I thought he meant. We crawled across the bridge. I was tempted to make some calls, but why should I? Everything was fucked up, and I'd only get more aggravated. At last, we arrived at the tollbooth before we entered into Manhattan. The driver got into one of the cash lanes.

He opened the Plexiglas window and said, "I need cash."

"You don't have an EZ Pass?"

"No, give me cash, please."

For those of you who aren't New Yorkers, allow me to explain the toll situation to you. You have two choices at tollbooths in the metropolitan area. One, you can pay cash. The cash line is always long and moves slowly. Two, you can subscribe to EZ Pass and drive straight through. A scanner charges your account without your having to stop the car. The EZ Pass costs nothing to own and it saves its users (and taxi passengers) a lot of time. In fact the cost of a toll is discounted if you use EZ Pass. The only catch is you must have a credit card to which the toll charges are posted.

Why in heaven's name wouldn't every person who lives in the New York area have an EZ Pass? It costs less and it's quicker. Why wouldn't a taxi driver who loses money when he's sitting in traffic have an EZ Pass?

"Why don't you have an EZ Pass?" I asked the driver.

Another dirty look, "No credit card."

"That's really stupid, you know."

He gave a more threatening look. "Mind your own business and I'll drive. OK?"

I whispered to myself, "Fucking dumbbell."

We pulled up to the curb and my odyssey from the airport was finally over. It took 90 minutes to fly from Chicago to New York, and 60 minutes to drive about 15 miles from the airport to midtown (not counting the wait on the taxi line), during which time I got at least ten dirty looks from the creep driving the taxi. The fare was $25, and I gave the driver a $50 bill. "No change for 50."

I gave him a dirty look and gave him two twenties.

"How much you want back?"

"$15, "another dirty look. I took the money and put it into my pocket.

"No tip?'

"Fuck you and your tip. You're a shit head. Do you know what that means? Get lost." He drove away and gave me the finger. Another typical New York City moment.

JOCK STRAPS AND FINALLY CLIPPED AT GYP

My health club is one of those executive spas that provides shorts, shirts, socks, and jock straps for its members (only male members are provided jock straps). You keep your own sneakers in a private locker. To be honest, I really have a problem wearing a jock used by another man. The shorts and shirts are bad enough, but a jock is too personal. There's a reason why you can't return bathing suits to retail stores.

Even though the club is expensive and virtually everyone is a businessperson, somebody might have the clap or crabs. If the wash doesn't kill the cooties, they could be passed on. If I came down with the clap, I'd much rather catch it from a woman, not another man.

Anyway, most of the people using the club are middle aged and out of shape. Most look like shit, and basically all they do is walk on a treadmill for 30 minutes and constantly take their pulse. The club owners want advance warning if somebody is going to have the big one.

What I really like about the place is that I always have the weights to myself and the hostesses are very good looking. They flirt with the old farts as an incentive to keep them coming back to the gym. One of them always talks to me and I figured I should ask her out at some point, given my new status. She always wears a sheer blouse (so I always know what kind and color bra she has on) and a short skirt. Unfortunately, she wasn't on the floor when I entered the workout area.

The place was nearly empty, and only few attendants were around in case someone needed to be revived. At lunchtime, it's a different story. The fatsos work out on a machine for a few minutes then leave and have a burger and fries, advantage cholesterol. By the way, the club has a number of male studs to cater to the old broads that use the place.

I used to belong to a hip club that had mostly attractive young and physically fit members. And the members wear their own workout clothes. The women invariably don tights and a thong on the outside. I'm not sure why they wear the thong, but it serves to accentuate the most important parts of their bodies. The tops are all low cut, so cleavage is abundant. Although stimulating, the club is logistically inconvenient, so I switched to the fat, ugly, and old fart club.

I hopped on a recumbent bicycle. It's one of those stationary machines, which keeps your legs and back straight. Because it puts less stress on my back, I'm able to exercise for extended periods of time and walk upright when finished.

I watched CNBC as I exercised. And there he was, my buddy Gil Richards. The news reporter confirmed everything I heard and read and expected. Gil had been indicted and arrested on numerous counts of securities fraud and grand larceny while I was trying to make out with Joy before our plane was expected to crash. He allegedly cheated the acquirers of Crucible by lying about the financial condition of Crucible before the buyout. The lies had to do with the status of the radar deal, which cratered, but was never taken out of the revenue and earnings forecasts provided to determine the sale price of the company.

To make a long story short, Crucible sold for $10 billion, but was worth substantially less without profit contributions from radar sales. The grand larceny charge related to a $5 million payment Gil paid himself, but wasn't approved by Crucible's Board. Marion Denning was cooperating with the authorities relating to the grand larceny charge. Apparently, she was covering her ass and/or getting revenge. You might recall that Gil banged Denning's daughter while on vacation with both of them.

I wondered how Gil would react if he found out that I had sex with his daughter, even if it was only for a few seconds.

The news people like to dramatize these situations by calculating the total number of years the accused would be in jail if convicted on every charge, received the maximum sentence, and was never paroled. Under those assumptions, Gil would be in the big house for 52 years.

Murderers are paroled in five years, so it was unlikely Gil would spend half a century in jail for white-collar crimes. And besides, he'd be 112 when he got out. What a crock of shit. All of a sudden, I didn't feel like working out anymore. So, I finished up, showered and walked to my office.

As I entered the hallowed halls of GYP, everybody stared at me. I ignored all of them and went directly into my office. Liz followed me in and said, "OK, lay it on me. What's going on?"

"You tell me. I saw Richards handcuffed and arrested on TV. They made him do the perp walk at a jail in Chicago. The media's going wild."

The perp walk is a walk of shame that arrested people are subjected to by the authorities, so the media can take pictures of them handcuffed and assassinate them in the newspapers and on television. It's unconstitutional in my opinion.

"Richards was crying and carrying on when he was arrested. They had to drag him out of the car. I always thought he was a stud, and then I see him bawling like a sissy. Business people are all wimps. But you shouldn't do the crime if you can't do the time." That's a line from the old detective series starring Robert Blake, who was recently on trial for murder.

"Speaking of crimes, did you do anything illegal?" I know Liz wanted me to say no with all her heart.

"Liz, you're not asking me that question. I didn't hear you. Of course, I didn't commit any crimes. I had no idea what Gil was up to. He told me everything was going well with the radar deal and the numbers we were using to structure the buyout were accurate. But it was all a big lie. The fucking radar deal was falling apart long before the Crucible buyout closed. That bastard lied to me and cheated his new investors."

"You're going to be implicated, aren't you?"

"I suppose I'll be accused of negligence. What the hell could I do? I've been doing business with Gil for years. We completed many transactions together. I thought I knew him and he screwed me."

"Cohen is going to be all over you."

"I know. All I can do is cooperate with the authorities."

"By the way, some man keeps calling you."

"Who is it?"

"He said to tell you the Don called, not Don as in Donald, but THE DON."

"Oh no. Now that's a problem. What time is it?"

"Five forty five."

"I have a meeting at seven. Make sure nobody bothers me. I have to make a few calls. Give me the Don's number." Liz left my office. I could see all my partners wanted to inquire about how I was doing, but stayed clear of my office as a courtesy.

I dialed the number Liz gave me.

"Yes."

"Is Don Vitello there?"

"I am Vitello. Who's this?'

"It's Stoke Spencer. You called me?"

"Yes, Mr. Spencer. I want to say how sorry I am that Gil Richards is in trouble with the authorities."

"Why are you calling me, sir?"

"I understand you witnessed a gruesome event outside of Salute."

"You mean a man being murdered? Why yes, I did see somebody being murdered."

"I'm sorry. You shouldn't have been exposed to that. But you must stay out of this business. It isn't your concern."

"The man killed was a consultant to Crucible, and Crucible is my client. Unfortunately, that makes his death my concern. Why was he killed, Don Vitello?"

"You don't want to know anything about the circumstances of his demise. You must not tell the authorities that you saw anything." He wasn't asking me.

"I don't know if I can comply."

"Mr. Spencer, you'll comply or someone will pay you a visit."

"Are you threatening me?"

"Yes. I'll have you killed if you're unwilling to heed my warning."

"I understand. Good-bye, Don Vitello."

"Don't force me to hurt you, Mr. Spencer." I hung up.

What else could possibly happen to me? A mafia boss was threatening me. I felt so frustrated. The phone rang and Liz picked it up. She told me that Cohen was on the line. "Yes, what can I do for you Norm?"

"You can get your ass over to my office now. We have a lot to talk about."

"Give me five minutes." I hung up.

As I was about to leave my office, Rob entered. "I have to see Cohen. I can't talk now." Viand had decided to leave the firm, so it wasn't a good use of my time to allay any of his concerns, as well intentioned as he might be.

"Wait a minute. You need to give me an update on the Crucible situation."

"Actually, I don't. You're leaving GYP and I don't have the time."

"How can you be sore about me leaving? I told you I'm running out of time. My life is passing by and I have no prospects for a family. Family is important to me."

"I'm not interested in your personal problems. I have my own issues to deal with. I'll talk to you tomorrow."

"Please, Stoke. Give me two minutes. You're my mentor. I wouldn't leave now while you're in trouble. I'm here for you."

"You mean it?"

"Of course. How could you think anything different? I worked on Crucible with you. How could I not help you?"

"OK. That bastard, Gil Richards didn't tell anybody that the radar deal was going south. He closed the deal, and now the numbers are shit. There's no way the company can service its debt without the cash flow from the radar sales."

"He didn't tell you this before the shit hit the fan?"

"No, I found out yesterday."

"I'll tell you one thing, his guys didn't have a clue that anything was wrong. The radar deal was the cornerstone of the buyout and they never let me forget it as we developed the financial forecasts. I spoke with the Chief Financial Officer last week and he told me the radar deal was going to work out fine."

"I hope you're prepared to testify to that. You're going to be involved in all this crap, you know."

"Don't worry, I'm ready. What about the grand larceny charge? Is it true?"

"Gil paid himself $5 million before the deal closed and didn't tell anybody except Marion Denning, the woman on his Board. She was Chair of the Compensation Committee before Crucible went private."

"So what's the problem? If she knew, how could he be accused of stealing from the company?"

"She didn't tell anybody else, and he was banging her."

"Get outta here. No shit. She's a fox. I saw her at a few Board meetings. I'd like some of that myself, even if she's a little old. Damn, Gil's such a swordsman. I think he's my idol."

"There's something else."

"What?"

"Marion has a daughter, and Gil was screwing her as well."

"Come on."

"Really, and she's even better looking than her mother."

"Then I want to amend my former comment. I'd like to do both mother and daughter, preferably at the same time. Gil didn't do them together, did he?"

"You're a pervert. I wish I were your age, so I could find some healthy perversion. When Marion caught Gil and her daughter in bed together, she went crazy. In fact, Gil believes that's the real reason why she went to the authorities about the payment."

Rob was rubbing his face in disbelief. "Terrific. Gil is banging the entire Denning family and mommy is Chair of the committee that determined his comp. Then he fucks his new investors by lying about the prospects for the company they were buying for $10 billion. Anything else?"

"There is something else."

"What else can there be? What the hell else could Gil have done beyond all this?"

"Apparently, the Mafia is involved."

"You're shitting me. No way. Come on, this is all a joke, right?"

"It's real all right. I've been threatened by a real Mafia Don."

"Stoke, you're pulling my leg, aren't you?"

"Nope. Did you hear about that guy who was killed in Chicago yesterday? He was a consultant for Crucible."

"So."

"I saw him take a bullet in the head."

"No."

"Honest. I did. It was the most frightening thing I've ever seen. Some wise guys beat the crap out of him and then shot him."

"What did you do?"

"We got the hell out of there."

"Who was there?"

"Gil, his daughter and me."

"Then what?"

"The Don, who I met a last night called me today to say he knew I witnessed the shooting and I should keep my mouth shut. Or else."

"What's the Don's name?"

"What difference does it make?"

"I'm curious. What's his name?"

"Don Vitello."

Ron started to roar. "You're bullshitting me. You really had me going. Don Veal. Get the fuck outta here."

"It's true." Rob stopped laughing.

"What are you going to do?"

"I'm meeting with a New York City DA tonight, a friend of Josh's. I need to get myself extricated from the murder thing. Then I need to convince the US Attorney that I didn't know shit about the radar deal coming apart before the buyout closed."

"You think the Don may try to whack you?"

"I think he might. Why are you talking like a mobster?"

"I guess I've been watching too many late night cops and robber movies."

"Cohen awaits. I'll see you later." I ambled over to Norm's office, and was tempted to walk out of GYP's offices forever. A bottle of scotch might help me get through all of this.

But I was in a mess and needed to clear my name. Cohen's door was closed. I knocked and walked in. The room was full of attorneys. Antun had two partners with him and Cohen invited GYP's General Counsel, a useless compliance guy who would add nothing to these deliberations. His principal job was to make sure GYP employees reported their stock trades to the company. Cohen referred important legal problems directly to Antun. "Should I have brought counsel to represent me?"

"Sit down, Stoke." Cohen responded.

"If this is an inquisition, I'm out of here."

Antun said, "Just collecting facts, Stoke."

"Is your firm representing me, Antun?"

"Not sure yet. Depends on what I hear during the next 30 minutes."

It's important to understand whom the attorneys are representing in a meeting before saying anything. "Norm, are you going to ask me to resign? If so, this meeting should not take place."

"Stop fucking with me, Stoke. You got us into a mess with that scumbag, Gil Richards, and we have to find a way to protect ourselves."

"You never complained about Gil when I was bringing in all those fees."

"Well, you're not going to get any more fees from Richards or Crucible."

"All right. What do you want me to talk about?" I decided to cooperate for a moment, anyway.

I knew Antun would lead the examination. He accurately assumed that Cohen and I would be incapable of having a civil conversation at this point. The tension was unbelievable. "Gil Richards allegedly lied to his new investors about the financial condition of Crucible. Is this true?"

"I found out yesterday that he wasn't forthcoming about an impending transaction with the military for radar equipment. The forecasts he presented in the prospectus included revenues and earnings from the sale of that equipment. The company's ability to service debt, much less give the new investors a compensatory return, is questionable without those sales."

"You helped Crucible create those numbers, right?"

"We generated forecasts based upon information provided by the company. We didn't create anything."

"Why didn't you uncover this in your due diligence before the buyout was completed?"

"Rob Viand and I conducted several months of due diligence. As you know, we're highly experienced in this process. Also, GYP has been doing business with Crucible for many years and we thought we were well informed about the company's current performance."

As expected, Cohen stuck his two cents into the interrogation. "Apparently, you weren't as informed as you thought. You fucked up. Gil bullshitted you and you took it hook, line, and sinker."

"Norm, you have two choices. One, you keep your mouth shut and I answer questions from Antun to give him a sense of everyone's liability. Two, I walk out of here if you interrupt me one more time. It's your choice."

Antun again, "Calm down fellows. Everybody is a little excitable right now. I'll ask the questions, if that's alright with you, Norm."

"Go ahead. But his insubordination is something we're going to discuss later."

"Fuck you, Norm."

Antun again, "Let's continue. Why do you think the due diligence process broke down?"

"Gil chose to keep me in the dark about the radar negotiations."

"Did you ask him how negotiation with the military was proceeding?"

"Of course, every time we were together it was on the agenda. As I said the buyout doesn't work without the sales and profits from the radar equipment deal."

"You blew it, Stoke. You were negligent." Once again, Cohen attacked me.

"If you open your trap one more time I'm going to stick my foot in it."

"I'm sick of you." Norm stood up and I went after him. Guess who stepped in between us, almost 300 pounds of Antun Smith.

"Sit down boys. I'm not going to tell you again. I'm an attorney, not a referee for the World Wide Wrestling Federation."

"Our due diligence was complete and the facts we used were true to the best of our knowledge."

"You know the investors are going to say you were negligent."

"I know, but there's nothing I can do about that."

Norm jumped in again. "Did you know that Gil stole $5 million from the company?"

"If you don't know the facts, you shouldn't be so accusatory. You haven't done a deal in years. Leave the deal making to professionals."

"Some professional you are. Gil knew you were a patsy. He knew you'd sign off on anything he put in front of you."

"Antun, this is the last warning. If that jerk off makes one more stupid comment, you can work through my attorney. Actually, I think I've had enough. I have a meeting to go to."

Norm responded, "I hope your meeting has nothing to do with the firm, because you're fired. You're out, Stoke. This is the last straw. My partners and I want your resignation by tomorrow morning."

"I'm going to sue GYP for terminating me unfairly. You better start thinking about a large severance package, because if you don't I'm going to put GYP out of business."

Antun commented, "Stoke, you have bigger fish to fry. You better focus on the US Attorney and the criminal charges he's likely to press, not a severance package."

"Don't give me any advice. I'll discuss all that with my counsel. You represent this asshole. Remember Norm, this firm is nothing without my contacts and fee generation. You're going to earn less money from here on out because your largest rainmaker is gone no matter how all this ends up. Eat shit and die, fellows." I got up and went back to my office.

Liz approached me, "How'd it go?"

"Cohen fired me. I want you to pack up my office. Do it quickly because Cohen may try to stop me from taking my files."

"Don't worry. I'll have it packed and shipped by this afternoon. I'll send it all to a storage place."

"Thanks, Liz. You're the best. I have a meeting to go to, so I'll call you or you can reach me on my cell phone." Liz walked away dejectedly. She knew her career at GYP was over.

I called home and SS answered. "Hello."

"It's me. I have a major problem at work and I wanted you to know about it before it hits the newspapers."

"I already heard about Gil Richards. His arrest is all over the news. Are you involved in that situation?"

"Yes."

"What happened?"

"I can't talk about it. I want you to tell the boys that I'll visit them in a couple of days to explain everything. In the morning, I'll come by to pick up some clothes. I'm going to stay at the Hyatt."

"Stoke, you can stay here."

"Look Sharon, I don't want to make our situation any worse than it already is. I'm giving you advance notice because I want you out of the apartment when I come by."

"What's your problem?"

"It's simple, I don't want to see you. I've had it with you, Cohen, and Richards. Our relationship is over."

"You need your family, Stoke. We can help you get through these problems. You'll be lost with no one to lean on."

"You should've thought of that long ago. You never supported me in the past, so I have no reason to expect you to help me now."

"You ungrateful bastard. You're ruining our lives. First you leave us and then you get into trouble at work. Did you get fired or something?"

"It's none of your business."

"You're very cruel."

"I allowed you to push me around too long. It's not going to happen any more. Just be out when I come by. I don't want to fight. The best way is for us to stay away from each other." She hung up.

I walked out of my office and Rob approached me. "What happened? There are rumors floating all over the place."

"I'm out. I'm going to take up residence at the Hyatt. I'll call you tomorrow. I suspect they're going to interrogate you today. You may get fired because of our relationship."

"No problem. I'm quitting in any case."

I exited GYP for the last time and headed towards Anderson's to meet Stan Forman.

Anderson's is an old time gin mill. It's not a restaurant and not a lounge. You go to Anderson's to drink and talk. If you get hungry they'll whip up a burger and fries or one of a few different kinds of toasted sandwiches. The place is dark and has tables along the wall if you need privacy. I consummated many transactions at this dump. It's a place where I've always felt comfortable and safe. Considering the subject of my conversation with Forman, security and privacy were paramount.

Josh told me Forman was a carrot top. He said you couldn't miss his orange hair, even in the dark because it glowed. I looked around the crowded bar and saw an iridescent head sipping clear liquid at the bar that probably wasn't water. I walked up to him, "Are you Stan Forman?"

"Yep. You must be Stoke Spencer?"

"I am. Let's take one of the tables so we can speak in private." He followed me over to the far end of the bar. The waitress was beside us before we sat down and took our drink orders, both gin.

"My buddy, Josh Aaron, told me you had a problem that you wanted to discuss with me."

"That's correct. The problem is getting worse by the minute."

"Maybe I can help you. Just so you understand, I'm in the business of prosecuting criminals. We receive leads from many different sources, so I'm assuming you have something to tell me regarding a felony, or something like that."

"I hope you can help me. It involves a crime that I witnessed yesterday in Chicago."

"Go on."

"I have a corporate client named Crucible. You may have read that the SEC is investigating the company. I've done business with Crucible and with its CEO, Gil Richards, for a decade. Richards has been indicted and arrested."

"What are the charges?"

"Securities fraud and grand larceny."

"Mmm, I see. You know that securities fraud cases are usually the bailiwick of the US Attorney?

I gave him a blank look, which meant I didn't know anything about legal jurisdictions.

"It doesn't matter. Tell me more."

"Richards falsified SEC documents during the buyout of Crucible."

"And the grand larceny charge?"

"The idiot paid himself $5 million right before the buyout and didn't notify his Board."

"Are you involved?"

"In a sense. I didn't know about the manipulation of the financial statements, but I did do due diligence on the numbers and uncovered nothing. So, I'll probably be accused of negligence. As far as the illegal payment is concerned, I had nothing to do with that. It's complicated because Gil was having an affair with the former Chair of the Comp Committee."

"Is this person a man or woman?" He asked the question with a straight face.

"Female. She knew about the payment and turned him in."

"Sounds like Mr. Richard's world is crumbling around him. So what's your concern?"

"Actually, the Crucible financial stuff is what it is. I'll be embarrassed and shamed, when all this is dragged through the media."

"Stop beating around the bush. What's the issue?"

"You don't like to waste time, do you?" Forman was treating me only slightly better than he would a common criminal. I guess that's the way DAs do business.

"No."

"I was with Richards last night. Apparently, the feds arrested him early this afternoon. We went to dinner at a restaurant named Salute located in a Chicago suburb. It's a Mafia joint."

"Why would you go to a place frequented by mobsters?"

"I didn't know its reputation until I got there. Anyway, we had dinner and I met a man named Vitello, Don Vitello, who's some kind of organization boss."

"How did you meet him?"

"Richards introduced me in a private room. But more importantly, after dinner I witnessed a murder outside of the restaurant."

"Did you report it?"

"No, Richards whisked his daughter and me away and warned us not to get involved."

"So?"

"The guy who was murdered is a consultant for Crucible."

"Is there any connection between Don Veal and the murderer?" Forman must eat at Italian restaurants and made an attempt at some humor. I didn't laugh .

"Actually, Richards told me the Don did favors for Crucible from time to time. He intervened when Crucible's unions caused trouble."

"That's it?"

"No. When I got back to New York today, the Don called me. He told me I better not speak with anybody about the murder."

"Did he threaten you?"

"Yes."

"What do you want me to do?"

"I think I need to inform the Chicago police or whomever is working on the crime that I witnessed it, and that Vitello is involved. I'd like you to act as a go between for me."

"Could be dangerous for you."

"It's already dangerous. But I'm not involved in anything illegal, and I don't want the cops knocking at my door at some time in the future accusing me of being a participant in a murder."

"I'll call my contact in Chicago tonight and discuss this with him. How do I get in touch with you?"

"You can call me on my office number. I got fired today, but my secretary is loyal. Or you can call me at the Hyatt tonight. Marital problems."

"You have a lot of problems, Mr. Spencer."

"I know." We chatted a little longer and went our separate ways.

HYDROPHOBIA

I checked into the Hyatt. I thought I deserved a good night's sleep. Maybe I'd wake up and find out the last two days never took place. I took off my clothes and had the urge to relax on the toilet. A *USA Today* was conveniently sitting on the coffee table. I'm sure I'd be charged for the paper. I instinctually avoided the business section, not wanting to read anything else about Gil or Crucible.

While on the throne, I felt a drip on my head. Here I am, paying 200 bucks a night and the toilet in the room above me is leaking on my head. I used the newspaper to shield myself from the liquid hoping it was pure water and not sewerage. I picked up the phone next to the commode (only expensive rooms have phones by the toilets) and called housekeeping.

A woman answered. "Ello, housekeeping. 'Ow can I help you?"

I hoped this person understood English. "I'm on the toilet and something is dripping on my head."

"Why doan choo move away?"

"Because I'm not done." What a discussion.

"Ees dee water clear?"

"You mean, is it urine or does it contain other things?"

"Yeas, dat's what I mean."

"I'm not sure. Will you please have somebody come up to fix the leak or get me another room."

"I no can change room sir. Choo have to speak with the fron desk."

"Then, why don't you just get your ass up here and fix the leak?"

"Choo doan have to be rude sir."

"You'd be angry if you were paying two hundred dollars a night and the toilet was leaking on your head."

"I spose choo're right. Someone be right up."

"Thank you." I figured I better finish my business. The repairman could arrive any second. You shouldn't rush on the toilet. It's not healthy. I already had enough problems, and didn't need a gastro issue.

In five minutes there was a knock on the door. I wasn't going to put on my suit after being spritzed with an unknown liquid, so I approached the door in my boxer shorts and looked into the peephole. And wouldn't you know it, the repairman was a repairwoman.

"Yes?" I yelled through the door.

"Maintenance. I've come to fix a leak."

I said to hell with it and opened up the door. "Come on in. The leak's in the bathroom."

The woman smiled when she saw what I was wearing and walked past me. These hotel people must have a million stories about the crazies that stay with them. She went into the bathroom and straightened up from the smell. What the hell, I took a dump a few minutes ago. "Sorry, I just finished."

"No problem." She rolled her eyes.

"Mind if I watch? Repair people fascinate me. I have two left hands and can't fix anything."

"Sure. Be my guest."

The woman was Hispanic with short jet-black hair. Thank goodness she spoke English. She was average height and her low rider jeans were really tight on her curvy hips and ample ass. She wore a white maintenance workman's t-shirt with her name, Maria, on it. Of course her name was Maria. I'll bet a quarter of the women in Spanish Harlem are named Maria. They all wanted to be virgin mothers and give birth to the next messiah.

Anyway, the shirt clung to her sizable boobs. And most striking were her large black eyes and beautiful lips colored dark red. She immediately spotted the leak stain on the ceiling.

"Can you fix it?" I asked her.

"I don't know yet." She had a look on her face that said how the hell do I know if I can fix it? I just got here.

"Can you imagine having something dripping on your head while on the toilet?"

"Must've been gross, especially when you don't know what's coming down." She said this without looking at me. She was a real professional and totally focused on her work.

She stepped up on the toilet and stretched to poke at the damp spot in the ceiling. As she did this, I got a wonderful view of her body. Her t-shirt came out from her jeans revealing a thong, which was above her waistline. It was black with a lace border (I liked it). I couldn't understand why a maintenance woman would be wearing Victoria Secret underwear to work, unless she wanted to be ready for unexpected action. But she probably didn't understand why I wasn't wearing any pants.

The woman lifted out a piece of the ceiling and peered into the dark space with a flashlight. "I have good news," she said.

"What's that?"

"The leak isn't from the toilet over this room. It's a damaged pipe joint in the main water line."

"So, sewage wasn't dripping on my head?"

"Correct. It's pure water."

"Can you fix it so I can go to sleep sometime before dawn?"

"Maybe." She gave me another one of those stupid looks. I stared at her ass when she turned away. It was pretty enticing. Making out with a female maintenance worker might be a fitting end to my day. I wondered whether she would respond to me.

With a wrench, she reached up exposing more skin between her shirt and jeans. I was starting to get aroused, although I was sure she wasn't doing anything intentionally to turn me on.

After a few grunts she said, "I think I got it."

I said, "Nice going."

She started to replace the ceiling tile and all of a sudden a rush of water came pouring down. I was stunned and Maria was drenched. Her white t-shirt was now see through. And what a set of knockers this girl had. Fortunately, I was able to dodge the surge of water from the pipe.

"Godammit," she screamed. She was wet from head to toe besides being totally embarrassed.

I was going to suggest that she take her clothes off, but she was intent on stopping the water before it flooded my room and all the rooms below it.

"Maria, I'm getting out of here. Good luck. I love your wet t-shirt."

She gave me one last look. I put on my pants and went down to the lobby. It was easy to pack up, since I just had my overnight bag. The desk clerk asked how she could help me. I told her what happened and she gave me another room. It was after midnight by this time and the lobby was empty. Ten minutes after I arrived in my new room, which was thankfully on the other side of the hotel, the phone rang.

"Hello," I said in an exhausted voice.

"It's Stan Forman."

"Pretty quick turnaround. What did you find out?"

"I'm afraid I have some bad news. Gil Richards was killed in a lockup as he was awaiting to be arraigned."

"Oh my God. What happened?"

"Some thugs beat him to death for no apparent reason. My contact suspects that the attackers are affiliated with the Chicago mob. This happened just a few hours ago. I'm not sure the press knows anything yet."

"Who told you this?"

"I have a friend who's an Assistant District Attorney in Chicago. He's not working on the case but was able to get me the scoop."

"Did you tell him about my involvement?"

"Yeah. He said the police are still investigating the murder of that guy. They know it was a hit and were able to deduce that the crime had something to do with Crucible. Your acquaintance, the Don, is in the middle of all this. He's a really dangerous man, a pretty senior guy in the organization."

"Has he been connected to Crucible?"

"It's just a matter of time. As you indicated to me, he helped Richards quell some labor problems in the past."

"What about the murdered man?"

"His name is James Digon. He was a procurement officer for the Navy. He quit abruptly about two years ago and went to work as a consultant for Crucible. It's not kosher to go from government employment to an industry job. To avoid legal problems he became a consultant, not a direct employee of Crucible. He worked on the development of the radar while he was employed by Uncle Sam."

"Is there any relationship between Digon and the Don?"

"Good question. No answer, but there must be been something."

"What am I supposed to do?"

"I told my buddy that you were there and prepared to help in any way. Also, I let him know you've already been threatened by Don Veal." Another joke, ha. "He said he'd tell his colleagues and they would contact you only if it was necessary. They understand the risk you took by coming forward. Richards' murder only serves to dramatize that point."

"You think the Don is responsible for Richards' murder."

"No doubt in my mind, based upon what I know."

"Holy shit. This is getting to be a really scary situation."

"Just sit tight. If I hear anything, I'll call you. My Chicago friend promised to come through me if he needs to talk to you. So, you won't be surprised by a visit from the cops."

"Thanks for everything."

"Good luck, Stoke." I hung up.

Trying to sleep after all that happened wasn't going to be easy. I showered quickly and got into bed. After an hour of tossing and turning, I clicked on the TV. My thoughts were with Sophie Richards. I wondered how she was doing and if I should call her in the morning.

Thinking of Sophie made me horny. It's hard to believe that I'd have sexual urges after a day like today but that's what happens to guys when they don't find relief.

I surfed the free channels and took a look at what was available for $12.95. The normal movies did nothing for me so I scanned through the porno titles.

I bought a dirty movie from the pay TV offerings. It was hard-core and very stimulating. As far as I can remember, I saw breasts, vaginas, penises, and sporadic penetration. At the conclusion of each sexual vignette, the picture faded away before the men reached orgasm. It was so interesting that I fell asleep in about ten minutes.

As usual, I woke up at about 3:30 to urinate. My prostate seemed to be under control the last few months, but that didn't really mean anything. The next time I go to the doctor, I could be in deep trouble. It's like a sword hanging over your head. You never know when it will fall on you.

When I returned to bed I couldn't fall asleep. I kept thinking about Gil and his tragic life. Gil Richards was an amazing man. He built his business from scratch into a giant company in his industry. His technical and managerial skills were unsurpassed by his peers. His instincts made him successful against the competition and with his employees. Crucible was known as one of the best paying companies in the aerospace industry.

I suppose greed overcame Gil, just like it does many businessmen. To retain men like Don Vitello to do favors for him, had to involve something unethical or illegal.

Then came the buyout, which was Gil's crowning success. The company was operating at full throttle and the profits from the radar deal would've propelled it even further. Without the transaction, Crucible still would've commanded a sale price of $6-7 billion, and Gil's take would've been in the $500 million range. But because of the expected profits from and longevity of the radar transaction, Crucible's valuation literally jumped to $10 billion overnight.

At this price, which was the price negotiated with the new buyers, Gil received $1 billion. I'm confused as to how Gil would think he could get away with deceiving the acquirers, unless he believed he could somehow get the negotiations with the military back on track. And using the Mafia to help close the deal was sheer insanity, although I really didn't know the Don's true role in the transaction.

Gil Richards had more money than he could spend in ten lifetimes. He had no cash flow problems. Relatively speaking, he wasn't a spendthrift like many other CEOs. He was so busy working and chasing women he didn't have time to keep a house in France and in Central America. Sure, he used Crucible aircraft to fly himself all over the world on vacations (I'm sure he reimbursed the company for personal use of the planes.). So, why the fuck did he rip the company off? Five million dollars was chump change to this man. Sometimes I just have to scratch my head and wonder why people do the things they do.

As far as GYP is concerned, we probably should have discovered that the radar deal was falling apart. If I had had additional conversations with the military procurement people, I might have been able to root out the extent of the problems.

But I'd been doing business with Crucible for nearly a decade. We did 20 major transactions with Gil and his staff and never had a problem with disclosure. Why should I suspect the guy was lying now? Cynics will say there were one billion reasons. Nevertheless, GYP and I were going to look incompetent for "allowing" this travesty to take place. The new investors would sue and it was going to take years to finally settle this situation.

So, Gil goes to jail and is killed. The man's dead. My largest client was arrested, which is staggering in and of itself. But to be murdered while in jail after just a few hours is beyond comprehension. When doing business with dangerous people, very bad things are likely to happen. And they did for Gil, Sophie, Crucible, its employees, and me.

Gil's demise would totally complicate the inevitable lawsuits that should start tomorrow or the next day. The crimes committed would never be fully understood without the principle player around to testify about this unfortunate drama. My world was getting more complex by the minute.

A SURPRISE FROM DOWN UNDER

I slept restlessly over the next two hours and finally gave up at around six. I ordered a large breakfast even though I really wasn't very hungry. In fact, I felt nauseous.

Maybe the delivery person would be a beautiful woman who'd spend the morning with me. For somebody who had been in the act of intercourse for a grand total of five seconds during the past two months, I sure had a lot of females to contend with. I didn't need to get involved with a waitress along with a judge, an heiress, a banking executive, and a bitch (SS). Even Maria, the maintenance lady, was in play.

I wondered how she had fared in her battle with the water pipe. I'll bet she was in my first room most of the night trying to stop the leak that became a waterfall.

Breakfast arrived in about 15 minutes. If I had waited until 7 a.m. to order, it probably would've taken 45 minutes. A male waiter arrived (damn) with one of those folded up rolling tables. Somehow he fit it through the door and set it up next to my sitting area. I requested a couch in the room and ended up with a mini suite, which also had a king-sized bed (just in case I got lucky, ha).

The guy was like a magician, pulling up the sides and drawing food out of small ovens somewhere from the bowels of the rolling table. It was all laid out for me, breakfast for three (I told you I ordered too much) in no time.

The waiter handed me the bill, which came to $75 including tax, plus an automatic $15 gratuity (20% for all you former English majors). I almost fell over. "How could breakfast cost $90 for one person?" I asked the messenger.

"You ordered enough food for three people and $30 per person in an expensive hotel is about right."

"Who are you kidding? When was the last time you spent $30 for breakfast?"

"I don't eat in places like this, so I never in my life paid so much for breakfast."

"This is totally fucking outrageous."

"Take it up with management. I just brought you your breakfast. I didn't set the prices."

"You don't even have to be a good waiter. Waiters automatically get a 20% tip? Suppose I hated you, or you acted like an asshole?"

"You oughta know that the tips are shared with the kitchen workers. I don't get the whole thing. But to answer your question, you pay no matter what you think of me."

"Nobody has to earn anything anymore in this country. Everything is an entitlement."

"Look mister, I don't know what you're talking about. What do you want from me? I'm just a working slob who rolled a meal up to your room."

"You're right. Sorry. Thanks for bringing up my breakfast." I decided to take the high road and stop ragging on the poor fellow and dismissed him.

My feast included orange juice, freshly squeezed. It had a lot of pulp in it. I love pulp, although I choke on it when I drink too quickly. Orange juice is supposed to be fattening because of all the sugar. I'd rather take the calories than risk coming down with scurvy. Then, there were two eggs, sunny side up. I hate eggs that are overcooked.

When we first got married, SS used to screw up my eggs every time, and just about every other thing she cooked for me. I told her to stop making eggs for me because they tasted like shit. She thought I wanted her to stop cooking everything and never made another home cooked meal again.

My pancakes had blueberries in them and were accompanied by a large container of maple syrup. Of course, both entrees had bacon and hash brown potatoes. And finally, a toasted bagel and lox came with a huge glob of cream cheese on top.

Then I saw it, the worst possible thing that can happen to food. A black hair was floating on my sunny side up eggs. It wasn't a straight hair that would likely come from somebody's head. Nope, it was a curly and black. I'd bet anything it was pubic hair.

Now, how the hell could a pubic hair find its way onto my eggs? Do the hotel cooks work in the nude? Are pubic hairs flying around the kitchen? Does this hotel's restaurants use pubic hairs as garnish? I felt nauseous again. I can't eat anything that has a hair on it, especially if the hair is from down under. I picked up the phone and called the front desk.

"Can I help you, Mr. Spencer?" A friendly woman answered. Somehow they know who's calling. I think it's a nice touch.

"I found a hair on my eggs."

"That's terrible. I'm so sorry. We'll cook you more eggs and send them right up." I liked this gal. She empathized with my problem.

"It's a pubic hair." I wanted to see how much more empathy I could extract from her.

"How do you know it's a pubic hair? All of our chefs are fully clothed when they cook. It couldn't possibly be a pubic hair, Mr. Spencer." My strategy backfired. I lost credibility.

I wasn't going to give up that easy. "Look, I know a pube when I see one. This thing is black and curly."

"Well, I am sorry. All we can do is send you another breakfast."

"I'm not hungry any more. I want this breakfast out of my room immediately, and be sure I'm not charged for it."

"Of course, sir. I'll personally come up to retrieve the food."

Five minutes passed and the doorbell rang. I put on a robe so I wouldn't frighten the young lady to death.

She entered. "It's over there." I pointed at the rolling table.

She could see that I hadn't touched anything. "Look at this." I pointed at the sunny side up eggs and there it was, the pubic hair lying across the yolk and white of the eggs. It was hard to miss because its dark color contrasted with the yellow and white of the eggs. If it had been a blonde pubic hair, I might not have seen it, and ate it.

"You may be right, Mr. Spencer. That looks like a pubic hair. But I can't imagine where it came from."

"I assure you it came from somebody's private area."

"I didn't mean that. I know where pubic hairs grow."

I looked her over. She was really cute. Her name was Ms. Johnson. She was a perky little thing with short blonde hair. Maybe she never saw a black pubic hair before.

She had on just a touch of makeup and pink lipstick. Her white shirt was starched and her tiny nametag covered her entire left breast. The length of her skirt was perfectly appropriate.

She was probably 30, but could easily pass as an 18 year old. OK, I admit it. I could've eaten her up for breakfast.

I suddenly felt bold and said, "Why don't you make yourself comfortable and we could discuss the mysterious pubic hair."

She smiled, and then stopped. "Sorry, Mr. Spencer, we aren't allowed to meet with guests in their rooms. You understand?"

"You sure are cute."

"Thank you. I think you're very handsome."

She knew how to handle assholes like me. I respect that. "Sure you don't want to stay a while?"

"Maybe some other time. I have to get back to work. Sorry about the hair. I'll take your table out with me."

I sighed. Too bad, I could've used a roll in the hay with a sweet thing like Ms. Johnson.

WHAT THE HELL IS NEXT?

Before Ms. Johnson departed with the food, I grabbed the coffee from the cart hoping it wouldn't contain any foreign objects. I poured a cup and started to think about Gil.

Stan told me he was murdered in a lockup. You always hear that organized crime can get to you even if you're in jail. In fact, it might be easier in jail than on the outside. I was tempted to call Stan and emphasize the possible connection of Gil's murder to the Don, but decided not to play detective and leave all that to the police.

Gil found himself on a slippery slope that had a tragic ending. He was so focused on business success and sexual conquest that he allowed his judgment to become clouded

How many material things does somebody really need in life? How many dollars are necessary to make a person happy? How many women does a man need to screw to be satisfied? Gil had all the money a person could dream of, even before the buyout. But he chose to lie to obtain even more.

Gil was the kind of person who gives successful people a bad name. He was the type of person whom the socialists and communists in this country scorn. He made a fortune and cheated to take an even greater share for himself. He personified greed.

Now, I admit I don't think Gil was that different from other CEOs I've met over the years. He was self-centered and more concerned about himself than anybody else. But he was fair to his colleagues and the senior officers of the company. Unions protect rank and file employees. He was a tough negotiator with union leaders, but never to the point of giving them a reason to strike. Of course, I don't know what role the Don played in Crucible's labor matters. Historically, labor peace is bought or coerced.

From a philanthropic perspective, Gil was relatively generous. Much of the donations attributed to him were actually paid by Crucible, so his direct stake in them was far less than it appeared. But he did authorize the payments.

So, what happened? Was Gil on a slippery slope? Was he so greedy that he broke the law and ended up in jail? Was his desire to have a billion dollar net worth the ultimate reason why he was killed in a jail cell like a petty thief? To a certain extent, I believe so.

Gil's relationship with the opposite sex was another reason his life ended on such a sour note. God knows how many women he seduced at work and elsewhere. Many of his conquests probably thought it was exciting to be with him. Others were sexually abused and regretted they had succumbed to his power and charm.

Personally, I hate unfair fights of any type. When a person as powerful as Gil uses his position to take advantage of innocent women, it's a crime. Rock singers, diplomats, presidents, athletes, and many others have used their celebrity to get laid. Some women are available and encourage those types of relationships. But some women don't and only go along because they feel they must.

I'm not interested in having sex with a woman who doesn't want to be with me or feels threatened if she doesn't yield. That's the reason why I didn't have sex with Sasha when she was lying naked on my bed.

Gil wanted every beautiful woman at any cost. He wanted Marion Denning and her daughter. That was typical Gil Richards. He was a predator and a sex maniac. And the more dangerous the tryst the more he enjoyed it. I'm sure his relationship with Marion's daughter was even more exciting after the mother knew. He probably wanted to have sex with them together. Actually, I'd enjoy that myself. Oops!

But Gil was dead. His company was in shambles. His daughter was probably an emotional wreck and my life was in the shitter.

I needed to snap out of this funk. I could feel myself sliding down yet another slope. The end of a slippery slope can result in many things, from financial ruin, to jail, to alcoholism, to divorce, to mental problems, to suicide. And it's possible to be on more than one slope at the same time. I knew I needed to start recovering from my problems now, even before I knew how serious they would ultimately be.

The glass must, at worst, be half full, and never half empty. I couldn't allow anyone or anything to ruin my life. People and events can make me unhappy for a minute, an hour, a week or a month. But they should never be able to make me unhappy forever.

In this regard, I needed to quickly end all contact with SS. She'd attempt to drag me down. I had to find a lawyer to act as a go-between. Direct conversations with SS would be unproductive from this point forward. She's spurned, and her meal ticket had expired.

If she didn't want to work again, she'd have to negotiate a good deal. And I'm sure there were plenty of attorneys who would be happy to help her try to fuck me financially.

I was, and still am, concerned about my boys. A sensible custody arrangement had to be negotiated, which would enable me to have an appropriate amount of time with them. Children get caught up in divorces in any number of ways. Even in the most "amicable" situations, problems arise continuously and bad feelings may last a lifetime. Kids don't forget.

If a divorced parent makes a small judgment error, a child may hold a grudge well into his or her adulthood. A divorced parent can never atone for the sins committed during a split. The best I could do was keep mistakes to a minimum. That would be possible only if both of us cooperated. If one of us acted like an asshole, the process would be destructive to everyone. I've seen this happen so many times with friends who are divorced. I might not be able to force SS to do anything, but I could control my emotions for the benefit of my boys.

GYP had forsaken me. Norm Cohen finally got an opportunity to force me out of the firm. He would now be able to assert himself without me to counteract his bad managerial skills. But it would be a double-edged sword and he might have placed himself at the precipice of his own slippery slope.

Until now, Norm has not been able to be a true autocrat. My influence politically and financially had curtailed his aspirations of total dominance. He was so concerned about my behavior that he left most of our partners free to do business and operate without too much interference, and the firm prospered.

In the future, I expect Cohen to be more intrusive and disruptive throughout GYP. He hadn't done any deals personally in a long time. My business acumen and revenue success made it possible for him to focus exclusively on administration.

Even though we despised each other, we were a good team, a Mr. Inside and a Mr. Outside. Prospectively, Norm would have to conduct business with clients and make some rain. My departure would result in a great void. Basically, he would have more control and less income, a dubious tradeoff. But some people thrive on power.

GYP would be implicated because of my actions. Cohen and Smith would attempt to blame the Crucible due diligence oversights on Rob Viand and me.

It's laughable because everyone on the Street (Wall Street, that is) knows Rob and I are the "straws that stir the drink" at GYP (a loose quote from that famous orator Reggie Jackson).

GYP might face litigation as a firm. It has insurance, but its reputation would be soiled and reputation is everything in investment banking. When the most successful dealmaker screws up, can the lesser players at the firm be trusted?

Then there's the issue of severance. No way would I allow GYP to kick me out without providing severance and buying back my interest in the firm. I own about 5% of GYP (as compared to 7.5% for Cohen).

A negotiation relating to the valuation of my interest in GYP would be brutal as the market is turning up. From a negative perspective, the company had the Crucible debacle hanging over its head and I'd no longer be bringing in fees. It would be an interesting few months.

I had to consider my future business aspirations. After the litigation and name calling subsided, I could probably get a high level position at another investment bank. It would be an uncomfortable experience, but most bankers in town know what I am capable of accomplishing.

I could do something new like write a book or get involved with charitable organizations. But in the end I'd suffer a serious reduction in my resources after I settled with SS. By the time I paid legal fees, I would need to get a real job, if I wanted the good life.

My legal problems were multifaceted. I needed counsel for my divorce. A lot of money was at stake, so I needed a street fighter. Sometimes I wondered why it was necessary to hire these people, as the New York laws are clear. I had to split the estate.

As divorce negotiations, problems arise for a few different reasons. In some cases, the husband doesn't want to give half of everything to his wife because he feels she hasn't done a damn thing to deserve it. It's more complicated than it sounds because what has been accumulated to date and what it will grow to in the future may be very different.

This aspect of the negotiation can be broken down into two parts, how much the husband earns each year and how much his assets will increase in value prospectively (like stock options). This all needs to be quantified and since much of a wealthy person's estate is in things other than cash and readily marketable securities, the calculations could be complicated and contentious.

Another scenario is that the wife really wants more than half, or gets to that point by valuing things incorrectly (on purpose, with the help of her attorney). This isn't legitimate from a legal standpoint, but the wife has weapons at her disposal.

You guessed it, the kids. She can apply pressure to settle unfairly by negotiating a lousy custody arrangement and/or by proposing outrageous child-care support. My negotiations with SS would be difficult and we'd both be unhappy, I was sure.

My other legal problems would begin to crystallize now, after the fall of Gil Richards and Crucible. An employer is supposed to protect an employee. But since GYP wanted to put all the blame on me, I was on my own. GYP couldn't disassociate itself from the fact that I was an employee, but its counsel would attach responsibility to me every time it couldn't quash a charge in another way.

So, I needed somebody to protect my interests. To hire the best, I would have to pay up and that's what I intended to do. I did nothing illegal, but the accusations might result in fines and censure. The latter was the most problematic because it would impact my ability to work in the industry.

The final legal issue related to the murder I witnessed. I trusted that nothing would come from it. But I had no way of really knowing. Accusations regarding murder are criminal in nature, so although they don't appear to be an issue, I would have to tread carefully. However, the specter of the Don putting out a contract on me was another kettle of fish. I just hoped my name didn't come up in all this stuff and that I never see or hear of Don Vitello again.

And finally, I had to consider the three new women in my life, Joy, Sophie and Sasha. What a fantastic menu. My relationship with Joy occurred because we thought we were going to die in an airplane crash. This was not really the best circumstance for two people to come together.

But when a person's life is on the line, everything happens in fast forward. I had run out of time to do the things I wanted to do, so I had to make decisions quicker. Being with somebody I loved in my last moments were comforting (I'm sure of it now). I'm not looking forward to the real deal, but that's how I felt when I was with Joy on the trip back to New York.

Interestingly, she seemed to have the same reaction and emotions, she was scared and needed someone to hold. If I were a troll, Joy would still have been attracted to me because I brought her some peace at a potentially violent moment. And I was hypnotized by her beauty, maturity, and charm.

Maybe she wasn't really like the woman I thought I met on the plane. Maybe she was a bitch like SS, although I doubt it. I wondered how SS would act under similar conditions. She'd probably demand the stewardess (sorry, flight attendant) bring her a blanket. Should I call Joy? The long term potential was questionable because of her age, but she sure looked terrific at the moment. It would be really interesting to be close to her.

Sophie was situated on the other end of the spectrum, not from a beauty perspective, but in terms of maturity. She had a lot of the same attributes as her father. She was a free spirit. She was rich, especially now that her father was gone. So, she needn't work or do anything productive with her life. She was as privileged as a person could possibly be.

Finding a man to make her happy would be an extraordinary task. In fact, an older and more experienced guy would be good for Sophie. Now, I fit that description. But I was afraid I'd never be able to live down my sub-standard sexual performance with her. If I were a woman and some guy got off on me after one stroke, I wouldn't be interested either. My desire to see Sophie again, I admit, was related to my damaged ego. I could do better in bed. My name is Stoke and I'm a stud. Yeah right.

Sasha offered me the best opportunity for a substantive long-term relationship. Granted we had only just met, but it was intimate, though not consummated. She was the right age. She was successful. She was really attractive. Sasha would understand the business problems I had to deal with. And most important, I had done the right thing. I didn't have sex with her when she was unconscious. Women usually appreciated that courtesy.

There was no reason to wait to start a new relationship because I was now unofficially a free man. I had three excellent possibilities and I was really horny. I'd make calls immediately.

Well there you have it, possibly one of the worst days in recorded history, excluding nuclear holocaust and famine. I had behaved badly at times and fairly well part of the time. Nobody's perfect. My life was in shambles from every perspective, but I remained optimistic that good things would happen to me.

COOKIE IN THE OVEN

My account of the fateful day is complete and three months have passed.

I never mentioned this earlier, but I had a fair amount of money stashed away for a rainy day. GYP paid me well over the years and I invested it with great success. Lady luck was kind to me, as I made the right calls and anticipated the stock market decline a few years ago. To make a long story short, I sold all my equity investments and reinvested them into high-grade tax-exempt bonds. So, while most investors were losing 40% of their money, I was earning 6%.

Additionally, GYP had an excellent group of guys who invested in private equity transactions. In the private equity arena, one gigantic success offsets many losers. The partners of GYP were able to invest in certain transactions and our boys scored big on one of them. I made a $250 thousand investment in one deal, and received 20 times back, or $5 million. My investment record wasn't perfect, however, I invested an additional $1 million and lost every cent.

In sum, I had almost $4 million. Additionally, I had cash and bonds of about $5 million. My Park Avenue apartment was worth about $6 million. And our country house in Lakeville, CT was worth about $3 million. From all this I'd pay all legal expenses and probably have to give SS half of the balance. One thing not in any of these numbers was any severance from GYP or the value of my stock in the company, which they'd buy back from me. The bottom line was that I could survive quite well beyond a divorce settlement.

A week or so after I collected my belongings at the Park Avenue apartment, I rented a two-bedroom place on East 72nd Street near the river. It had quite a few amenities and was big enough for my sons and me. My boys were angry and a lot of work needed to be done to get them straightened out. Sometimes these situations never get corrected, but I intended to do the best I could.

SS wasn't particularly helpful, as she tried to turn my sons against me. On the day I went to collect my belongings, SS was waiting for me. She chose to ignore my request to be away when I arrived. Unfortunately, I ended up speaking with her for about an hour. During that time she ran through the whole spectrum of emotions. She cursed me. She tried to convince me not to move out. She threatened me. She told me what a caring father I had been.

I'm ashamed to tell say this but she seduced me. I knew it was a really stupid thing to succumb to but she was all dolled up when I arrived. She had a plan and executed it perfectly. The best way to a man's heart is through his penis. The seduction resulted in wild sex. I redeemed myself from the episode with Sophie. Whew!

After we finished copulating and doing all sorts of other things that SS hadn't done with me in years, she asked me if I had changed my mind. I wondered if she thought I was that shallow. I told her it was too little, too late, but I thanked her for an enjoyable morning. If SS were more like she had been in bed that day, maybe we wouldn't have all our problems. But one sexual encounter changed nothing. I still hated her and wanted my freedom. I heard something smash against the door as I walked out with my things.

From time to time, SS tries to call me and usually I don't return her calls. If I happen to pick up the phone, I cut our conversations short.

The day after Gil's death, I phoned Sophie. She was a complete wreck and appreciated my concern. I asked if there was anything I could do and she asked me to attend Gil's memorial service.

I flew to Chicago and arrived at the church just in time for the funeral. Amazingly, the place was almost empty. Gil Richards had impacted thousands of people during his career, and practically nobody came to pay their last respects. It was a sad commentary on our society. When you're in a position to help people, you're the most popular person. When your career is over, you never hear from the same people who were kissing your ass months before. Gil's situation was different because he cheated, but we must forgive and forget. Not even his family had the decency to attend.

I walked up to the front row of the church and sat next to Sophie, Gil's only child. She kissed me and thanked me for coming. The young woman was beautifully dressed in black, without makeup and with tears in her eyes. I looked around and maybe fifteen others were in the great cathedral, most of whom worked at Crucible.

After the ceremony, I spoke privately with Sophie. She apologized for being so mean to me, and I apologized for being a lousy piece of ass. She started to laugh at the remark through her tears.

I asked her whether she was going to come out of the whole mess with some money. She told me that her father had established two huge trusts for her long before all the problems started. Sophie added that the trusts were protected from litigation according to her attorneys. All of Gil's other assets were at risk, including his homes and considerable outside investments. In the end, the millions Gil was supposed to receive from the buyout might end up being zero. But he had earned so much prior to the buyout that his daughter would be well cared for. We agreed to speak in the future and I departed.

I met Joy for dinner a few weeks after our nearly tragic plane ride. We went to a very romantic restaurant on the upper Westside. She told me about her career and her family, and I did the same. She read a few stories about my problems relating to GYP and Crucible and empathized.

After dinner we went back to her place for a drink. A depressing air hung over our conversation. I sensed that Joy was feeling her age and saddened that life had passed her by. She told me that she had always wanted to have children, but had no time for it. Right after saying those words, she started to cry hysterically. I hugged her for a long time. My life was turning to shit, but I felt sorry for her. Inevitably, we ended up in bed kissing and touching each other tenderly and consummated our date in the sweetest manner.

I thought I should be in love with this woman, but was unable to do it in the traditional way. She was a pathetic person who regretted giving up a "normal" life for the life of a successful person of the bench. It really bothers me when people make perfectly acceptable life decisions and then whine about their decisions later.

I tried to convince her that her life was a great one and she should be proud of her many achievements. It was a waste of time. She wanted to be a wife and a mother and it was too damn late for her. Nevertheless, Joy appreciated my appreciation of her career achievements. We agreed to visit in the future and silently came to a decision not to pursue a romantic relationship.

I called Sasha the day after Cohen fired me. We got together for a burger and a beer late that night, as Sasha was working on a deal. The first thing she wanted to get off her chest was her feelings about our encounter in my hotel room. She kept saying that she felt really stupid about going to my room, getting drunk, and passing out. But she was complementary about my behavior.

Her experiences with men would have her believe that there wasn't a man alive, except me, who would've passed up an opportunity to have sex with her while she was in a drunken coma. I told her that it took every ounce of strength for me to walk away, and I wanted to look into her eyes the first time I made love to her (What a great line!). She joked and said that that was impossible the last time because she couldn't open her eyes.

Well one thing has led to the next and I'm crazy about this woman. She's helped me with my legal problems (other than those dealing with SS). We're enjoying our time together and I think our relationship may develop into something special.

When the news of my departure from GYP (and involvement with Crucible) hit the newspapers, the reaction in the investment community was as expected. Some bankers love to see the competition have problems and actually hope they die of a terrible disease. Others seize these opportunities.

I had been successful against so many competitors over the years that many were really interested in recruiting me. They had two questions in mind: what was the extent of my legal problems and were my clients willing to do business with me prospectively? The answer was that my legal problems were not as bad as I had anticipated. In fact, Crucible's acquirers had concluded that Gil was the perpetrator of the fraudulent numbers and I was duped just as they had been. It appeared I'd suffer no long-term legal problems in that regard.

As far as my clients were concerned, they had depended on me in the past and wanted me to work with them in the future. Literally, every one of my clients called to wish me well and a speedy return to the business.

I rented space in midtown with Rob Viand, who Cohen had fired the minute I walked out of GYP's offices. We immediately signed up five of my old clients and received retainer fees of several million dollars. After much conversation, we decided to name our new company PYGLET Partners. Get it? Rob's working hard to find the Greek woman of his dreams, now that his hours at work are much more reasonable.

Gyp quickly offered to end the dispute with me regarding my severance. I believe Antun Smith was behind the generous offer that was made. I don't know how Antun was able to convince Cohen to settle, but he did it. The deal was to pay me $5 million up front and $4 million for two years. These amounts represented my severance and a buy back of my GYP stock. I immediately accepted the offer and withdrew my $25 million suit against GYP. I plan to whip my old company's ass in the marketplace every chance I have and take all my old clients to PYGLET.

Oh, just one more thing. I received a phone call from Sophie a week after seeing her at her father's funeral. The conversation follows.

"Hi Stoke. It's me, Sophie."

"Well, hello. Is everything OK?"

"Yes, we're fine."

"What do you mean we?"

"I'm pregnant."

I said to myself, no way. "Congratulations, who's the lucky father?" Please, please not me, I said to myself.

"You."

"Get out of here. You're kidding. You're not pregnant. This is a joke, right?"

"Stoke, I don't know how it happened. I can't believe you did this with one stroke, but you did."

"I don't know what to say. Are you sure the baby is mine?"

"Has to be. I didn't have sex with anybody except you for several months, and I use the term sex loosely."

"Are you going to keep the baby?"

"If you mean, am I going to have an abortion? No. If you mean, am I going to put the baby up for adoption? No. I couldn't do that. The baby was conceived at the exact moment my father died. It's a sign."

"I think that's wonderful, Sophie. I can't wait to meet our new…"

"Son. It's a boy."

"Unbelievable. Of course I'll do whatever I can to help, and get to know our son."

Well that's the end of the story. I'm not going to go into any details about Sasha's reaction to Sophie's condition except to say that she was pretty cool about it. However, I think she figured out that the child was conceived on the same night I didn't make love with her.

116038